God
Speaks to Me

God
Speaks to Me

Stories of Triumph over Tragedy from
Women Who Listened to God

Valerie Love

URBAN CHRISTIAN

www.urbanchristianonline.net

URBAN CHRISTIAN is published by

Urban Books
1199 Straight Path
West Babylon, NY 11704

ISBN-13: 978-1-60162-951-7
ISBN-10: 1-60162-951-6

First Printing: Novemebr 2007
Printed in the United States of America

10 9 8 7 6 5 4 3 2 1

This is a work of fiction. Any references or similarities to actual events, real people, living, or dead, or to real locales are intended to give the novel a sense of reality. Any similarity in other names, characters, places, and incidents is entirely coincidental.

Submit Wholesale Orders to:
Kensington Publishing Corp.
C/O Penguin Group (USA) Inc.
Attention: Order Processing
405 Murray Hill Parkway
East Rutherford, NJ 07073-2316
Phone: 1-800-526-0275
Fax: 1-800-227-9604

DEDICATION

This book is dedicated to five beautiful embodiments of God's love: Cory, Alana, Varonika, Ronnie Sr., and Ronnie Jr.

ACKNOWLEDGMENTS

One would think that writing is a solitary affair, but it is actually a synchronistic melding of the time and talents of many individuals in order to produce and distribute works that inspire others. One of the most important persons I'd like to thank is my husband, for he puts up with me writing even when he'd rather have me sitting next to him watching a movie. He understands my passion and mission, and he lovingly supports and promotes my work. I love you, Ronnie, God continue to bless you richly.

I am so very grateful for the guiding hand of my agent, Audra Barrett, from the beginning of the path to publication for this book, down to the finished project. Her enthusiasm for this project has been the catalyst for great things to occur.

In addition, the enthusiastic support for this project from my editor Joylynn Jossel at Urban Christian has made this book the labor of love you now hold in your hands. Joylynn championed this book and I am so very grateful for her faith in the spirit of what is written on these pages.

Again, writing is not a solitary affair. It is a harmonious joining of minds and hearts. For all the minds and hearts who have joined mine on this project, thank you and may you continue to see all the ways you are richly blessed by God.

"There is a lesson in any and every experience that I have. The question is: How can I learn it with the least amount of pain, suffering and lack?"

Rev. Jim Webb
Takoma Park Metaphysical Chapel

NOTES

Please note that all references made to the Higher Being or Universe refer to God. God has many names. Feel free to substitute whatever name you desire.

Also please note that names have been changed to respect and protect privacy.

TABLE OF CONTENTS

INTRODUCTION

This is not a religious text insomuch as it is a spiritual text. It is written to illustrate how extraordinary God is as a teacher and counselor, and how we are continually guided in every possible aspect of our lives. God is in constant communication and communion with each one of us.

The question is: Are you listening?

God can teach us using anything, anyone, at any time, in any place. The Creator uses our experiences—the great and the seemingly insignificant—to lovingly teach us our eternal lessons. Each day, something magical and wondrous is happening: the Universe is continually transmitting to you an immeasurable amount of wisdom and guidance. Most of the time, we're simply not paying attention.

Regrettably, we are often not cognizant of the gem hidden within each experience or encounter—the sacred lessons that, if mastered, would enable us to manifest more of our divine nature. In fact, moments of pure revelation occur more often than we may think possible or even probable. There is an admonition: *we gain the most benefit from these sacred lessons if we are fully present, spiritually aware, and conscious enough to have invited Divine guidance into our lives*.

Over the past four decades, I've been in school. I didn't always pay attention when God spoke to me, but I've still been able to assimilate quite a few valuable lessons.

One of the major lessons in my spiritual life was the

direction I received from a fellow author a couple of years ago. He recommended that I begin a practice of writing down the lessons I learned from God. He convinced me that this simple but profound practice would catapult my spiritual growth and save me from repeating the same mistakes over and over again.

His advice sounded wise, so I decided to heed it. I began to pay more attention to the lives of those around me and to my own life, and then I began to record some of the lessons I was learning. I wrote down lessons friends and family shared with me that they had learned as well. I can't say that I recorded every lesson on a daily basis, but I can say that whenever I was particularly moved by an experience, it went into my journal. The journal became the net that captured beautiful but fleeting gems of wisdom from every day occurrences. Each of these precious morsels of wisdom was intended for my spiritual growth and development. The results of that commitment and ongoing process is the book you now hold in your hands.

My practice of recording events and their related meanings and messages revealed several commonalities that appear to be present when each of us learns a sacred lesson. I've listed these themes below, which may prove helpful to you while reading this book.

1. ***Few lessons are revelatory.*** Many lessons are simply reminders of something you've heard before, or know intuitively to be familiar and true for you. You begin to recognize the familiarity of some sacred lessons simply because they keep repeating themselves. They are reiterated either because you have not yet mastered them, or because you have not yet responded to the guidance they offer. With each successive sacred

lesson you master, you will emerge a more spiritually aware learner.

2. **Sacred lessons are not always monumental or life-changing.** Some of our lessons seem insignificant, miniscule or just plain unimportant. However, our divine lessons are cumulative in nature; a small skill mastered today rests upon a foundation of previously mastered spiritual skills. Never underestimate the power of even the smallest, simplest lesson—it could be the foundation cornerstone you need to successfully master a much bigger challenge later on.

3. **All lessons are for our eternal benefit, especially the painful ones.** God desires only the absolute best for you, now and in your future, and God is gracious enough to equip you with everything you need to get it. Never retreat in fear from a painful lesson. Mustering the courage to face it with grace and faith will become an excellent and necessary tool for your continued spiritual enlightenment. → *having the power to produce a desired effect*

4. **God is efficacious.** Each lesson prepared for you is precisely and perfectly what you need to produce the desired result. Nothing more and nothing less. Remember, God is the master physician who prescribes exactly what we need when we need it. You can be absolutely sure that the dose you are getting is precisely what you need, regardless of what you may want.

5. **God is always on time.** Each of our sacred life lessons is presented to us at the ideal time, whether we appreciate the moment or not. There may be situations that cause you to question the timing of a life lesson while you're immersed in it, but hindsight will eventually confirm its timeliness.

The universe doesn't consult you as to when
would be a good time for you to fit a sacred lesson into your schedule. They just show up,
seemingly out of nowhere. Though we have summoned these lessons through our thoughts and
emotions, we may not always be aware of the
process, nor do we always remember what we've
summoned. When the lessons show up, it's up to
us to honor them and pay close attention.

6. ***Some sacred lessons become public for the benefit of others.*** If you're wise, you won't have to
   complete every spiritual class yourself. Why not
   look around you and see what you can absorb
   spiritually from the experiences of others. Many
   of my learnings came from careful observation of
   what was unfolding in the lives of those around
   me. I realized that if I paid attention to what God
   was teaching someone else, I could make different choices for myself, which could prevent me
   from making some of the same costly mistakes.
   My late grandfather (who, it has been revealed to
   me, is now a guide to my youngest daughter, Varonika) used to say, "Keep your eyes and ears
   open and you'll find out everything you need to
   know." His advice has proven itself both sage
   and advantageous.

7. ***God is love.*** Every lesson you learn will be cloaked
   in love and motivated by love.

Search for these themes in this book, in your own
life and in the lives of others, always asking the question: How and what can I learn from this? The answer
will be golden.

A CHALLENGE TO YOU

The mind's capacity to remember every event that happens in life is grossly limited. You've probably noticed that if you don't write down certain ideas, thoughts or experiences as they occur to you, your ability to remember them diminishes quickly with the passage of time. However, there are countless experiences and sacred lessons placed in your path that are too critical to trust to memory, lest they be forgotten forever. A written record of such important discoveries could support and expedite your spiritual progress substantially.

As a result of heeding the beneficial advice given to me over two years ago, I can state to you with complete certainty that chronicling my sacred lessons has been both spiritually fulfilling and deeply enlightening. With that in mind, I want to extend the same invitation to you to journal your personal sacred lessons. Don't be overly concerned if you're not accustomed to writing in a journal. There's good news: Journaling is easy to do and doesn't require much money, time or creativity. Simply write down what happens to you, and then write down what you've learned from the experience. If you're under time constraints, writing in a journal doesn't have to be a daily affair; you can write every other day, or 2-3 times each week. Or, you may choose to do as I did and write down only the experiences that touch your soul in a special or profound way.

After you've recorded your experiences and what

you've learned from them, revisit your writings regularly. You'll be astounded at your journal's content, but you'll be even more amazed at the spiritual transformation your journal effects. There will be an added benefit: You will be less likely to repeat the same painful experiences over and over again. Though some reiteration is certainly necessary and beneficial, life on this earthly plane is too short for needless or mindless repetition. If you're like me, you've had the experience of circling around and around in a painful, repetitive loop of the same problems. This happens simply because *you haven't learned the lesson yet.* This is not the easiest path to follow, or the most desirable. The best path is to learn the lesson well the first time it is presented, so as to not get "left back" and have to complete the same lessons again. Keeping track of certain sacred lessons you've learned brings your awareness to the process, which will provide you with greater success.

One of the grandest benefits of the journaling process is a new awareness of what is mystically unfolding in your life, *every day.* The more aware you are of what is unfolding in your life, the more you are growing. Awareness prevents you from plodding through life's events completely oblivious of the gems of wisdom they contain. You'll learn more quickly, effectively and effortlessly than you ever have before. You'll also become more *present* than you've ever been, which—if being present in the moment becomes a habit for you— will produce a deep, unparalleled and profound joy.

My desire in writing this book is to share with you personal sacred lessons from my life and those around me. My prayer for you is that you will allow God to work wonders in your life through your acceptance, appreciation and application of the sacred lessons our Creator patiently teaches you each day. May you bask in God's loving guidance and prosper exceedingly!

God Bless You,

Valerie Love

God Speaks Through Relationships

"When people show you who they are, believe them
the first time."—Maya Angelou

Sandy's Saga

"Yes, Ma'am, your husband's here. He's being held for bank robbery and possession of controlled substances."

Sandy, an outgoing young woman with a quick wit and a warm heart, made a personal vow that she would not sleep with John until they had plans to marry, or at least until she had a diamond ring on her finger and a definitive wedding date. Since he was not yet ready to make that commitment, she decided that their relationship would remain platonic. She knew he was intimate with other women, and that he needed more time to work them all out of his system. When he was ready, and if she was still available, they would join in a monogamous relationship that would proceed down the path to holy matrimony. Until then, Sandy was firm: no cohabitating in the meantime!

John understood and had no choice but to comply. So they set about building a friendship, an essential key to any stable marriage. It was easy to build the friendship considering their shared interests and deep regard for each other. He was the proverbial "perfect gentleman."

But, despite the comfortable friendship, the long conversations on the phone, and the easy way they cliqued, Sandy had doubts about John. She couldn't pinpoint exactly what it was, but something just wasn't *right* about him.

Soon enough, Sandy's subtle, uneasy feelings were swept away by the excitement of blossoming love. Within a few short months, John's feelings for Sandy forced a decision: it was time to pick one woman to spend his life with. That woman was Sandy Mason.

The wedding was beautiful, and after the nuptials, he moved into the condominium she had owned and lived in for years. They planned to buy a home together after they'd spent more time together and saved more money.

But something was amiss. It wasn't long before John's behavior reminded Sandy of those strange and increasingly familiar gut feelings she felt from time to time before she and John got married. John's negative patterns with money and his ever deteriorating employment situation only heightened the stress level. Every so often, money would be missing from her purse.

Initially, Sandy ignored John's financial woes, even though they were bleeding into her own financial affairs. She rationalized away her feelings as to why and how he systematically lost every cent he got his hands on. In her gut, there was an ugliness hanging around about him that she just couldn't shake off.

One year of marriage elapsed, and it was time to celebrate their first anniversary. Sandy and John decided to take a leisurely drive to Atlantic City, New Jersey for the weekend to mark the occasion. They planned to leave on Friday around noon and return on Sunday evening. Atlantic City was a short two and a half hour drive from their Maryland home, so it would be a pleasant, albeit short, getaway. That morning, Sandy and John both had errands to run. They agreed to complete their errands separately and meet back home by twelve noon to get on the road to Atlantic City.

At about 11:45 a.m., when Sandy was just about done with her errands, John called her from home. It was getting close to noon and he wondered where she was and how long it would take her to get back home. Since it wasn't quite noon yet, Sandy thought it strange that he sounded so urgent. She told him she was on her way back and would be there within just a few minutes.

Surprisingly, when she got there, he wasn't home. Once again, Sandy was slightly perplexed, considering the phone conversation they'd just had in which he'd told her how anxious he was to get on the road. She dismissed the oddity: *he must've forgotten something and had to run out at the last minute.*

She waited a while for him to return, and when he hadn't come back by 12:30, she called him on his cell phone to find out where he was. No answer. An hour passed. Then two. Sandy was worried and completely baffled. In the meantime, she had placed several more calls to his cell phone, all in vain. She called his friends—none of whom knew where he was nor had seen him that day. Even his mom had no idea where he was, which was a rarity.

Sandy's mind and heart raced. Where was he? Why had he disappeared when they were both so eagerly looking forward to their anniversary getaway?

At 3:00 p.m., the phone rang. It was John's mother. "Sandy, I know where John is . . . he's in jail."

Sandy's heart jumped to her throat. "What!?!? Why?!?! What do you mean, he's in jail?!?!?"

Amidst Sandy's internal panic, a dichotomy arose. While she desperately wanted to believe that this was some horrible mistake, there was a part of her that believed John could have done something that would land him in jail.

She fought hard to quell her frenzy. At this point, it took all she had. John's mother answered soberly. "He robbed a bank, Sandy."

The words punched Sandy in the stomach.

Before she could utter a word, John's mother added, "He was caught on the bank's surveillance cameras. They could see him clearly since he wasn't wearing a disguise. When the police caught up with him, he had $200 from the bank and heroin on him. They arrested him on the spot. If you want to see him, he's in the county lock-up until his arraignment."

Sandy tried hard to digest John's mother's words. "Robbed a bank . . . caught on the bank's surveillance cameras . . . wasn't wearing a disguise . . . heroin . . ."

Try as she might, the words were too much to digest. She quickly got the details and decided to call the jail where John was being held. As she dialed, a strange thought about John's mother darted through Sandy's mind. How was she able to deliver a message like this with such composure? She seemed a little too calm. In that split second, Sandy became convinced that John's mother had been through this type of drama with her son before. Sandy didn't know any mother who could have had a conversation quite this calm about her son being arrested for bank robbery and drug possession. There was only one exception she could think of: this was a repeat performance. John's mother, having been through this before, was no longer surprised or alarmed by her son's actions.

After speaking with the law enforcement officers,

Sandy got off the phone and raced down to the county lockup as fast as she could. Upon arrival, she received more specifics of the day's events.

She heard about how her husband had strolled into the bank, stood on line for his turn in front of the teller, then politely pushed a note toward her requesting that she fill his bag with twenties.

He was not wearing a disguise, not even a cap.

After receiving the cash, he picked up the bag, quietly turned around and left the bank.

He climbed into his white SUV that he had left parked right outside the front door of the bank and drove away with no more ado than if he'd been in the bank withdrawing his own funds. He was as calm and collected as he would've been going to the cash machine. One would suspect that he wanted to get caught.

When Sandy was allowed to view the bank surveillance tape, she was dumbstruck—there he was, in plain view, robbing a bank.

I can't believe I'm watching my husband rob a bank!

But that wasn't all. As she had deduced from the conversation with John's mother, this wasn't his first infraction. He'd been arrested several years earlier for the same crime—bank robbery. Nine different bank robberies to be exact.

Later, in answer to Sandy's query as to why on earth he had robbed so many banks, John made a startling, but truthful, confession. "I rob banks because that's where the money is."

As if this latest barrage of information wasn't quite enough, there was more.

Years ago, after serving two years of a five year prison sentence, John was released; presumably and hopefully to become a productive member of society. This he was able to accomplish for a few years, until he happened upon a few old buddies, one of which went by the name heroin.

After being clean for five years, he was drawn in by the spell and became an addict again. A low key addict, but an addict nonetheless. The kind of addict who can halfway hold a job. The kind of addict who can marry someone, live with them, and then work night and day to hide the addiction.

It almost worked, except for the fact that addictions have a terrible way of coming undone and breaking out of their prescribed hiding places. No matter how hard John tried to contain the monster, the addiction reared its ugly head—determined to make its presence known. And once John's monster was out, there was no way he would ever be able to get it to go quietly back into the closet.

The jigsaw puzzle finally all fell together; Sandy's strange gut feelings about him, his elusive behavior, his inability to hold a job for more than a few months, and his frequent and long stays in their guest bathroom, the bathroom he never allowed her to enter (in her own home). The constant long sleeves, even in the blistering summer heat. The missing money from her purse and her bank accounts. The bad checks. The air of anarchy their lives had taken on right after they were married.

Mystery solved.

Now, the painful truth of John's barely hidden, thinly veiled heroin addiction fell on Sandy's head like a ton of bricks. She could no longer ignore, escape or excuse it. No rationalizing this time.

While Sandy sat at the county lockup being regaled by the police detectives with stories about John's sordid past, every negative emotion imaginable rushed in on her. She felt angry, betrayed, humiliated, hurt. So many emotions swirled about, picking one that was perfect for the occasion was almost beyond her ability.

Stunned won. It was the emotion that suit her best now, although later she would decide that betrayal and anger would be a better fit.

She finally saw John. He looked a pathetic soul. There was nothing he could say that made any sense to Sandy or could console her.

After the initial pain of the discovery dulled, Sandy searched herself for answers about what she would do. A steady stream of tears was a constant companion.

One day, she ventured into the second bathroom, the one he proclaimed as his private bath, the room whose door was always closed. There she found the paraphernalia that took him to the high places that were his escape from reality and all its expectations.

She vacillated between feeling sorry for him and being infuriated with him. How could he do this to her? Regardless of his fate, she would have to decide what to do with her own life. The answer came swiftly. She would divorce him, as soon as she possibly could. A clean break was best, she thought, like severing a gangrenous foot.

He pleaded. Begged. Tried his best to get her to reconsider, to stay with him, to wait for him while he served his time so they could begin their life anew once he was released. Neither was sure how many years that might be.

Amid his vehement protests and desperate begging, Sandy made it clear to him that whatever they had was over. Forever.

So she set about the work of cleaning him out of her house and her system. He made it easy for her with the conflagration he had started. The more drug paraphernalia she discovered in her own home, the more she affirmed her decision to leave him to rot right where he was. And that's exactly what she did.

After more than two years of healing through prayer and reconnection with God, and with the support of loyal friends, Sandy met a wonderful, hardworking, fiscally responsible man whom she grew to have a deep affection for. He felt the same way about her. Their love was real. She had no inner secret worries about what he was doing or where their money was disappearing to. Her inner voice confirmed that "all is well with this man."

Sandy and her new love eventually walked down the aisle to marital union. They remain together and happy as of this writing.

In retrospect, Sandy has made peace with herself about John's betrayal and the pack of lies he employed to keep his heroin addiction and past incarceration concealed. She realizes the detrimental choices she could have made had she not listened to God. When it became clear that John was a criminal, Sandy decided to end their relationship. Had she not followed her internal guidance from God and continued in a relationship with John while he was incarcerated, she may have never met her current husband.

God was speaking to Sandy from the very beginning of their marriage. The beauty of this story is its reminder to us to always be attuned to Divine guidance.

Sandy looks at the time spent with him as a life-changing school; and is thankful to God for the grace, love and protection that surrounded and filled her throughout her ordeal.

God Speaks

What were Sandy's sacred lessons from her tumultuous time with John?

Sacred Lesson #1: Your Intuition Is Really God Sending You a Private Message

The tiny inner whisper of truth you often hear is God speaking to you in a voice and language only you understand: your own. That little voice at the core of your being—commonly referred to as "intuition" or "gut feeling"—is God sending you a very private and beneficial message.

There are two challenges related to this internal source of wisdom that is innate to us all.

The first challenge is that this internal voice usually whispers; especially the first time it sends you a message regarding a certain situation, person or event. If we're not aware, the much louder daily commotion of a fast-paced, high-tech, high-stress world could cause interference or static, rendering the message from God almost imperceptible.

The second challenge arises when we *do* hear the voice (as it tends to get louder and louder the more negative a situation becomes). After hearing it, our first reaction may be to discount it, or to try to ignore it altogether. Worse yet, we decide to argue with it; creating an internal dialogue that can escalate to a full-scale personal battle.

Let's address the first challenge: not being able to hear our internal wisdom and guidance. Many attendees of my workshops and classes tell me that they don't know what to do in their lives that would make them happy. They don't hear or feel God talking to them as much or as strong and clearly as they'd like.

The answer to this malady will sound incredibly simple, because it is:

Be silent. Be still. Listen.

That's it. I do not seek to oversimplify this issue or trivialize the challenge many feel about their commune with God. I seek merely to tell the truth of my experience and that of many others; indeed truth is never complicated.

Silence is simple, but it is far from easy. The world we live in is very noisy. In general, our society has difficulty becoming and remaining quiet for an extended length of time. There is an actual disdain for silence: we walk into a silent room and complain, like my 16-year old daughter. "It's too quiet in here." We turn on the radio or TV even when we're not interested in what's on just to "break the monotony." We even dread silence in a conversation with someone else. If the conversation lulls, rather than just sitting quietly in the presence of another, we become nervous and are quick to add fill-in dialogue just to "keep the ball rolling."

The reason many don't treasure quiet solitude is because sitting in silence forces us to be alone with our thoughts—some of which we'd rather not be alone with. I've heard it said that the mind is a dangerous place that you don't want to visit alone.

When the mind is full of thousands of noisy and opposing thoughts, it becomes almost impossible to decipher God whispering to us above the commotion. It's little wonder that Buddhists call this the "monkey mind."

There's only one remedy for taming the "monkey mind": a regular practice of silent meditation and prayer.

If you can't hear God's voice speaking to you, shut up and listen!

To avoid suffering and pain, invite God's guidance in through prayer and meditation every day. One way to tap into this voice is to meditate and pray each morning and each evening, and at tiny meditation respites during the day. Learning to practice the art of silence at regular intervals is an essential step in recognizing God's voice in every situation. A meditative practice helps us attune to and heed our Divinely-inspired inner voice. Taking treasured time to meditate every day in quiet solitude forces us to dismiss the noisy chatter that is constantly playing in our minds. With the suspension of noisy chatter, the path is cleared to reaching higher levels of communication and communion with God, the angels and the Holy Spirit. During meditation, we are able to see how the pathway to the Divine connects directly to our inner core—the voice deep within that gives us a steady stream of life-enhancing and life-saving messages, large and small.

A regular meditative practice will also enable you to decipher God's wisdom even when you're in the eye of a personal storm and things are not quiet around you. I have a practice of meditating each morning, but even when I'm not meditating, I hear God's voice more clearly than I did before I started the practice. It's as if meditation is an amplifier that turns up the volume on your God-voice within. The daily time I spend in the company of God, the angels and the Holy Spirit through prayer and meditation is *unparalleled.* There is *nothing* I could do that could elicit the identical feelings of joy, serenity, bliss, tranquility, peace, harmony, love and compassion as my morning ritual spent in the presence of God.

Invest time in becoming quiet enough to listen to your Divinely-inspired inner voice of wisdom, and invite God to speak to you even more intimately and often than through daily prayer and meditation. Doing so will cause you to experience the depth of peace and happiness that can only come from God.

The second challenge is no less damaging than the first: hearing the voice, and then ignoring it or fighting with it. Have you ever noticed that a little voice inside you may pop up with a tiny bit of helpful advice, such as, "Don't forget your keys", and your mind immediately forms a rebuttal: "I don't have to take my keys now; I'll remember where they are." Later on, you can't find your keys, or you've left them locked in the car. Then you say to yourself, "Something told me not to forget my keys". I've had this experience so many times that I gave up fighting with the voice and now I just listen to what it tells me, the first time.

What's the alternative? Well, you could go on ignoring this wonderful internal stream of help and guidance, but, let me warn you: ignoring and silencing this voice is not without its consequences. The habit of suppressing our intuition creates a detrimental, vicious cycle: when we ignore our gut feelings, we weaken our ability to correctly and swiftly intuit what would be best for us at any given time, no matter where we are, or whom we're with. The weaker we *perceive* the link between us and God, the less powerful we are. We lose our ability to navigate through life safely, wisely and productively. When we shut down our intuition, we lose our guiding light.

Observation of the animal kingdom can teach us a poignant lesson on gut feelings. Animals are completely attuned to their internal guidance system and instinctively know to trust it fully and do so by responding instantly. It was reported that in the days and hours leading up to the tsunami that hit Southeast Asia and Africa in December of 2004, the wild and unfettered animals started moving away from the shore and into the mountains and other remote areas. When the tsunami hit, even though it reached over a mile inland, they were safely out of harm's way and survived. The domesticated animals that were tied or confined to the houses of their owners were the animals that were devastated by the tsunami. We can't help but wonder where those domesticated animals would've been if they weren't tied up or confined. My bet is, they would have been hanging out with their wild animal counterparts somewhere safely outside the reach of the tsunami. The other question that comes to mind is: what were the humans doing? With no disrespect to the victims of the tsunami, let's ask honestly, did they watch an exodus of animals and think that everything was normal? Obviously not. The animals served as an early warning system, triggering strange gut feelings in humans. Later we would read about the people who thought it unusual that the animals all seemed to be migrating at the same time, in the same direction. People reported that they even saw snakes moving inland to higher ground. If the humans had followed the animals, even though this may not have made "common sense", perhaps some of them may have been spared. There was a time when humans lived in close contact with the earth and all its creatures; which served to give us increased awareness of all earth's cycles and changes, especially the most violent ones.

If God gave animals the ability to safely navigate in any situation, including potentially life-threatening ones, wouldn't He have given us abilities that are at least as powerful, if not more so? Could these abilities be developed to a very high degree to keep us safe, happy and content? The answer to all of these questions is a resounding YES!

I had an unforgettable experience with regard to heeding my instincts on the streets of New York City in the 1980's. I was walking home from worship service one dark, chilly fall night. I was accompanied by my younger brother and sister, who were about seven and five years of age at the time. I held each of them by the hand, one on each side of me. There was a walk of six city blocks from where we were on 151st Street and Broadway—on Manhattan's Upper West Side—to our home on 158th Street. On the way, there is a two block stretch of darkness, where few people walk at night. It is the walk past the graveyard. We had grown accustomed to walking there at night as we'd been doing it for years. We were never afraid, and strangely enough, nothing untoward ever occurred. Until that night.

Before I started the walk home with my brother and sister in tow, a little voice told me, "Go back. Wait a while before you walk home; then go with a larger group of people." As you might imagine, I didn't listen. I wanted to get home, and since nothing had ever happened before in years of traveling those city streets, I pressed forward unafraid; completely ignoring my inner voice of wisdom.

Sure enough, as soon as we were about a quarter of the way down the dark street past the graveyard, two thugs appeared out of nowhere behind us. I could hear fast footsteps running up from behind, and I instantly felt panicked. I swung around, children still at my sides. There stood two young muggers, one with a gun in his hand pointed squarely at my chest. The other one yelled, "Give me your purse!" I imagine he asked me for it because it was strapped across my body as women in New York City frequently wear their purses, and for precisely this reason. Unbelievably, I said "No!" Don't ask me why. To this day, I don't know where that urge came from, but it popped out of my mouth before I could think about what I was actually saying. There was only $15.00 cash in my purse, along with credit cards. Nothing irreplaceable, and certainly nothing worth risking life or limb over.

The one with the gun didn't say a word. Oddly, he stood completely still, gun still pointed straight at me.

The one giving the orders yelled again, "I said give me your purse!" This time, he didn't wait for me to respond. He lunged at me and yanked my purse off my body in one fell swoop.

The mugger with the gun stood completely motionless and quiet.

The other mugger turned and ran away with my purse.

The mugger with the gun continued standing, completely motionless.

The yelling mugger must have realized that he didn't hear the footsteps of his partner accompanying him, so he turned back to see what was going on. When he turned around, he saw his partner in crime standing there, with a gun in his hand, completely paralyzed and staring off into space.

It suddenly dawned on all of us that the gunman had been standing there for the entire time, immobilized, and apparently now incapacitated as well. He looked as if he were staring at something awesome just behind me. I dared not turn my head to see what he was looking at, not with the gun still pointed in my direction and my brother and sister so close.

We stood for one very surreal moment, which appeared to last an eternity: me, my brother and sister, staring at the gunman who was staring at something behind me—the sight of which rendered him dumbstruck.

The unarmed mugger, with my purse in hand, ran back to his partner and shook his arm. He yelled again, "LET'S GO!" The gunman, finally shaken free of his trance, turned and ran away with his counterpart.

We heaved a deep breath, a heavy sigh of relief. To this day, I know the gunman was stunned by angels at my sides and back. He was motionless, paralyzed, entranced. The gun never moved. We could've been shot on the streets of New York City that night. There would have been a certain irony in dying right in front of a graveyard. But it was not to be. The angels of protection showed themselves mightily that night and stupefied the young gunman.

There are many lessons I could share with you from this life-changing event, but the one I'll focus on in the context of this discussion is the fleeting flash of insight I received just before I started out on the walk home that night. In a second, a Spirit communicated to me, to go back. That tiny voice of wisdom told me to wait, to walk with other people who were going in that direction; that we'd be safer if we traveled with a group. All of that information was conveyed to me by God in an instant.

If I had heeded my internal warning system that night, I would not have subjected myself, my brother and my sister to looking down the barrel of a gun. It is a sight I will never forget.

At just 20 years of age, I had not yet learned the lessons of how valuable that inner voice was; nor had I learned that a sudden flash of insight from God is always worth obeying—or at the very least—is deserving of immediate careful attention.

Let's take a moment to look back at Sandy's situation again. God spoke to her on several different occasions, warning her through her inner voice and gut feelings that something wasn't right about her husband-to-be. Despite those feelings, she was reluctant to accept the truthfulness of her inner voice and to *act on its advice*. Though hindsight is always 20/20, it's worth noting that a marriage may have never taken place had Sandy followed closely her internal guidance system. She admits that she would've made different choices had she fully trusted the counsel of her inner voice.

This guidance from God is not only reserved for major life issues (such as marriage) or life-threatening events (such as a tsunami or a robbery at gunpoint). God offers help on the mundane aspects of life as well, *if we are listening*. How many times have you heard a little voice inside say, "Go the other way," or "Be careful on the steps," or "Watch your purse," or any other helpful little tidbit of information that makes your life easier? When we don't take heed, we usually wind up saying: "*Something* told me not to do that, but I didn't listen and now look at this mess!" That *something* you keep hearing is God speaking to you from within.

This brings us to the solution to the second challenge mentioned above. If you have a tendency to ignore, argue with or rationalize away the first instinctive flash of insight you receive in any given situation—which is a startlingly accurate assessment and a gust of guidance—pray to God asking for the courage to follow your internal voice and feelings. This is difficult to do, because the inner voice may call upon you to do *something different than what you are accustomed to doing.*

For example, the voice may tell you that the man or woman you're dating right now is not good for you. If you were to heed that voice, it would mean leaving that person. This could be painful, because you feel that you are in love with this person, and you think that you may not find another person who is compatible and fills your needs like this person does. Besides, if you let this person go, you rationalize: who knows how long you may have to wait before another suitable partner comes along, which means that you may be alone for a while.

If you are about to get married to someone you know you shouldn't, this voice is probably yelling at you right now. If you heed it, it would mean calling off a wedding. It may mean losing money. Or worse yet, you may fear looking bad by calling off a wedding after your friends and family have been invited.

If you notice, rationalizing takes a long time. A flash of intuitive insight happens in a split second. We could spend all day rationalizing away a one-second bad gut feeling. But, in the end, the one-second bad gut feeling will win, hands down, over the day-long rationalizing. The flash of insight carries an unparalleled, pin-pointed accuracy.

Rather than rationalizing your way into marrying someone you know you shouldn't, why not pray to God for the courage and strength to heed your internal spiritual guidance and do what is right for you in the moment. Forget what everyone else would think. Will everyone else be married to this person, or will you be?

This internal spiritual guidance works in the arena of work and finance also. Let's say that you're looking for a new job and have been called in to interview with a company you'd really like to work for. However, your fleeting gut feeling on the job interview might tell you that the new boss you would have if you took this job—who is slightly demeaning on the interview—may make life on this job unpleasant. You get the feeling that you would be subjected to an insecure boss who micro-manages you. But, you rationalize, "I need the money, and this is the only job prospect that looks good right now. If I don't take this job, how am I going to pay my bills? I don't know how long it would take to find another job. Besides, this is the company I'd really like to work for." When he offers you the job, you hear yourself saying, "When do I start?" rather than saying, "No thank-you, this isn't the position for me." After you take the job, you become increasingly unhappy with your boss's demeaning attitude. Eventually, you start looking for another job.

Could you have saved yourself the time, trouble and energy expended by just listening to your gut?

These examples illustrate why we find it so difficult to act on our inner voice of wisdom: it takes immense courage to do so. It calls on us to break through a barrier of multiple, imaginary fears. The fear of, "What will people think of me if I did that?" The fear of, "But I'll lose him/her (or something else) if I do that." The fear of, "I won't have enough (money, time, energy, fun or whatever else you think you'll be missing out on) if I did that."

For Sandy, listening to her internal guidance system from the beginning concerning John may have meant not marrying him at all.

After getting married, heeding that internal voice would have meant facing a painful reality for Sandy:

*My husband is a drug addict who is stealing
from me and growing more desperate every day.
He has demonstrated clearly to me that he will do
anything to get his next heroin hit. Even though
we just got married, I must make a tough decision
if he does not seek help and permanently change,
which he presently exhibits no desire or inclina-
tion to do. If I don't take action, I will continue to
endanger my health, happiness and security, and
perhaps my life.*

Sandy wasn't ready to accept the painful reality,
though all the signs were present, because it would've
called upon her to make a frightening and huge
change. Change is difficult. Change can even be downright painful.

Just like Sandy, we've all been reticent, at one time
or another, to face the honesty of the messages our
inner voice delivers, because *heeding the guidance
could mean changing the path of our entire life.* Most
of us don't generally accept a nasty truth about a loved
one until it is hoisted upon us in such a manner that
we can no longer ignore or deny its reality; just as
Sandy's situation culminated in events she could no
longer ignore.

Again, courage is called for so that we can make
wise decisions with the best possible timing. In order
to do this, we must develop a practice of honoring the
inner voice as soon as we hear it. How many times
have you heard a tiny voice inside tell you to take a
certain action but you ignored it? What was the result?
How many times have you found yourself in a negative
situation because you chose to rationalize away that
uneasy feeling in your gut? Had you heeded the warn-

ing, might not a negative situation have turned out more positively or avoided altogether?

Today, try this exercise: when you wake up in the morning, before jumping out of bed, take a moment to breathe deeply, pray to God, silently sit there and do nothing. Listen. See what your intuition tells you about what you should do today at work, or in your family, or how you should handle certain people. Throughout the day, before reacting to what people around you say and do, take a quick second to check in with your inner voice and then make a conscious decision to follow whatever it's telling you to do.

It may say, "Don't go to lunch with your usual friends, go for a walk outside instead." When you go outside, you run into an old friend or meet someone who can help you accomplish an important goal you've been reaching for.

It may say, "Drive a different route to the office." Later, you find out that there was an accident on the road you normally take and traffic was backed up for miles. You arrive to work safely and earlier than your workmates because you tuned into the frequency inside you.

Or the voice may say, "Call your grandmother today". You call her and find out that she's been thinking of you and is delighted to hear from you. You have a lively conversation that uplifts both your spirits.

If you have a meeting today at work, when you walk into the room and greet the other attendees, take a moment to look around and see what your intuition is telling you about each person there. All of us are projectors; we project outside of us what we are thinking on the inside. It isn't difficult for your internal guidance system to pick up on the energy and frequency of each person in the room and then determine how to approach each one. Just let it work for you. You'll be amazed.

Never underestimate the power of this tiny voice to make dramatic shifts in your health, family, work, worship and your overall outlook and approach to life.

If you're unaccustomed to listening to your inner voice in this fashion, it will take time, practice and dedication to attune to this little voice, especially if you've stuffed it down repeatedly. However, no matter how much you've ignored this voice, or argued with it in the past, it is ever present, and ready and able to help you in every situation. It will take work for you to consistently attune yourself to it, but be assured that it is well worth any effort. Seeing how your life will start to spontaneously work out exceedingly well will convince you that you're on the right path. Christ taught that a tree is proved righteous by its fruits. You will taste the sweet results of following your inner Divine guidance, if you make it your intent and determination to do so.

Happily, Sandy now enjoys peaceful contentment in her current relationship, and her life, through honoring her inner voice—the voice that comes from God.

Sacred Lesson #2—God Protects Us Even When We Don't Know We Need It!

One of the things Sandy marveled at as she told me her story was God's powerful, constant hand of protection. We can't count all the ways Jehovah-Jireh protected her, because no one knows for sure how much danger she was in, or how often. Mentioned here is only part of the story; the parts where Sandy knows God maneuvered events for her safety and protection:

- Sandy was grateful that she wasn't in the vehicle when the police caught and arrested her husband. If she had been, she's convinced that she would have been arrested as well and charged with being his accomplice. Indeed, it would've been extremely difficult for her to prove in a court of law that there was no collusion between she and him if she'd been caught in the getaway car with him, the stolen money and the drugs on the way to Atlantic City; crossing multiple state lines in the process (reminiscent of Bonnie & Clyde). Under such circumstances, the outcome for her could have been disastrous. Sandy feels that God prevented her from being in the vehicle with him when he was arrested, and is filled with gratitude that she was protected even when she didn't know she needed protecting. The Universe always supports and protects us.
- Her husband was never violent with her. Sandy knows—in hindsight—that living with a drug addict placed her in a highly volatile setting. Yet, the volatility in their home never reached the "boiling point" where John became violent with her. God protected her in her own home for an extended period of time from any ill-will John may have directed at her.

There are far too many ways to enumerate how God's hand rested on Sandy to give her security in an insecure circumstance, *every day*. Suffice it to say that she is forever appreciative of God's ever-present, watchful and loving protection.

Sacred Lesson #3: ". . . for the tree is known and recognized and judged by its fruit."
Matthew 12:33b (AMP)

"When people show you who they are, believe them the first time."—Maya Angelou

Maya Angelou's powerful words sum up Sandy's story amazingly well. When someone shows you who they are, believe them the first time. Though every person is inherently good, since we were all created by God, there are some who still need to do more spiritual, emotional, mental or physical work on themselves. As Christ so lovingly taught us, no one on this earth is better or worse than anyone else, each of us is just at a different stage of spiritual growth and development.

There are those who have done considerable work on themselves to improve and evolve spiritually, mentally and emotionally, and are highly developed in these areas.

Then there are those who have not recognized their need to grow and develop, and are presently stagnant and stunted. Eventually, an event or life experience may shake them awake. In the meantime, spiritual growth and development may not be high on their priority list.

Then there are those who have not learned to cope with life's challenges, and turn to external crutches such as drugs, alcohol, food or any other thing they've transferred their power to. They may be seeking relief from emotional pain or a way to cope with life's twists and turns. In time, use of and reliance on an external crutch such as drugs, alcohol, sex, money or power, be-comes an addiction.

Sometimes we fail to pay attention to negative or destructive behaviors when we detect them in others, especially if they are exhibited by someone we are in-fatuated or in love with. When we fail to accept the stage of growth an individual is in, we may be setting ourselves up for enormous disappointment. When the object of our affection exhibits negative or dangerous patterns of behavior, such as substance abuse, verbal or physical abuse, or any other form of "red flag" behav-ior, some tend to rationalize:

"He's in a bad mood, I shouldn't have said anything to him."

"She didn't mean it."

"I'll overlook his abuse because I know he really loves me."

"He's under so much pressure, he didn't mean to do it."

These are lies ingeniously constructed by the ego-mind to relieve ourselves of the responsibility to take action. The truth is, when a person exhibits negative or even dangerous behavior, consider it a gift. They've just made known how they operate and what they're about, providing you with valuable information. You can take that information and use it to make wise choices in the future with that particular person. As Mom says, "Get me once, shame on you, get me twice, shame on me."

After all, if a tree—as Christ so succinctly put it—is known and recognized by its fruit, then what are the fruits of the people around you saying about them? If you have a partner who is exhibiting that they are sour like a grapefruit, why are you trying to make them into a sweet watermelon? If someone shows you that they are a bitter lemon, why should you proceed as if they are a delectable and juicy pineapple? Just look at the fruit. What are they producing in their lives? We are all known and recognized by the kind of fruit we produce. If you don't like the fruit the person is producing, why would you move further into a relationship with that person?

If you're wise and you recognize bitter fruit in someone around you, know that the fruit and the tree that produced it cannot be separated. If the fruit is of a certain kind, the tree is identical. A peach tree cannot produce apples, no matter what you do to it.

Therefore, since you see what kind of fruit a person is bearing, if that isn't the fruit you want in your life, then you have some decisions to make. For me, the decision making process has been distilled down to three simple steps. The steps are always identical whether it be a romantic encounter, or one of the less intensive types of relationships: Step 1—read, step 2—believe, and step 3—heed.

The simple steps of reading, believing and heeding any "red flag" warnings, (or rotten fruit) would end abusive relationships before they've had an opportunity to begin. It would prevent you from relationships with someone who is addicted to money, sex, drugs, alcohol, power, ego, or any other personally destructive vice. It would prevent you from getting into a relationship with a pathological liar. It would end many first dates right there, leaving them no room to become any more damaging than that: a bad first date.

Sandy's saga epitomizes the value of believing others when they show us who they are and what kind of fruit they're producing—*the first time.*

Her story also boldly illustrates how the inner voice of wisdom from God will save us from pain in every situation if heeded. Our internal voice is God speaking to us with only one motive: to make our lives more loving and fulfilling and joyful.

How beautiful!

"And so faith, hope, love abide [faith—conviction and belief respecting man's relation to God and divine things; hope—joyful and confident expectation of eternal salvation; love—true affection for God and man, growing out of God's love for and in us], these three; but the greatest of these is love."

1 Corinthians 13:13 AMP

Chocolate Cake Don't Love Me

It was 8:00 a.m. on a warm Saturday morning in June. Jade rapped loudly on his door, an air of desperation swirled about her like a mist. *Where the hell is he?* At first, there was no answer. She knocked again, a little louder this time. Suddenly, the door swung open: there stood Tom, in all his manly glory, wearing not a stitch of clothing. He stared at her as if he could see right through her. After a few seconds had slipped by, he calmly asked, "What do *you* want?"

Jade couldn't believe it. There he was, standing at the door wearing only what he came into the world with, and asking her, with no small amount of audacity, what did she want?

After surveying him, Jade's eyes darted inside and landed on the couch—she could see a woman's purse and a dress draped over the sofa like a tell-tale throw. She felt heat rising within; her emotions began to boil like a kettle of stew.

She fought her animal instincts and tried her best to remain calm. *What if one of his neighbors hears us and opens their door, only to get a gander at this crazy man standing in the doorway of his apartment butt naked?*

After collecting herself, Jade finally demanded answers from him, "Where have you been? I've been looking for you since last night! We had a date!"

"I was busy." The tone in Tom's voice along with his nonchalant, defiant attitude spoke volumes, not to mention his stance in the doorway, sporting only his birthday suit.

I remember where I was and what I was doing the day I got the stress-filled message from Jade. I was returning from a speaking engagement I had done at a church on Maryland's Eastern Shore. My 16-year old daughter and I were now riding home after having just finished lunch. I was standing at the gas station filling our rental car with gas for the ride when I turned on my cell phone and noticed I had several messages. The most urgent one was from Jade.

She was upset; I could hear it in her voice. The message sounded sad and restrained, with a charge of emotion just beneath the surface.

"Valerie, you'll never believe what that man did this morning! It's Jade, call me as soon as you can."

Hers was the first call I returned. As she related the events of that morning to me, questions came up in my mind one after another in rapid succession: *I thought they broke up; what were they doing going on a date? Who's the other woman? And why in the world would this man open the door and stand there wearing nothing more than the skin God gave him? How crazy is that?*

I settled on asking her the first question that had bounced into my head.

"What were you two doing going out on a date anyway? I thought you guys broke up weeks ago."

"We were trying to give it another go."

Obviously, it hadn't worked out as she had hoped and planned. The reason for that was clear: she wanted another go at the relationship, but Tom had already moved on. Jade still loved a man who no longer loved her.

Tom and Jade had met in the early 90's during a rough patch in Jade's life as a single mom. During that period of time, she didn't have a car. He was a kind and concerned workmate, so he offered to give her a ride back and forth to work each day until she bought a car. It seemed innocent enough, except that Tom began to feel drawn to Jade sexually and emotionally, and she was beginning to fall for him too. They spent lots of time together in the car, back and forth to work, talking and laughing for hours each day. After a while, the ride home was extended to an invitation inside Jade's home and a glass of wine.

There's an interesting phenomena that sometimes takes place between women and men that I refer to as the "Hero Factor." The Hero Factor is when a man does something unusually kind for a woman, or rescues her from some sort of adverse situation or condition, and she becomes emotionally (and many times sexually) attracted and attached to him. She envisions him as her hero, her savior, the one who rescued her from the lion's den. What usually prompts the man to do the rescuing in the first place is a strong attraction to the woman and a desire to elevate himself in her eyes. Before the "rescue," the woman may or may not have been attracted to the would-be rescuer. But after the rescue—when the "Hero Factor" has fully kicked in—the woman takes a dive for the man. Usually the fall is hard and fast.

Tom's desire to become a hero in Jade's eyes was no doubt prompted by his immediate attraction for her, considering the beautiful woman that Jade is, in appearance and in personality.

Jade's fall for Tom is an example of the "Hero Factor" in action. She finds herself in a predicament where she can't get to work each day without an undue amount of struggle. She's a single mom of two children and her life without a car isn't easy. Tom steps in and carries her to and from work each day, and even devotes a little extra time to help her run errands. The situation works splendidly for both of them—he's becoming a Hero and she's being rescued.

As I stated earlier, a woman who falls for a man due to the Hero Factor usually falls hard and fast. This was exactly the case with Jade. She quickly fell in love with Tom, and he fell deeply in love with her. Everything would have worked out perfectly, and you probably wouldn't be reading this story right now, had it not been for one significant detail: at the time, Tom was married with two children.

As the story goes, Tom's wife, Eleanor, probably knew very early on that her husband was having an affair. Women seem to be masters at sniffing out other women, even if something in their psyche causes them to ignore or deny their innermost feelings. Eleanor never had to actually catch Tom with Jade—Tom's absence, both emotionally and physically, was all she needed to deduce that something was amiss. One day, Tom and Eleanor were in the middle of an argument when Eleanor shocked Tom by yelling: "Stop calling me Jade!"

Eleanor knew. And now Tom knew that Eleanor knew. And of course, because Tom knew, Jade knew.

Despite the knowledge, things carried on in the same

fashion for years. Tom swore to Jade that he no longer slept with his wife, that she had exiled him to the living room couch. So it came as quite an unwelcome surprise to Jade when Tom revealed to her that Eleanor was expecting the couple's third child. Up until then, Tom's story had always been, "As soon as our two kids are old enough, I'm leaving so we can be together." And because they were in love and Jade had no reason to disbelieve him, she continued in the relationship. She viewed Tom as a man to be empathized with, a person who was trapped in a relationship with a wretched wife whom he no longer desired, yet couldn't leave because he couldn't bear to turn his back on his kids while they were still young and living at home. The addition of a new baby to the equation would certainly set Tom's freedom date back several more years. Jade was not happy.

Ironically, one of the tools Tom used to hold onto Jade was insisting that she not speak to, or keep company with, any other men. Tom was adamant about maintaining control over her interaction with the opposite sex. He frequently told her that if any other man tried to get next to her, he would hurt him or, if he had to, he would kill him. Whenever Jade was approached by another man, whether she was attracted to him or not, she would immediately let him know that there was no possibility of them getting together. Fear was an active and essential ingredient in their relationship. Tom used it to keep Jade away from any man who might treat her better. Most of the time, it was Tom's only weapon. If he was home with his wife and children and could not monitor Jade's movements, he felt he had to resort to threats and temper tantrums as a way to keep her in line while he was absent. Without being physically present, he had to make his presence known and felt somehow. This he managed to do by enforcing an inordinate amount of rules of engagement and behavior on Jade (which she complied with), and by threatening her into not interacting and communicating with other men.

Months later, Eleanor gave birth to a bouncing, healthy baby boy, and Tom was delighted to have his first son. The birth of Eli changed Tom's story. "I can't leave my son." Jade became even more furious; not so much because of the birth of the child (which was a happy event), but because Tom was exposed for the liar that he was. He had always maintained that he hadn't touched his wife sexually in years, that he was deprived of all love and intimacy in his own house, and that his wife had completely shut him out emotionally and physically.

Obviously, there wasn't as much sleeping on the couch as Tom had claimed. Or maybe he had company on the sofa. Either way, his story was missing one vital factor: the truth of his active sexual life with his wife.

In a way, Tom was living what could be considered a dream for some men: having two women at his disposal.

Jade's pain was partly because of Tom's lies and partly because of imagining her man in the arms and bed of another woman, even if that woman was his wife.

Over time, Jade got over the shock of Eleanor's pregnancy and had no choice but to accept the joyous birth of Eli and Tom's delight at having a son. She wished the baby and his mother well, but she couldn't help but feel deceived. Even still, she continued on in her relationship with Tom—their love was strong.

When Eleanor became pregnant yet again, Tom knew the news would send Jade packing, or at least he thought it would. So he decided to withhold the news from her for as long as he could. Since Jade and Tom worked at the same place of employment, news of Tom's wife's pregnancy eventually spread to co-workers and Tom knew he couldn't keep the news suppressed any longer. Jade found out and she blew the roof off. By the time Jade found out, Eleanor was five months pregnant with the couple's fourth child.

If ever there was a perfect time for Jade to walk away from Tom, this would have been it: his only son is now about two years old, his wife is pregnant with their fourth child, and he's making no moves whatsoever in the direction of leaving his family for Jade. All clear indications to Jade that Tom was staying right where he was.

However, Tom's story to explain away this latest pregnancy was that he only slept with his wife once, and that the pregnancy was a result of his slip-up in a weak moment after having had too much to drink—he was overcome with alcohol and had made love to his wife.

You know things have become somewhat convoluted when a married man feels he has to explain to someone else why he made love to his own wife.

Tom explained and explained, and placated and placated, until he felt that Jade was okay. Eventually, Jade got over the shock of Eleanor's fourth pregnancy for the couple and second pregnancy since she and Tom had begun seeing each other. Four months after Jade found out, Eleanor gave birth to a beautiful baby girl.

Tom definitely was not leaving his wife, his two older children, his toddler and his new baby girl. "I can't leave now", he told Jade.

To remain in the relationship, Jade had to hang on to what little shred of hope she had left that Tom would ever pack his bags and leave. The rope she hung onto was getting thinner and thinner by the year, but Jade wasn't quite ready to give up yet.

It did mean, however, that Tom had to have a vasectomy. At Jade's urging, he agreed to get neutered. That was the only solution that ensured he wouldn't get his wife pregnant again.

In the process of all these happenings, it became clear to Tom that Jade definitely was not leaving him.

A couple more years passed, with Jade and Tom still in their relationship when something unexpected happened: Eleanor left Tom.

She packed up all four of her kids and walked out on her adulterous husband. The rumor was that while Tom was tipping out on Eleanor, Eleanor had another man of her own.

In addition, for some years, Eleanor had been in school. Now, with a freshly earned Masters degree in hand, and a new high-paying position to go along with it, Eleanor had been working to set herself up rather nicely while Tom was out running around with Jade. Eleanor's children were now a little older, so she saw it as the perfect time to make her move; a move she had no doubt been planning for years.

After Eleanor left Tom, it seemed that nothing stood in the way of Jade and Tom moving in together and being the happy couple they always wished they could be had it not been for Tom's wife. Much to everyone's surprise, Tom decided he didn't want to live with Jade. He needed his own space after being in a marriage for so long, he told Jade. So he got his own apartment.

Jade told me that as soon as Eleanor left, there was an unidentifiable loss in her relationship with Tom; something had changed for the worse and could not be regained. Both she and Tom had felt it, though neither could name it. Thus began the irreversible decline of what Tom and Jade had had for over a dozen years.

Jade knew that it was the beginning of the end.

Tom now had to fulfill his parental duties during visitation with his children on certain assigned week-ends. Eleanor forbade Tom to have the couple's children around any other women, especially Jade. Tom complied, much to Jade's chagrin. Thus, Eleanor was able to set the parameters for Tom's behavior even when she wasn't around. According to Jade, when Tom would protest, Eleanor's histrionics quickly put him back in line. So Jade and Tom saw less and less of each other since Jade was not welcome at Tom's house on the weekends when he had his children; and he had not mustered the balls to tell his soon-to-be-ex-wife that who he welcomed into his home was his business, even if their children were there. Whether Tom went along with Eleanor's demands because he didn't have the balls to do otherwise, or because it was a convenient way for him to ease Jade out, we may never know.

Clearly, Eleanor's abandonment of her husband was not the boon to Tom and Jade's relationship they had expected it would be.

Jade was clearly no longer happy with the relationship and had other suitors who were anxious to have the opportunity to be the man in her life that Tom could no longer be.

Since Tom and Jade had experienced an immediate and noticeable decline in their relationship after Eleanor left, and now seeing less and less of each other because of Tom's visitation with his children, Tom became restless. Not restless in the normal sense of the word, but restless to see what may be out there waiting for him. After all, he had been married for almost 20 years. Surely the world and all the women in it had changed during those decades. Suddenly, Tom felt as if he had a lot of catching up to do.

So he began to hang out at night without Jade. He ran with his boys, with workmates, and with anyone else who would accompany him; and when no one could or would, he'd go by himself. His new found freedom in living on his own for the first time in over 20 years afforded him the delicious opportunity to go out anytime he desired and to return anytime too. *Not being monitored nightly is a beautiful thing for a newly separated man,* Tom probably thought.

Of course, all of Tom's hanging out with the boys and having fun without Jade started to rustle her feathers. She didn't understand his sudden apparent urge to relive his youth, and she certainly didn't understand why he was doing it without her. He told her he just needed a little time to himself since he had been married for so long. After he had been separated for more than a year, Jade began to pressure him to get started on his divorce from his wife so that they could move forward and, hopefully, get married. Though he never came out and said it, Tom wasn't interested in that proposal, or a proposal of any kind. He didn't file for divorce from his wife in what Jade thought was a timely fashion, so she gave him an ultimatum to get it done by a certain deadline. When the deadline came and went and Jade was still there, it was clear to Tom that, once again, he was off the hook.

The turn of events soured their relationship further, and eventually Jade noticed evidence of other women in Tom's life; not that he was trying to hide the fact that he had become sexually active with other women. He didn't really seem to care if Jade found out. He began to become more and more aloof, and she continued to question him about their relationship and where it was headed, since it was clearly not headed for the altar.

The answers were not forthcoming because Tom probably didn't know himself where their relationship was headed; after all, he barely knew where he was headed. He just knew he was hanging out, having fun, and enjoying being unencumbered for the first time in two decades. Other than that, he had few answers.

Tom did eventually file for divorce from his wife, and Jade was happy. But Jade's happiness was short-lived, because the divorce did not pave the way for them to get married. Tom told her that he just wasn't ready for marriage, and that he felt they should each date other people. He was doing that anyway.

So Tom and Jade parted ways. The parting was partial, however. Tom had already moved on in heart and mind, but Jade's heart was still in the mix with Tom. Her love for him had not fully evaporated, though it had taken a pretty bad beating and was declining rapidly. Thirteen years of company with a man is not easy to walk away from. So when there was an opportunity for her and Tom to rekindle their fire, she seized the chance. She and Tom decided to try to get back together and give it another go. He said he was tired of running around and was ready to settle down, again. So they made plans to go on a date that Friday night. Jade was excited and Tom probably was too. They had planned their evening, and he was to pick her up at 7 p.m.

When he hadn't arrived by 7:00 or even 7:30, Jade didn't think it strange. She figured he was just running a little late. She started calling him, but got no answer. By 10:00 o'clock that night, she was livid. Not only had he not come, he hadn't called and it was obvious that he purposely wasn't answering his phone.

The next morning, since he still wasn't answering the phone, she decided to pay him a visit. So she got up early, got dressed and arrived at his house at about 8:00 o'clock in the morning. She knocked and knocked. No answer. She banged.

Finally, he opened the door wide and stood there, as nude as the day is long. After looking at him and trying hard to find her composure, Jade glanced inside and saw a woman's dress and accessories lying on the sofa. *What a dog,* she thought.

"What do *you* want?" Tom asked, his tone defiant and insolent.

"What do you mean, what do I want? We had a date! What happened to you?"

"I was busy."

Apparently.

Right then, Jade knew in her heart of hearts that this man was not for her, and that she needed to just walk away. She had known it many times over the past 13 years, but she had never been able to bring herself to do it. Now, it was almost as if he was being so insolent and hurtful that she would have no choice *but* to walk away.

In a way, his standing there in the doorway with no clothes on was somewhat of an allegory: for 13 years he had exhibited brazen behavior and lack of concern for others. Any man who would openly call his wife by his mistress's name probably had definitely passed the bounds of decorum. This was just another example of the code he had been living by for so long.

Happily, Jade has moved on. Her heart is still making the transition, but she states frequently that she knows she should have left him long before she did. She is realizing what a beautiful woman she truly is, and how desirable she is as well. Many men have pursued her over the past 13+ years—as she is an extremely attractive woman—but she never gave them a passing thought. Now, she is open to the notion that she can be in a loving relationship with a man who truly values her for the gem she is. Jade is no longer willing to invest her time, effort and heart in a man who doesn't love her.

She is living in her new home, happy and whole.

God Speaks

What Sacred Lessons were revealed to Jade during her 13-year relationship with Tom?

What is true love—how does it look, act, speak and otherwise manifest?

Sacred Lesson #1: Learning to love ourselves well and first is critical to a successful romantic relationship.

Before you can love another, you must be in absolute and unconditional love with yourself. You cannot love someone else fully if you do not love yourself fully. Your love begins with you, of you and within you. The success of your romantic relationships is contingent upon you being able to accept, love and nurture every aspect of yourself. Jade's experience was a valuable lesson in self love.

Once we practice self love, it becomes easier for us to love others. Our partners in relationships can only show us as much love as we exhibit to and for ourselves, and we only attract to us those who love us as we love ourselves.

The amount of love you receive will be in direct proportion to the amount of self love you are able to develop. Conversely, you will accept just as much abuse from someone else as you heap upon yourself, and not a stitch more.

Jade is a beautiful woman, in body, mind and spirit. However, she did not see the extent of her own beauty and value, and hence was okay with someone else doing the same. When we don't treat ourselves lovingly, we open the door for others to treat us in ways that are unloving. Jade's experience underscores how critical self love is. Self love would have prevented her from being in a relationship with a man that was not available to her on many levels: mentally, spiritually, emotionally, and often times, (because of his family engagements and obligations) physically.

Jade has learned to honor and nurture herself, thus demonstrating to any potential partner that they must treat her with dignity, respect and love. As she nurtures herself, she will naturally attract men who nurture her, and are available to her.

Self love protects us from those who are unloving.

When you love yourself, you simply will not tolerate (or be in relationship with) other people who don't feel the same way about you.

When you love yourself fully, you become a powerful mate in any relationship you enter into. When you love yourself without reservation, you become more lovable and irresistible to others. When you love yourself and treat yourself as the valuable jewel that you are, others will see your value also and will treat you accordingly. Those who do not see your value simply will not be able to hang around you if you exhibit a high level of self-worth and self-value.

Self love is the key to getting and keeping the love we desire. It is the key to being lovable. The basis for loving ourselves is to remember God's unconditional love for us, which is total, complete and everlasting. Any time you are tempted to doubt your lovability, just take a moment to reflect on how much God loves you. When you do, you will see that you deserve only the best of love, including the love you give yourself.

For Jade, her lesson in self love has been well learned.

Sacred Lesson #2: Chocolate cake don't love me.

On many occasions, Jade wanted to leave Tom, but she was not able to. Her inner guidance told her to exit, but she didn't. Why not?

Every time Jade expressed to me that she knew she needed to leave Tom, she would end the discussion with the same sentence, "But I can't leave that man, it would tear my heart out."

When a woman loves a man so much that she feels parting with him would be like parting with a slice of herself, she will invent reasons to stay with him, despite all the evidence and Divine guidance to the contrary.

It's never easy to walk away from someone we love deeply and madly, even when the person is not treating us with honesty, dignity and respect. Jade is no different from me or any other woman who has loved a man that is not good for her. I call this common malady "Chocolate Cake" syndrome. Here's why.

I love chocolate cake. It's been one of my all-time favorite desserts since I was a little girl helping mom in the kitchen with her baking. I got to lick the mixer blades and the icing spoon. The whole affair sent me to my own little version of heaven. So it is deeply ingrained in my consciousness to love chocolate cake. Even today, I still believe chocolate cake is the best way to end an excellent meal. A meal isn't complete without chocolate cake at the end. I'll take chocolate cake with vanilla ice cream, with coffee, or all by itself. Chocolate cake doesn't need any company for me to be happy. I simply love chocolate cake.

Here's the dilemma: no matter how much I love chocolate cake, chocolate cake doesn't love me. It puts fat on me where I'd rather have muscle. It raises my cholesterol. It gives me a sugar high and, a few hours later, a sugar crash. It wants to clog my arteries. It wants to sit on my thighs for years in the form of cellulite. It has become abundantly clear to me that chocolate cake doesn't love me.

So then, why do I love something so much that doesn't love me, never has and never will? Why do I want to continue to enjoy and indulge in something that means no good for me other than a fleeting sweet and delectable taste on my palate? Where is the self love in that equation?

My love of chocolate cake and the fleeting sweetness it brings does not outweigh the lasting damage it causes. This is why it is wise for me to avoid it most of the time, and when I do choose to indulge, I use moderation.

The same is true of some men. There are certain men who are no good for the women who love them. Such a man may be eye candy, truly a pleasure to behold. He may be sweet tasting and delectable. He may even be smooth and rich. He may offer moments of intense pleasure. He may offer a love high, but a crash is sure to follow.

Such a man can be compared with chocolate cake because the lasting damage he can inflict outweighs any momentary pleasure he supplies. Just like chocolate cake.

Tom was Jade's chocolate cake. Yes, Tom loved Jade immensely, and he loved her for many years. However, somewhere along their mutual walk, he stopped loving her with the same intensity and fullness as he had formerly. In addition, Tom's love was coming from a place of dysfunction from the beginning because he was trying to make himself feel better because of his failing marriage. Jade's problem was that she continued to love Tom as a romantic partner even after his love for her had begun to fade away. As stated earlier, she frequently commented to me that leaving him would rip her heart out. "I can't do it, Valerie. It would break my heart." On more than one occasion, I admit that, as a friend, my heart was almost broken observing her trying to prevent her heart from being broken.

I felt her pain because I have had the same pain. I've been in love with a man who didn't love me as much as I loved him, or so I thought. And it hurt. It was a hurt I thought I would never recover from. It was a hurt that made me cry until my eyes and head stung with pain. And just when I thought I was over it all and couldn't cry anymore, I would see something, or hear a song, or smell a fragrance, and all the memories would come rushing back to me and I'd be in a heap on the bed again.

So the question for all women is: how do I avoid the pain of being in love with a man who doesn't love me the way I love him? How do I know true love when I see it, a love that will nurture my soul?

Sacred Lesson #3: How to recognize true love.

Recognizing true love can be made easier if we have a road map, or a guide, to show us what true love looks like, and how it manifests in our lives. Use the following guide when testing your love for yourself, and then your love for others. Also, hold any potential partner up to this test to see how loving they are truly willing to be.

1. True love endures.
Today it is common for folks to get married and, be-

fore the wedding is completely paid for, they've filed for divorce. Most people today are not committed to a relationship of any kind, especially when the relationship becomes "difficult." It is precisely at these times that we must remember a key component of true love: endurance. The word **endure** has three pertinent definitions:

Definition 1: ***To remain firm under suffering or misfortune without yielding.*** Tom was in a marriage that did not satisfy his needs and wants, or those of his wife. He had once been committed to his wife, but when they came upon hard times, he was no longer committed. Tom would have benefited from practicing endurance.

The word endure in this sense would have meant that Tom would have continued with his wife, faithfully, without yielding to internal pressures or desires. He would have been able to remain firm under suffering. What does that mean? It doesn't mean that we should suffer in silence when we are unhappy in our relationships. However, when a marriage is in trouble, the solution is not to throw in the towel, nor is it to go out and have an extramarital affair. The solution is to find ways to regain the loving relationship both parties in the marriage desire. This loving process requires time, work, energy and desire. The process requires endurance.

Endurance in a marriage that is not happy can mean working to do our best to improve ourselves, which will ultimately improve our relationship. After all, if we are not happy in the marriage or relationship, do we not have responsibility and ownership of our own state of being, and whether or not we are happy? We must own our share of why the marriage is not happy and seek ways to correct whatever behaviors we are demonstrating that serve to lessen the level of happiness. It is easy to stand and point a finger at a spouse or mate who seems to be the problem. Few of us are willing to stand in the mirror and point a finger at the one who stares back at us. However, the person in the mirror is truly the only one who can effect a change in your life, not your spouse.

It is vital to our own state of happiness to look within at our inner thoughts, feelings, ideas and beliefs to find what may be contributing to an unpleasant relationship. Surely, if we look long enough, we will uncover much within ourselves that could give rise to unhappiness in our romantic relationships. No one is exempt from having inner turmoil, and that turmoil makes its way to the surface and manifests itself in the form of turbulent marriages and unhappy partnerships. Turning within to find the cause and root of unhappiness in our relationships is the most loving thing we can do for ourselves and for those we are in a romantic partnership with. Indeed, it is the most loving course for us to take with regard to every other person in our lives, not just those we are romantically involved with.

The process of turning within requires time. It takes time for us to uncover our internal disorder, and even more time for us to get it in order. The process requires endurance.

In addition, when we meet a person who could be a potential romantic partner, we want to examine that person closely for the quality and level of endurance they've been able to master. Ask your Self:

- *How has this person handled pressures in previous relationships?*
- *Have they had (or do they have) a tendency to run away every time problems arise?*

- *How do they handle the heated situations that invariably arise in relationships?*
- *Have they endured when called upon to do so?*
- *Is my inner Divine guidance telling me that this person will endure through difficult times with me while remaining faithful?*

Another way of looking at endurance is to substitute the word "love" for the qualities that endurance displays. Thus, another aspect of love could be defined as:

Love remains firm under suffering or misfortune without yielding.

True love means your partner will stay with you and remain firm under suffering and misfortune without yielding. It doesn't mean that we endure anything and everything, but we learn to recognize the difference between what we need to endure and what is not for us by listening to the voice of our inner wisdom from God. Though there are many lessons to be learned from being in abusive relationships, I am not advocating this path. Make sure that you use your spiritual discernment to determine who you should endure with. If a person treats you with little regard and does not honor you, is this the person you should be in an enduring relationship with? Only you will know the answers based upon the guidance you receive from God speaking to you.

Definition 2*: To regard with acceptance or tolerance.* Each mate must endure the less desirable traits of the other in order to have a fulfilling relationship. The key to doing this is to know your own internal issues that require your spiritual work and attention, and to give these parts of yourself what they need in order to become whole. While you are working on these internal issues, there is a need for you *to regard* *yourself with acceptance and tolerance.* There is a need for you to endure with you.

Once you have learned to accept yourself—all of yourself—there is now room for you to accept the less than desirable traits of your mate. If you have accepted the desirable traits about yourself, and, more importantly, the less than desirable parts of yourself, you are well on your way on the journey to wholeness.

Of course, acceptance and tolerance have limits. In each relationship, there are, what Dr. Phil calls, "deal breakers." A deal breaker is something you will not put up with in a relationship, and you have clearly articulated that to your mate. I have a few deal breakers, or reasons for me to leave a serious and committed romantic relationship: a partner who would continually cheat on me, a partner who decides to settle our problems with a raised hand aimed at me, a partner who becomes addicted to drugs or excessive alcohol, or a partner who thinks crime is a viable option. These represent a few of my personal deal breakers, and since I do not conduct myself in such a fashion, I would not attract a partner that acts in such a fashion. These deal breakers represent factors, situations and circumstances that I will not allow into my life. I will not abide a man who consistently does not honor his word, nor one who would purposely harm me in any way; nor a man who thinks that alcohol, drugs and crime are an acceptable mode of operation. Though I can love such a man, I would not be in a relationship with him. We are required to love all, but we are not required to be involved in a partnership with all.

Your personal list of deal breakers may be different from mine. We each have a list of conditions we know would cause us to walk away from a relationship. Usually, these comprise a short list.

Outside of the short list of deal breakers, while our partner may have certain habits and attitudes that we find irksome, they do not constitute a reason to give up on the relationship. We must regard our mate with acceptance and tolerance while we give them loving feedback and the room they need to improve.

However, what seems to happen most often in relationships is that small habits and differences that have not been effectively addressed can eventually lead to a deal breaker. For instance, if a man or woman is consistently ignored by his or her mate, it could lead to him or her casually building a relationship with someone other than their mate. The relationship may seem casual and innocent at first, just as Jade and Tom's relationship started out. Over time, the person may find that they are emotionally drawn to the new friend, which leads to a deeper level of connection. In time, it could turn into a romantic entanglement that neither party was prepared for. Such was the case with Jade and Tom. Tom was not seeking an affair, nor was Jade seeking to have a relationship with a married man. However, one thing led to another, and before they knew it, they were between the sheets.

Cheating is never the answer to an unhappy marriage or relationship, as cheating is an act of dishonesty and betrays a lack of integrity. If one will lie to oneself, one will lie to everyone else. Cheating also betrays a lack of courage on the part of the cheater because they haven't stood up in their relationship and effectively addressed what they want and expect, and how they'd like to get it. If the cheater doesn't work on their relationship, but instead chooses to sneak around to get what they want, they've robbed their mate of the opportunity to improve and grow in the relationship. If we do not clearly communicate to our partners our perception of what's wrong in the relationship, and what we would like to get from it, whose fault is it if we don't get what we want? It certainly isn't our partner's fault. Once again, it would pay dividends for us to look in the mirror.

This aspect of endurance calls for us *to accept ourselves and others as they are.* The purpose of our relationships is not for us to fix or repair our partner. We are not there to make them into a different person, or to overhaul them. We are not there to make them do anything they don't want to do. Acceptance means that we love our partner as they are right now, while simultaneously holding the vision of all they could be.

In short, we are called upon to exhibit this definition and facet of endurance in two important ways:

1. First, there is a need *to regard yourself with acceptance and tolerance* while you work on your own personal areas in need of improvement.

2. Second, there is a need for you *to regard your partner with acceptance and tolerance* while you lovingly communicate your desires to them and afford them the space and time they require to address their own internal areas that are in need of improvement.

Once again, let us substitute the word "love" in our further definition of endurance:

Love regards oneself and others with acceptance and tolerance.

Definition #3: ***To undergo (as a hardship) esp. without giving in.*** This definition adds yet another layer to endurance: to stay in a relationship, even when it is rocky, without giving in or giving up.

You've probably heard, "If you can't stand the heat, get out of the kitchen." My version of this saying is, "if it gets hot, stay in the kitchen and finish cooking."

Endurance dictates that we stay in the kitchen, even when it's hot.

Today, it is almost fashionable to quickly give up on committed relationships and just walk away.

The value in not giving up when your relationship gets rocky is that you will discover things about yourself that need to be acknowledged, addressed and ultimately healed. There are parts of us buried deep within that will only arise when put under the heat and pressure of a relationship. Essentially, we need to go into the kitchen of our lives to see what's cooking. When the heat of relationships causes our undesirable issues to surface, view it as a blessing. The event, no matter how dramatic or painful, can be viewed as a golden opportunity to begin important and vital work on that particular part of our internal landscape that needs healing.

Many times we ask the wrong question when a mate does something that we feel angers or upsets us. The question we tend to ask is, "Why are you doing this to me?"

The more beneficial question to ask would be, "What can I learn from this?"

The former question casts us in the victim role, with no way out except for someone else to stop doing something to us. This view takes control and power away from us. It causes us to look outside of ourselves for the answers to what would make us happy. This is a horrible position to be in because it means that we will never be happy unless someone else does something (or stops doing something) to us. There is no power in that position; it makes us the unhappy effect and someone else the controlling cause in our lives. Apart from being an undesirable idea, it is purely false.

You and only you are the boss of your life. No one else is in control of your life except you. The sooner you are able to realize and accept this truth, the sooner you can be about the business of getting your life on course for where you'd like it to go. The longer you choose to play a victim and give someone else power over the level of happiness you will experience, the longer you will remain unhappy.

This definition of endurance says that we must be willing to undergo a hardship without giving in. A victim gives in. A victim has no power. You are not a victim. You hold the power and sway over your life, and hence over *all* your relationships. The only thing left for you to do is realize that fact and act in accord with it. When you do, and you decide that you will be happy, then you will be happy. Remember that your true power lies in you knowing that you have the power.

Asking the latter question, (what can I learn from this?) gives room for you to grow in new, and sometimes surprising, ways. You see, each difficulty—if viewed as such—has within it the potential to teach you something valuable about yourself. The hardships that arise in relationships help us to see where we are being rubbed the wrong way and alert us to an internal issue that is the true cause of the pain. In order to answer the question, "what can I learn from this?", we'll have to take the focus off any external factors or persons and direct it where it ought to be: within.

Be determined to stand in the face of hardship without giving in. When you don't allow yourself to play the victim role (which seems to come easy), you are showing self love. You are retaining your power rather than giving away the keys to your happiness by blaming someone else. When we love ourselves enough to not give in to victim mentality and we stand firm through the hardship and learn from the experience, we have triumphed. The next time that situation presents itself, we will behave a little differently. These incremental steps toward being a better person yield great results over time. During the process, the most loving thing we can do is to simply endure.

Love doesn't run when hardships come. Perfect love throws fear outside, so what would love be running away from anyway? Love doesn't fear anything or anyone, so it has no reason to run. A person who runs from you every time hardships arise does not display love. You would do well to ask yourself if they should be considered as a serious partner. The times when we most need our partner, and other loved ones around us, is when things are not going well in our lives. It is at those times that we may look to those we love in our lives to stand strong when we are not able. Their loyal encouragement can help us recover sooner and get back on our feet. Conversely, you will do the same for them when their difficulties arise.

If the person you love most runs at the first hint of trouble, do they really love you? Let's explore this question.

If a person is only willing to be around you when all is going well in your life, and when you experience hardships they disappear, you must question yourself about their ability to be a true and lasting friend, confidant and companion. There are some folks who are only in our lives to take from us, and don't presently show a capacity to give. They only stick around when we are giving to them, but when we are going through a difficult time and are not in a position to give as much, they are absent. When you notice this type of pattern with someone, especially a person who claims to be in love with you, you have two choices.

One option is that you can continue moving forward in a relationship with this person. If you do, be prepared to be disappointed frequently. Understand that you will never be able to rely on this person to be in your corner when you need them to be. This person has already shown themselves to be a deserter. Until they learn to conduct themselves otherwise, they will continue this pattern. A deserter is like a person who works on a cruise ship, but who does little work and is always busy eating or enjoying the cruise. When the cruise ship hits upon a rough patch and begins to sink, the person quickly grabs a life boat and escapes alone, selfishly leaving all others behind.

If you choose this person, you are also giving up your right to complain about them. You already know what you're getting yourself into, so when they desert you, as you know they will, you have no right to talk about them to your other friends or anyone else. You chose this relationship, so accept it and shut up.

One day you will discover that you deserve to a have a mate, and friends, who will stick with you during the times when your life gets a little ugly (or even very ugly), without immediately darting out of the first open door or window. When you come to believe and accept that you are good enough and worthy to have such a mate, you will ditch all the deserters in your life.

Your second option is to lovingly let this person go and not accept them as a mate. You can still send them love, but keeping your distance may be the wisest approach; which may very well be what your inner guidance is indicating to you about this person anyway. This is especially true if the person has deserted you on more than one occasion.

How many times would you let a dog bite you before you decide that the dog is dangerous?

While we do not expect others to rescue us from our difficulties in life, we know true love by its ability to stand with us even when it is not easy; to accept us even when we are exhibiting what some would call unacceptable behavior; and to be willing to undergo hardships with us without giving up or giving in.

Remember to substitute love in this definition of endurance as well:

Love undergoes hardship without giving in or giving up.

True love endures.

2. True love is patient.

Patience is defined as:

Bearing pains or trials calmly or without complaint. When a person is patient with you, they are showing you another aspect of love. When we are patient with others, or "not hasty" (as another definition of the word states), we give them one of the greatest gifts one person can give another: time and attention. When we patiently allow our mate the time they need to grow and evolve in all aspects of life, we are displaying love.

There are few shortcuts to a happy union. Patience is required for a loving relationship to continue to blossom, mature and nurture both parties. In the beginning of most relationships, each of the partners feels excitement and the exhilaration of a new love. After a while, the neophyte stage of the relationship is over and the couple settles into a different stage. This stage is not as exciting as the neophyte stage and may cause the couple to not pay as much attention to each other as they did in the beginning.

After Tom and his wife had been married for many years and they'd had two children, things began to cool off. There wasn't much excitement anymore, which caused Tom to become restless and ask himself what else was out there.

Patience would have helped Tom stay faithful to Eleanor. Patience is not hasty, but allows time for others to grow. So even if a marriage does not have all the zest and zip it once had, patience would enable the mates to work on their relationship and, over time, restore it to a level of excitement and exhilaration both mates enjoy. If we've held negative patterns in our relationships for years, we may not be instantly able to change them. Patience is required.

This definition of patience says that we would bear pains or trials calmly, without complaint. Let us understand an important distinction between putting up with certain behaviors we may not like, and becoming a doormat for someone's feet.

There is nothing about patience or love that requires us to bear someone else's negativity, meanness or abuse. There is no need to remain with a person who would abuse you in any way, including mentally, physically or otherwise. There is no reason to continue with anyone who does not honor you in the way you desire to be honored.

On the other hand, there are, once again, habits and attitudes that our mates may exhibit that we do not like. These habits do not pose a threat to us, but our reaction to them may be annoyance, irritation or anger. We do not like what they do, so there is a need for patience in these instances. We may really feel like punching the person in the face, but then we realize that that would not be a good idea. There is a need to bear trials calmly. There is a need for patience.

In addition, this definition of patience means that we do not complain. There is a saying that fits here well: "Complainers are always heard, but they are never respected." Complaining is one of the worst possible things you could do with your mouth. It takes the power out of your hands and affirms the power in the problem. Complainers don't usually take action to change anything, as their energy is expended in blowing hot air. The complaining spirit also infects anyone who listens and seeks to poison them also. Complaining also acts as a magnet to attract to you more things to complain about. It is unhealthy and useless to complain about anything, and will only damage your relationships.

The antidote to complaint is to give thanks. We will never be able to change a situation if we continue to repeat the problem's hold and power over us in the form of complaining. However, if we affirm thanks for all we do have, we miraculously cause those positive aspects of our relationships to grow and the less desirable parts to wither and eventually die. The more thanks we give, the less we will have to complain about.

We know true love by its ability to stay calm and not complain even when things do not go well, or when there are trials that arise in the relationship.

Love bears pains or trials calmly and without complaint.

3. True love is kind.
There are two definitions of "kind" that we will focus on here. The first is:

Affectionate, loving. Affection is defined as a tender

attachment or a fondness. True love treats ones self and others with tender attachment and fondness. This does not mean that every person expresses affection and love in the same way. While leaving room for individuality, true love, or kindness, expresses itself. Even though there are variations in how kindness and affection are expressed, and there are degrees of expression as well, we know when someone is treating us kindly, with fondness, and when they are not.

Though he was affectionate and loving toward Jade, Tom did not treat his wife with kindness.

There is only one reason why you would tolerate any person treating you with a lack of love in the form of kindness and affection. That reason is because you do not lavish yourself with kindness and affection. Once again, the quality of love—in the form of kindness and affection—that you are able to attract is an exact representation of the kindness and affection you gift to yourself. Consider the following questions, which will provide you with a barometer of how much kindness and affection you heap upon yourself.

Ask yourself:

- ***Do I take good care of my body by providing it with high quality, healthful food, regular exercise and plenty of fresh water?*** The way we treat our bodies is a prime indicator of how much affection we have for ourselves. Show affection for your body by giving it the best quality of food you can afford, exercising adequately, and drinking half your body weight in ounces of water each day. The amount of affection you have for your body is being displayed to others every day by the way you look. Perhaps there is room for improvement in this area for you, as it is for me.

- ***Do I get enough rest to restore my body and to
  dream sufficiently?*** Each body has its own needs
  for rest, and you show love to your body by giving
  it the rest it tells you it needs. Your body speaks to
  you all day long, and all night long too. When you
  rest well, your mental faculties are sharper, and
  your day proceeds with less stress. When you rest
  deeply, you are able to enter the dream state, which
  is where you can receive many important messages and guidance from God.

It has been noted by scientists that a lack of sleep, especially the dream state of sleep, will cause a person to
become mentally imbalanced within days. God created
the dream state for each of us to enter each night. When
you do not sleep well enough or deep enough to reach
this important level of sleep, your mind, emotions and
body suffer. Show affection for yourself by getting all
the rest your body needs.

I've had challenges with this, as it used to be my pattern to attempt to achieve an inhuman amount of tasks
in one day. This pattern of behavior caused me to miss
out on a lot of sleep and I rarely ever power napped.
The longer I went depriving myself of needed rest, the
more it became evident to everyone around me that a
crash was coming. Sure enough, after a period of time
of running around wildly without sufficient down time,
I found myself in bed, not being able to get up. After
going through this cycle many, many times, I began to
realize that I was not giving myself enough love and affection. It caused me to tune in and listen to my body.
Now, when I feel tired, I go and put my feet up and take
a brief power nap to recharge myself. I go to bed when
I feel sleepy rather than trying to cram one more thing
in before retiring. I've learned that tomorrow is another

day. A useful affirmation for you if you have established a pattern of trying to do everything in the world
before going to bed is:

I am enough. I am complete. I am whole.
I am enough.

Repeat this series of affirmations several times and
then go to bed without worrying about a single thing
that you didn't accomplish.

- *Do I get regular bodywork done, such as mas-
  sages, or chiropractic adjustments?* This may
  sound like a luxury, but aren't you worth it? If you
  believe you are worth it, you will find the time
  and the money to get it done. It will become one of
  the essential ways that you heap love, kindness
  and affection on your body.
- *Do I take good care of my hair, skin and nails?*
  This too is a measure of how well you treat—and
  show fondness for—yourself.
- *Do I wear the best quality of clothing that I can
  afford?* Wearing attractive and appealing clothing
  does something to the psyche of the wearer. When
  you look good and know it, you feel better and
  you walk taller. Treat yourself to clothing that cel-
  ebrates your personality and lifts your spirits! Buy
  the highest quality of clothing that your wise and
  carefully considered fiscal plan will allow.

If it is your sincere intention and desire to do so,
there are many ways to show affection and fondness
for yourself, you need only use your creative energies.

Certainly, if you are in love with yourself and you
show it by lavishing yourself with the highest quality
care, and affection, you will naturally attract others

who will treat you in the same way. This is why self love is so critical. Not only does it sustain you, it also enables you to become a magnet that will attract the best and highest quality of love from others.

To help you even further along on the road to passionate self care and self fondness, reflect for a moment on your awesome and wondrous body. The body God gave you when you came into this world is an absolute rhapsody in motion. Appreciatively consider some of its most amazing features:

- Your Brain—the most powerful super computer ever designed and implemented. Even the most sophisticated machines that humans have been able to devise are crude and rudimentary when compared to the seemingly endless capacity of the brain and its ability to perform complex computations easily and effortlessly. The sub-conscious mind is actually a powerful super computer that remembers *every single thing that has ever happened to you,* including your life in the womb.
- Your heart—which has been beating non-stop since you were only a few weeks old in the womb of your mother. It works incessantly for you around the clock. No matter what you are doing, it is beating. Even if your heart doesn't work perfectly, give thanks that it's gotten you this far.
- Your internal organs—which perform thousands of functions per day on your behalf with no conscious direction from you. Your liver, kidneys, gall bladder, pancreas and all of your other organs function without you telling them what to do. They operate under the direction of a beautiful and harmonious system that keeps you alive every day. Even if your internal organs do not function at op-

timum levels, be thankful for what they are able to do for you every day.

- Your limbs—which do your bidding all day long, many times without your acknowledgement or appreciation. Every so often, stop and contemplate how much your legs, feet, arms and hands do for you; then give a silent prayer of heartfelt thanks.
- Your skin—which is your body's largest organ, works tirelessly to keep out of your body what shouldn't be in and keep in what shouldn't get out. Your skin is never at rest, letting sweat out to cool your internal organs (which would all cook if you exercised and were not able to release the heat through sweat), and keeping you protected from any number of dangers that you are not even aware of. Your skin is one great big barrier that is able to keep you safe in the face of a daily onslaught from attackers, some miniscule and others that are not so small. You may not love the color or condition of your skin, but be assured that it is a perfect gift from God; a gift you couldn't live without. Today, thank God for the skin you're in and rejoice in whatever it looks like.

There's so much more to you than what is listed here, but this list is a good start to help you see the value of the treasure you carry around every day in the form of a flesh, blood bone and body. Don't take it for granted or carelessly forsake it, which is tantamount to a mild form of self-hatred. Rather, nurture and care for your body in a program of passionate self-care. Once you make extreme self care a non-negotiable habit, you will begin to attract others who feel the same way about themselves, which means that they will more than likely have the capacity to feel the same way about you.

The second definition of the word "kind" is:

Of a forbearing nature, gentle. To understand this aspect of kindness—which is also an aspect of love—we must first understand forbearance. Forbearance is defined as:

A refraining from the enforcement of something (as a debt, right, or obligation) that is due. This is quite a powerful concept; in essence it means to let someone off the hook. To extend forbearance denotes extending mercy and grace to another. As we've already discussed, before you can extend mercy and grace to another, you must gift yourself with mercy and grace by letting yourself off the hook. Many of us feel we owe a debt to someone for something we may have said or done. Some of us feel that we have an obligation to others in our lives, and that obligation may interfere with us living at our potential or living the life we desire.

Kindness, in the form of forbearance, allows us to let ourselves off the hook for whatever debts we may be carrying around. God has offered us an "out" when it comes to obligation and debt, and that is to allow the Holy Spirit to bear our burdens for us. We have grace and mercy extended to us right now whether we realize it or not.

Since God has extended grace and mercy to us, does it matter if anyone else does or doesn't? If God has already granted us forbearance by showing love through kindness, how is it possible to still feel indebted or obligated to another human being for something we may have said or done? Though it is loving and wise to make amends if we are wrong and to correct our mistakes as soon as we make them, to wallow in self-pity, shame and guilt is unloving and unkind.

There is a significant distinction between commitment (which is positive) and obligation (which may not be positive). Commitment means that you voluntarily decide to stay with someone in a relationship and you state your intention to do so. Obligation denotes being constrained, or restricted. We do not want to be in relationship with others because we are obligated to do so. We want to be in loving relationships that feed and nurture our soul. When our soul is well fed, we are ready to commit, but we are not obligated to do so.

Kindness does not obligate, constrain, restrict or bind. Kindness lets us off the hook, which means that we lovingly allow ourselves to soak in the fullness of God's grace, mercy, compassion and forgiveness that are already in our possession. Kindness lets others off the hook too by helping us to remember that no one owes us anything. The more you resonate with this truth, the happier you will be.

You will know true love by how kind it is, as expressed by affection, gentleness and forbearance. *Love is kind.*

4. True love is not envious nor does it boil over with jealousy.

There is a mistaken belief among some women that if a man behaves in a jealous fashion, he is demonstrating how much he loves the object of his jealousy. This belief, as mistaken as it is, has managed to hold many women captive in relationships that are unloving because the mate is extremely jealous of everyone their mate comes into contact with. A jealous person doesn't need evidence, they assume the worst.

One of the synonyms for envy is malice. The word malice implies an intent or desire to hurt another. Considering this definition, envy and jealousy are equal to causing hurt or pain to another intentionally. Though we may not think that envy and jealousy are driven by a motive to hurt someone else, as you can see from the word association, they are.

In the case of Tom and Jade, there are several points in their story where envy and jealousy played a role. Tom was intensely jealous of Jade, to the point that he would threaten any man whom he felt wanted to get close to her. He would threaten Jade by telling her that he would hurt any man she talked to. This behavior can be identified as unhealthy at best, and malicious at worst.

Jade's fear of what Tom would do to any man who showed an interest in her usually kept her from pursuing a relationship with any man who was interested. Jade, being the attractive woman that she is, was often approached by available men who wanted to date her. Her habit was to immediately turn down every man who ever approached her, as Tom was always on her mind. Part of her reluctance to see any other man was Tom's flair for throwing tantrums and becoming overly demonstrative about his feelings when it came to other men. It caused Jade to become fearful of what may happen.

Love and fear cannot co-exist. They are polar opposites. Therefore, if you are in a position where you feel fear in a relationship because your mate is overly jealous or envious—to the point of threatening you or others—you must question whether your relationship is built on love or on fear. If you are in a fear-based relationship, or if jealousy and envy are recurring themes in your relationship, it is unlikely that the relationship will last in its current state. Envy and jealousy are like handcuffs that keep one imprisoned to the fears and insecurities of another. If you are in such a relation-

ship, seek God's guidance through prayer, and follow
the lead of your inner voice.

*Love is never envious nor does it boil over with
jealousy.*

5. True love is not boastful, vainglorious or haughty. It is not conceited, arrogant and inflated with pride.

When we love another, we decide we will not exhibit excessive pride in our romantic relationships. A
level of personal pride is necessary for excellent self
care and nurturing, but excessive pride is unloving.

One way we can experience more love in our relationships is to keep them absent of excessive pride,
haughtiness and boastfulness.

Pride has a tendency to set us up for a big fall. Have
you ever had a humbling experience right after thinking you were the best thing since sliced bread? I've
been embarrassed more times than I care to remember,
and the humiliation usually came on the coat tails of
me exhibiting some kind of overly prideful behavior.
There are times when we know we look good, and
things are going our way all day, and we have a little
extra swagger in our gait. It can be uplifting to feel this
way, which can be positively reinforcing. However,
when we feel we are better than others, and that others
are inferior to us and we look down upon them, we are
setting ourselves up for a fall, and it probably won't be
pretty. Thinking we are better than the next person is
prideful and haughty. "Pride before a crash" was a saying I heard frequently while growing up. I didn't fully
understand what it meant then. Now, after many help-
ings of humble pie, I can better understand what the
saying means.

There is no person on this earth who is better than

any other person, as we are all created in the image and likeness of God. We are all special, we are all gifted, and we are all precious to God, without differentiation. To recognize and acknowledge that every single person on this earth, from beggar to king, from pauper to prince, is a unique and priceless creation of God's is the most loving way to view every other person on this earth.

Such a loving *world view* would prevent bigotry, as bigotry has at its roots feelings of superiority. Conceit has feelings of inferiority at its roots, which is equally unappealing.

This loving *world view* would also prevent all war, crime, abuse and hatred, as each of us would recognize the other as the precious creation of God that we all are.

This view would likewise cause our relationships to flourish, as we gaze at our mates and see God's creative expression in human form. How loving.

God is not a respecter of persons, so how could we be?

True love is not boastful, haughty or inflated with pride.

6. Love is not rude, and does not act unbecomingly. Rude is defined as: offensive in manner or action; discourteous; uncivilized, savage; coarse, vulgar.

When Tom stood in the doorway of his apartment in his bare skin, without a shred of clothing or concern for himself, Jade or anyone else, he exhibited the height of unbecoming and rude behavior. When he questioned her insolently, asking her what she wanted, even Jade, who had known Tom for over a decade, was caught by surprise at his rude and blatant manner. Tom's choice to act with rudeness toward Jade further illustrated his

lack of love. Love is not offensive, discourteous or vulgar, all of which Tom personified that Saturday morning, much to Jade's shock and dismay.

When we stand in the face of love, there is no rudeness or vulgarity—we see only kindness, compassion
and consideration.

Love is not rude nor does it act unbecomingly.

7. Love (God's love in us) does not insist on its own
rights or its own way, for it is not self-seeking. One of
the most significant ways we can recognize true love is
by the absence of ego.

A threat is an interesting thing: it only holds power
if the one threatened believes it. If the person who is
threatened does not believe the threat (or chooses to
stop believing a threat that they had previously believed), the threat immediately loses all power. A threat
needs fear to survive. Without the mechanism of fear
in place, a threat is completely powerless.

I read a long time ago in a book on child rearing that
screaming at a child is never effective. Firstly, when a
parent yells at a child for their misdeeds, not only does
it portray a lack of self-control on the part of the parent, but it also tells the child that no further action will
be taken. The child comes to see that when the parent
yells, they are not doing anything else, including punishing them. Some parents resort to yelling at their
children often, most of the time spewing meaningless
threats. The child quickly begins to realize that their
parent is full of hot air when they yell, thus the yelling
becomes ineffective.

The same thing happens with adults. When a person
threatens another person, rarely do they want to follow
through with the threat. They are usually hoping that
the fear and intimidation will keep the person in line,

giving the threat its power. If the person who is being threatened decides to push through their fear, they would probably find that the person who was issuing the threats would not follow through.

Only ego, with its fears and insecurities, thinks that resorting to threats is a good idea to keep one's mate in line. It is a form of control, which is another trick of the ego and betrays a gross lack of love.

For Jade, it became evident that their relationship was more about Tom and his insecurities than it was about love.

Love never threatens.

Love also does not insist on having its own way. I've heard many times that, in relationships, we can choose to be right, or we can choose to be happy, but it is unlikely that we will be able to accomplish both at all times.

As with all other aspects of your relationship, it is up to you to choose what supports you and what doesn't. If you are in a relationship with a person who is self-serving, consistently and persistently rude, or who threatens you into doing what they want you to do, is yours a loving relationship?

Remember, love doesn't need to be right. It doesn't need to insist on its own way. It doesn't need to do you in so it can win. Love has no need to win.

True love is not self-seeking.

8. Love is not touchy or fretful or resentful.

Touchy is defined as: ***marked by a readiness to take offense on slight provocation.***

If you grew up in a home with siblings, you no doubt know how touchy children can be. Siblings can take offense with the slightest provocation. One of the favorite annoyances of children is to point a finger close to their sibling's face without actually touching them. As an older sister to two brothers and a sister, I know what it can be like to be provoked. When we were growing up, it seemed that my younger brother had as his life's ambition to annoy and irritate me. He was excellent at his ambition.

However, as we grow and mature, we learn to not take offense at every little provocation. It becomes too taxing on our spirit to respond to every little annoyance or to take offense at every little thing. Most of the little things people do that irritate us would best be ignored. This is especially true in relationships, where close quarters and familiarity could cause us to become easily annoyed and irritated at our mate.

What I love about love is that it does not rush to take offense. This connotes that love would rather give a person another chance than get irritated and angry. It also means that love is faithful and trusting, as it believes that there is no malice involved in the slight irritations we experience in life. Love doesn't desire to get angry, upset or take offense.

Fretful is: *to become vexed or worried, to become agitated.* Here we have wise counsel in taking the loving path, which is a path free of worry and agitation. Though folks around us may not always act the way we would like, and though our situation may not always be desirable, love would help us remain free of worry and agitation. Relationships are fraught with opportunity to become worried or agitated, but we have an opportunity to express self-love when we refuse to worry. Worry causes stress in the mind and in the body, which quickly leads to illness and disease. We usually worry about things that may never happen; rarely do all of our worries come to pass. To worry is to display a lack of faith and trust that all things work together for our good. When we worry or become fretful, it means that we do not have faith in our own internal coping mechanisms which God granted each of us, and which have the potential to rise to meet any adverse condition that may occur in our lives and help us through it with grace.

Worry and fret betray a lack of self-love. Being loving and kind to ourselves means that we learn to walk faithfully with the knowing that all things will work out well, and to be thankful for God's presence in our lives, which can help us overcome anything. There is never truly a reason to worry. There is nothing positive that can issue from worry. Be kind to yourself, don't worry, and don't fret. God's got your back.

Resentment is defined as: **persistent ill will at something regarded as a wrong, insult or injury.**

Resentment is one of the worst emotions we can harbor. It takes a toll on the body and causes all manner of illness and disease, not the least of which is cancer.

When we resent others, we carry a heavy load. We are harboring ill will in our mind and spirit, which, if released, would make more room for God's spirit to flow within us. Resentment is like a sore that gets infected and festers. When we resent someone, the resentment tends to grow over time, and gets progressively worse if we do nothing to release it. Just like an infected sore, it is ugly and threatens our good health.

There is only one solution to resentment, and that is to flood it with love and forgiveness. Even if you resent someone who may have done terrible things to you, you are called upon to forgive. It may take years to actually accomplish, but the important thing here is that you have the intent to love, forgive and release all resentment toward them. The person who is the object of your resentment is not being hurt by it, you are. The resentment you harbor doesn't teach anyone else a lesson, it only teaches you how to be hurtful to yourself.

It is interesting to note that the definition says to "harbor" ill will. A harbor is a place of security and safety. Some folks actually protect their resentment by harboring it, giving it a safe place within to grow and fester. When resentment is afforded a safe place within us, we become unsafe and unstable. When we allow resentment to set up a home in our hearts, we spend more time replaying the old movies of how we were hurt than we do getting on with the business of life. If there is anyone in your life you resent, you may have noticed that you've played a rerun of the hurt they caused you over and over again in your mind, hypnotizing yourself with it each time you watch.

You can see how unloving resentment is. Not only is it not loving to the person who is the object of your resentment, but most of all, it is not being loving to yourself. Give yourself a healthy dose of self-love today and decide that you will release all resentments you harbor. When you make the decision, you don't need to know how you will release all of your resentment. All you need to know is that you have decided to no longer allow resentment to set up a home and have a safe harbor in your heart and mind. As soon as you make that decision, God starts moving to help you release what you've been carrying that doesn't serve you. All you have to do is take one little baby step, and God will take the other 99.

Give God permission to take out your mental and emotional trash. Surrender and allow God to come into your heart and mind and flood it with love and forgiveness. The only reason you still have resentment is because you are holding on to it. Just let it go, with no "buts".

You may want to visit a counselor, therapist or spiritual advisor who specializes in helping their clients heal and release past hurts, especially hurts from childhood, which tend to be the most damaging and lasting. This is the most loving course to take, to gradually free yourself of each and every old pain and resentment you've been harboring.

As you release resentments, you will find that your vital energy will begin to increase. You'll feel better and lighter. You will no longer be carrying around a heavy burden and you will feel the difference in your body, mind and spirit. When we relieve ourselves, we often say, "That's a load off my shoulders," or, "I'm glad I got that off my chest". These sayings indicate that our souls know on a deeper level that the resentments we carry around today in the mind will manifest tomorrow in the body.

Love has the power to heal any pain, hurt or resentment. It is said that healing is the act of applying love to those places within us which erroneously believe that love is lacking. Love is never truly lacking, though our perceptions and beliefs may tell us otherwise.

To release and let go of all resentment is to move to another level of spiritual maturity and allow yourself to experience greater joy, fulfillment and happiness. Isn't that yummy?

Love overlooks the small hurts—it isn't touchy, nor is it fretful or resentful.

9. <u>Love takes no account of the evil done to it [it pays no attention to a suffered wrong].</u>

The ego mind in humans has a tendency to keep score; not just in sporting events, but in life. The ego wants to keep score when others hurt us or when we feel we've been wronged. Usually, keeping score isn't enough. The ego mind also seems to want to recount all the ways that hurt has occurred, and wants to continue to play a mental picture of it over and over again to ensure that we do not forget and move past it. Of course, this does nothing but deeply instill the pain, making it more difficult to heal.

Love is different. Love doesn't keep score of every hurt. Love is forgiving, allowing hurts to pass by. Love recognizes that each person is only doing the very best they can in the moment based upon what they know and feel.

When you are able to forgive yourself, you are able to forgive others. Rather than keeping score of every act you've ever done that you regret, why not decide to let go of your mental scorecard and stop keeping score? Not only stop keeping score on yourself, but stop keeping score on other people also. You will find that you are much happier when you no longer focus on the ways others have hurt you. When you focus on all the times you've been hurt by someone, it naturally creates a cycle of getting hurt again and again, as what we focus on expands. Self-love means that you will begin to release your scorecard.

Love takes no account of the evil done to it.

10. Love does not rejoice in iniquity but rejoices in the truth. One of the most loving things we can do for one another is to overlook faults and remember the truth about who we really are: powerful creative beings, made in the image and likeness of God. When we remember the truth of who we are and the truth about who others are, we will no longer believe what our eyes tell us. What do I mean by that? We will no longer

look at the minor, surface differences between us and others and use it as a basis for interaction. No longer will we believe what our eyes tell us.

Our world has become focused on what is different between people, rather than what is the same. Essentially, every human being on this earth is the same as every other human being on this earth. We are each and all made in God's image, we are each and all powerful representations of God's love and creative power, and we are each and all able to accomplish magnificence. What is the same about us is radically more apparent than what is different about us. Yet, the problems that plague mankind are all related to the lie that we are separate; separate from each other and separate from God.

Love calls upon us to remember and rejoice in the truth. What is truth?

Truth is remembering who you really are; a divine creative being who came here to experience joy, happiness, love, spiritual transformation and fulfillment in every regard.

Truth is remembering who every one else is too; a divine creative being who came here to experience joy, happiness, love, spiritual transformation and fulfillment in every regard.

Truth is living up to and walking in your divinity. Truth resides in your knowing that God is expressing through you at all times and seeks to express through you to an even greater degree in each moment. Truth is allowing God's grace, love and goodwill to overtake you by staying present in each moment and simply remembering your connection to the Omnipotent One.

This truth shall set you free.

Love rejoices in the truth!

11. Love bears all things. There is not a single thing you could do to turn off God's love for you. You can't scare God away from loving you. You can't will God to stop loving you. You can't convince God to stop loving you.

There is not a single thing you could do to turn off God's love for you.

The beauty of God's divine love for us is that it is fully present in every second, in full measure, and is always completely unconditional. You can't do anything to be more loved than you are right now because you are already, and always have been, loved in totality by God. Even when your parents or your family or your friends didn't treat you lovingly, God's love was fully present in you, supporting you. Even when you behave in ways that are unlovable, God's love is fully present. And every time you thought you were completely abandoned and had nowhere to turn, *God's love was always fully present.*

The only reason we do not always feel the presence of love is because we are seeking it from the outside. If we are seeking love from another person, it is easy to feel unloved. Seeking love from another human being as our only source of love puts us at risk of feeling unloved because at any time that person could decide that they no longer love us. And in that instance, we would feel unloved.

However, part of remembering the "truth" is to know that God *is* love. We know God as love; and that love abides within each and every one of us at all times. God's love is so deeply imbedded within us that if we just sit in the silence, we will feel the presence of God's love within us, and we will come to see that there is nothing more powerful. When we know how complete and unconditional God's love is for us, we no longer seek love from others as our only source of love. And if another person decided that they don't love us any more, we are not dismayed because we know the truth; that God could never stop loving us.

God's love bears all things. Though humans may abandon or disown us, God's love for us bears any and all things we may do, be, or encounter. God's love for us doesn't have a breaking point. Divine love flows to us unconditionally, in every second of every day, no matter what we think, do, say or feel.

Divine love reminds us that we don't truly need another human being to love us in order for us to be happy. God already put enough love inside of you for you to love yourself and take excellent care of yourself, with or without the presence of a loving mate. We often forget this vital truth.

God is the source of all love. If we truly want to feel loved, all we have to do is remember that God's love is within us and surrounding us in perpetuity. We are never in a position where we must seek love from the outside, even though we often do. If you have a refrigerator and pantry full of food in your home, would you go outside seeking food? Probably not. If you did, would you get angry if you happened upon a person who didn't want to share their food with you? Probably not. The answers to these questions are obvious because you would be walking with the knowledge that you have a hefty store of food right in your own home. If someone didn't share their food with you, you certainly wouldn't go hungry or do without. You would simply eat from the more than sufficient supply you already had within your possession.

The same is true of love. You are full of an unending source and supply of love from God. That stream of love from God flows to you and is perpetually springing up within you. If someone else decided that they didn't want to share their love with you, would it really matter to you if you fully remembered how much love you already have?

Just remembering how much we are loved in every moment would help us to bear all things.

Nothing is unbearable. Victor Frankel, a survivor of the holocaust, suffered unimaginably while incarcerated in a concentration camp at the hands of Nazis. He lived to tell his story, and there was something most unusual about his viewpoint of what he had experienced. He stated that he did not have liberty to move about as he desired, but he had freedom. Liberty is a state of the body, while freedom is a state of the mind. Though he was captive, he still considered himself to be free. His body was imprisoned, but his mind was not. In the most horrific of circumstances, Victor Frankel was free.

One would think that the conditions of a concentration camp would make it absolutely unbearable. However, the power of God's love, and the resources God has put within each person, can enable us to survive, and indeed bear up under any circumstances.

Remembering the truth sets us free.

When we are hurting, it's easy to seek to blame our hurt on someone else. And even when it appears that we should be angry or hurt because of what another person has done to us, it is in that precise moment that we are called upon to remember God's unending, undying, unconditional love. If we are able to remember, in the most painful and difficult times of our lives, just how much God loves us, we would see that we are able to bear all things. There is not one thing that has happened to you—or that can happen to you—that you

cannot bear. You may think that a particularly painful
set of circumstances is unbearable, but within you are
all the resources you will ever need to bear everything
that will ever happen to you, all because of God's love.
How wondrous.

Love bears all things.

12. Love is ever ready to believe the best of every
person. There is nothing that you could do to get God
to stop believing in you. Even if you don't believe in
God, God believes in you.

God's love believes all things because all things are
possible with God. There is nothing that is impossible
with God. Therefore, even when a situation we may be
presented with appears hopeless, believe that there is a
way out. Believe that there is a way to transcend the
pain of today and create a joyful tomorrow. Believe
that all things work together for your benefit. Believe
that you are always taken care of, even when it doesn't
seem so. Believe that all is well, even when it appears
not to be.

This is the essence of love: to be able to look beyond
any unpleasant current conditions and see the brighter
picture which is sure to unfold as we train ourselves to
focus on it continually. Love can help us believe in a
better set of circumstances even when the circumstances we are in are unsettling or painful. Shifting
your focus from the pain of the moment to the beneficial lessons that the pain is there to teach you is necessary. Look back at all the painful times you've had over
the course of your life. Was there a lesson for you in
every painful scenario? If you got the lesson, you were
able to graduate. If you didn't get the lesson, you've
had to endure many similar painful experiences. The
sooner you learn what the pain is there to teach you,

the sooner you can rid yourself of the pain and advance to joy. Believe in this process, and believe that **all** things, especially the painful events, work together to transform and complete you.

When you hold this kind of solid belief that all is well, and that all things work together for your good, you are then able to believe in others. Believing in others doesn't mean having blind faith, nor does it mean being gullible. Our own inner spiritual discernment is always at our disposal to assist us in determining how much trust we should place in any individual. However, when you know you are dealing with a person whom you love and who exhibits true Godly love for you, then you are called upon to believe in that person. What does that mean?

When we believe in someone, someone whom we have a deeply loving, spiritual relationship with, we want the best for them. We want their hopes and dreams to be fulfilled, and we pray for positive outcomes in their life. We encourage them to do all they can do to bask in God's love and grow to being the kind of person we know they are capable of being. Truly, we see the gold in them when they are not able to see it for themselves. When we believe in someone, we tell them about the gold we see in them, and we encourage them to be the most magnificent version of themselves that is possible. We do this encouraging work without holding any judgments about where the person should be in their life and what they should be doing. Indeed, judgment is always about the person who is judging and never about the person who is being judged.

When we believe in someone, we encourage them to be the best they can be, without predetermining what their personal best should look like.

When we believe in someone, we see the best in

them, we see the gold in them, and we remind them of it often.

When we believe in someone, we do not make assumptions about them. In relationships, it is easy to assume certain things about our mates. I have fallen into the trap of jumping to conclusions and making assumptions about my husband and what I think a certain behavior of his might mean. Most of the time, my assumptions turn out to be completely inaccurate. Assumptions are unloving as they do not allow room for our mates to tell us what they are truly thinking or feeling.

When others believe in us, it helps us reach new heights. It's almost as if that belief becomes a gust of wind at our backs that keeps us moving forward in the right direction. Granted, we could move forward without the wind at our backs also, but it is easier to move forward when encouragement and support for our dreams are present from someone we deeply cherish.

Love yourself enough to believe that all things you go through, no matter how painful, no matter how tragic, no matter how unwanted, are there to teach you valuable lessons in this thing called life. Believe that all will work out for your benefit in the end. This is one of the most self-supporting beliefs that you could hold, and indeed is a belief that will see you through the darkest times of your life. When you truly believe that all is always well, you can face anything with faith and confidence.

Love yourself enough to believe in you. God believes in you. That is reason enough for you to believe in you. You'll find that the more you believe in your own dreams and abilities, you will naturally attract to yourself others who believe in you too.

When you look at yourself in the mirror, look deep into your eyes and see the spark of the Divine that lies in the heart of your soul. You are made in the image and likeness of the Creator. Believe that you are a spark of the Divine made manifest in a flesh and blood temple.

When you look at others, see straight through to the spark of the Divine which resides at the core of their being. See the God in every person you encounter.

Love is ever ready to believe the best of every person.

13. Love hopes all things. The scripture quoted at the beginning of this chapter states that hope is "joyful and confident expectation of eternal salvation." What a wonderful thought! We can joyfully and confidently expect to be delivered from anything that would threaten us.

When hope is present, anything is possible. When hope dies, desperation and depression set in. Hope enables us to see a brighter tomorrow, even when today is not very encouraging. Hope in your relationships allows you to see the brighter days that are just around the corner from the bad days.

Love hopes all things because all things are possible with God, so there is always firm reason to hope for what we desire to see in our relationships. Along with hope, we do the mental, emotional and spiritual work to create the relationship we desire. When combined with spiritual work, hope is a most powerful creative tool.

Love hopes all things.

14. Love endures everything [without weakening]. Recall the 3 definitions given earlier for the word endure:

- **To remain firm under suffering or misfortune without yielding**
- **To regard with acceptance or tolerance**
- **To undergo (as a hardship) esp. without giving in**

It is said that the cause of all suffering stems from not accepting what is. When things are one way, and we desire them to be different, we suffer if we continue to fight and resist against what is currently present. Endurance means that we accept what is.

Acceptance does not mean to settle for less than what we truly want. Nor does it mean to allow others to do anything to us that they want while we just accept their bad behavior. Self-love does not allow us to accept others infringing on our personal rights or overstepping the firm boundaries we have set in place for how others will treat and interact with us.

However, when we do not accept a person for who they are right now, and we try to change them, we are sure to meet with resistance on the part of the person we are trying to change and we will cause frustration within ourselves. Acceptance and tolerance are two of the most loving positions we could take with regard to another, especially our mates.

Let's be honest, every one of us has issues. Some of our issues are big, and some of our issues are small, but we all have multiple issues that we're dealing with. We all have idiosyncrasies. There is no person alive who doesn't have issues and idiosyncrasies. Since we all have them, wouldn't it be wise and loving to accept others for who they truly are, even with their issues and idiosyncrasies? Don't we want others to accept us for who we truly are even with our issues and idiosyncrasies? Do we not desire others to see the very best in us while being tolerant and accepting of the rest of us that isn't so pretty?

True love accepts others for who they truly are while seeing them as the very best they could be.

Remember that to endure also means to not give in when the road is rough. When our lives are most painful, we are growing and transforming the most. When someone triggers us into unloving behavior, that person is our greatest spiritual teacher at the moment. Spiritual growth and transformation take place more rapidly when we have resistance and difficulty. If everything in your life was perfect at all times, what lessons would you learn? How would you grow? You would quickly become stagnant.

However, when you are in relationships with other people, the closest of those relationships will begin to test your resolve to be a loving person. The people who are closest to you will begin to show you what you need to work on. They do this by saying and doing things that trigger you to have emotional responses, some of which may be unpleasant or unloving. When this happens to us, we frequently say that that person made us mad.

I am here to tell you that no one can make you mad. No one has the power to make you happy or joyful or sad or mad. No one has the power over your emotional responses. The *only* person who is in control of, or has ever been in control of your emotions, is *you*. Other people simply do not have the power over us to make us feel a certain emotion. No matter what your reactions to people have been in the past, no one has the power over you to make you feel a certain emotion.

However, people do come along and do or say things that are unkind, unloving and careless. People do come along and act as triggers. We then choose a certain emotional response, such as anger, sadness, irritation or frustration. However, that person is only a mirror showing you a reflection of your current inner state of being. The only reason that something someone says or does would trigger you to choose to have an emotional upset or trauma is because there is something in your inner world that identifies with what that person said or did.

I'll give you an example. Picture a small group of beautiful and slim women walking down the streets of Beverly Hills doing some shopping. The women are all very accomplished and each of them has developed high self-esteem. They are feeling particularly good about themselves that day and their shopping excursion. They are laughing and shopping and having a ball together. Imagine that a person ran past the group and yelled, "You all are fat and ugly!" Now if none of the women has any inner feelings of being fat and ugly, the comment would likely cause them to laugh and/or completely dismiss the person as a nut. It is not likely that the women would be triggered to have an emotional trauma in this scenario.

Now picture the same scene, except that the group of women walking down the street are recovering from anorexia. Though they may be slim, their inner feeling is that of being fat and ugly. If a person runs by who yells at them that they are fat and ugly, there is likely to be a painful reaction on the part of these women. They may argue that they are not fat and ugly, or they may yell abuses back at the person. They would likely walk away from the whole affair with rather unpleasant feelings.

The stimuli in both scenarios is exactly the same, so why the difference in reactions between the first set of women and the latter? The difference is simply this: the first set of women had no inner feelings of being fat and ugly while the latter group of women did. So when a person comes along who says anything about being fat and ugly, it has no effect on the first set of women because there is no fat and ugly thinking or emotions within them to be triggered. However, because the second group of women harbor thinking and emotions within them that they are fat and ugly, when someone comes along and calls them that, they are negatively triggered and choose to have emotional trauma.

Is the emotional trauma the fault of the person who makes the insensitive comment, or is the emotional trauma in the domain of the person having the trauma?

The answer is that the emotional trauma is in the domain of the person having the trauma. Though the person who is the trigger is being unkind, unloving and insensitive, the person who has the upset must still take full responsibility for their own emotional state at all times, even when being triggered. It doesn't matter how unkind, unloving, insensitive or intolerant someone else is being. *We are each still able to choose our response. We were created that way, and nothing will ever change that.*

When a person says or does something we don't like, we know, deep within, that we have a choice before us. There is a split second, let's call it "the gap", where you have a very brief opportunity to choose how you will respond. Most times, the gap is so fleeting that it is almost imperceptible. The gap appears in an instant, and if we are not aware of it, could completely escape us. However, all possibilities exist in the gap. All possible responses exist in this space. It is a gap of potential, therefore, anything is possible. It is in this gap that we choose our response.

From my observations, it appears that we tend to choose responses that are historic for us; we repeat the same responses over and over again. This cycle continues until we say to ourselves one day that we desire something different. This decision to make a different choice usually comes after we've suffered enough in our old patterns that we know we must change something, even if we don't know exactly what to change, or how to change it.

The gap is the answer. Whenever we are confronted with the unkind, unloving, rude or abrasive behavior of others, we naturally dip into the gap. As mentioned earlier, the problem is that we come out of the gap with the same old responses that we've used before. This was because we entered the gap unconsciously, and therefore responded unconsciously.

Now that you are becoming conscious of your thought patterns and behavior, and now that you are aware of the gap, you can make a different choice. You can dip into the gap and come out with a response that is completely new and different for you. You can come out of the gap with a response that makes you feel good about yourself, no matter what anyone else is saying or doing.

In the split second that we dip into the gap, we can choose a response that is either loving or reactive. We can choose a response that is either retaliatory or compassionate. We can choose a response that is either inflammatory or peaceable. There is no limit to the amount of choices in the gap, just as there is no limit to the responses you could choose to have to any particular stimuli.

We can choose how we will respond to any person or to any set of circumstances at any given time. This is what makes human beings such a high form of life, because we have, in every situation, the power and ability to choose our reactions and how we will respond to the stimuli in our environment. We have the ability to become aware of, comprehend and fully and consciously utilize the gap—that split second of infinite possibilities.

You've probably seen evidence of the gap at work, over and over again. I'll give you an example. Have you ever witnessed a person who, in the face of rude or unkind behavior, decided, in a split second, to lash out and have an angry response? Perhaps the angry response caused the person to do something that they later regretted. Maybe the angry response landed the person in very dire circumstances. The news is full of stories about men and women who caught their mate being unfaithful and, in a moment of uncontrolled fury, hurt or killed someone. It's interesting that we call these acts "crimes of passion." In the heat of the moment, the person dipped into the gap and came out with a response that was concurrent with their level of consciousness. It is wise to heed what the Holy Scriptures teach: be slow to anger, and quick to forgive. (Psalm 103:8)

In an instant, the entire course of a person's life could be changed, all because of a split second decision to react inappropriately.

There's good news: we can widen the gap. When we are faced with a potentially explosive situation, or one that we know could cause us to react explosively, it helps to slow everything down. Take your time. When events and reactions move slower, time is allowed for emotion and passion to subside and for reason and good sense to surface.

The next time you feel provoked by your mate, or by anyone, slow yourself down by taking several deep breaths, or turning away and saying a short prayer, or by immediately leaving the situation and going outside for a quick breath of fresh air. Whatever is appropriate for you to do to slow everything down, do it.

Then, go consciously into the gap, and choose a response that reflects loving kindness and compassion.

Remember that we are responsible; able to choose a response.

Here's where endurance comes in. When you are in a spiritually loving and committed relationship, you know that, at times, you will be presented with unkind or unloving behavior on the part of your mate. As we've stated, in that moment, you can choose love, or you can choose to be unloving. If you consciously dip into the gap and continually choose loving responses each time you face unloving behavior, you have the ability to transform yourself and lift your relationship to new heights. Your proactive application of love can also set the pattern of behavior that your mate will likely begin to follow, so that when you are acting unkind and unloving, in that moment, your mate will consciously dip into the gap and begin to choose loving responses to you also.

There's more good news: each time you dip into the gap and come out with a loving response, it becomes easier and easier to choose loving responses each time you are presented with a situation that has the potential to rustle your feathers.

This process requires endurance because it is not likely that you will be completely transformed overnight, or that all of a sudden you will choose to have only loving responses all the time. I have been working on this spiritual practice for years and I still don't have it mastered. I've made significant progress, but I am still working on this facet of myself and my responses to outside stimuli. However, I have learned that the hard times are giving me more opportunities to perfect my spiritual practice.

Endurance means that we go through these hard times so that we can reach the higher state of consciousness that is always the effect of undergoing a tough lesson and learning it well.

Endurance helps us to understand that even though our mate may love us, and we may be in a truly spiritually transformative and committed relationship, that person will still do things on occasion that could have the potential to rub us the wrong way. To expect that our mates will never do anything unkind or unloving is unrealistic and sets us up for failure. We are all humans. We all think and say and do human things. This is a part of life. So when the humaneness of your mate comes to the foreground, let your spiritual nature come to the foreground and allow you to practice endurance.

One of the factors in Tom's decision to cheat on his wife was the lack of endurance. He was not prepared or willing to endure in the relationship with his wife and find suitable answers and solutions to why they had the problems they did. His answer was to have an extramarital affair. While this may be a thrilling solution that feels good for the moment (or it may feel good for years as in Tom and Jade's case), it is not the answer to marital discord. The two people who are in the marriage have a responsibility to choose what they will think, do and say in the relationship to create marital harmony for themselves.

In today's society, it appears that divorce is the norm and having a long, happy and mutually satisfying marriage is the exception. If you are in a relationship with someone you truly want to be in relationship with, and this person suits your idea of what you want in a mate spiritually, mentally, emotionally and physically, then the hard times should be viewed as an opportunity for you to work on yourself and become an even more loving and patient person. The hard times are not there for you to exit at the first opportunity. There is no relationship that will stand the test of time that will not have hard times. If you are seeking a relationship that will never have any hard times, stay out of a relationship until you have a more realistic expectation of what relationships are all about. Hang around several couples who have successfully navigated rough times in their relationship and are still happy and thriving after many, many years. Ask them what makes for a successful pairing, and find out how they handled the difficult times. Every couple I've ever interviewed about what makes for a long and happy union attested to the fact that the hard times resulted in a stronger bond between the two. Each and every couple I know who have been together for many years, and who are still happy in their relationship, all said that the hard times were extremely difficult, and both parties had experienced pain. However, they also said that the difficulties made them stronger and made their love grow deeper.

The pastor of the church I attend has been married for over 20 years. He and his wife appear to have an excellent relationship, and they have several children who also seem to be quite happy and well adjusted. He frequently comments on his wife and their relationship and the fact that the road to marital bliss is paved with difficulties and pain. He stated one Sunday that he and his wife decided early on that divorce was not an option. So, he said, when the hard times came, they never even considered divorce. He stated: "Murder, on the other hand, we have considered on many occasions, but never divorce!" This humorous statement resonated with me because it showed me just how hot the kitchen can get in even the best of committed relationships.

Those who are able to endure through the hard times find the pot of gold on the other side of their troubles. And they are more resilient and ready for the next round of hard times, which is sure to come. One of my spiritual teachers taught me that relationships speed up our spiritual growth and transformation because they provide us with friction and resistance, which are opportunities for us to see where we still need to heal and grow. We can then go straight to the areas of ourselves that need the most help and work on these areas. Without that friction, we may live on our own for years and feel quite happy and content, but we may not experience the dynamic and increased rate of spiritual growth that being in close relationships affords.

This is why endurance is so crucial to a loving relationship. God says love endures all things. Not some things. All things. When we are truly in a loving relationship, and each person cares for, honors and respects the other, then we can endure all things. God's love helps us endure.

Love endures all things.

15. Love never fails.

To fail means to lose strength or weaken.
God's love never loses strength or weakens.
To fail means to fade or die away.
God's love never fades or dies away.
To fail means to stop functioning.
God's love never stops functioning.
To fail means to fall short.
God's love never falls short.
To fail means to be or become absent or inadequate.

God's love is never absent or inadequate.
To fail means to be unsuccessful.
God's love is never unsuccessful.
To fail means to disappoint the expectations or trust.
God's love never disappoints, nor is it ever below expectations.
To fail means to miss performing an expected service or function for.
God's love has never missed a performance.
To fail means to be deficient in, to lack.
God's love is never deficient nor does it leave anything lacking.
God's love is whole, perfect and complete.
To fail means to leave undone; neglect.
God's love never leaves anything undone, nor does it ever leave us neglected.
Love never fails.
It doesn't matter what other humans do. It doesn't matter who loves you and who doesn't. It doesn't matter how many times your heart has been broken, or who broke it. It doesn't matter whether or not you think you'll ever find your true love. None of that matters.
The only thing that matters in this moment is God's unconditional, perfect love for you. This love cannot fail.
Love never fails.
A man or woman may love you today, and be gone tomorrow. God's love is omniscient and omnipotent; present in all at all times and all powerful.
Remember this truth, and it will set you free.
Love never fails.
This is an eternal truth that has the power to change our entire outlook of the world around us. If we love others with the love of God, truly loving them from the heart, we can never fail. Even if the object of our affec-

tion does not reciprocate the love we show, we still do not fail. Love that is extended to others is always returned, though it may not come back to us from the same person we extended it to.

Make it your life's work to emulate God's love. Seek to develop within yourself the kind of love that God is. We may never have perfect love with another person, but we have perfect love within us from God right now.

Love is the highest quality we can display, and is the highest regard we can show for and to ourselves and others. Every one of us needs love. Even babies cannot thrive without love. Love is as natural and innate for us as breathing. Cultivating the best possible love for yourself and for others is the best use of the time you have here on this planet. The time you spend growing, widening and deepening the breadth and quality of your love is never wasted. The more pure, Godly love you radiate, the more pure, Godly love will be returned to you.

Find someone who needs love today and remind them of the eternal wellspring of love that bubbles forth from within them. The fastest way to transform a life as all healing is to simply apply love to the places within us that thought love was absent.

God's love never fails. Hold on to that thought the next time you experience "heartbreak". Hold on to that thought the next time you experience tension, friction or hardship in your relationship. Hold on to that thought the next time your mate says or does something that you find unloving and you are tempted to respond in an unloving fashion.

Hold on to that thought every night as you close your eyes and drift off to sleep.

Love never fails.

One of the reasons I'm able to speak with authority on the subject of adultery and am able to identify with Tom and Jade is because I, too, was an adulterer. I understand the subtle changes in committed relationships which occur over time that cause a mate to think that what he or she needs and wants is outside of their marriage. Nothing could be more untruthful. When problems and difficulties arise in committed relationships, there are solutions. What each mate needs is honest, open and frequent communication about all things which weigh upon their minds. Sharing what you like and don't like in a relationship is loving, and gives each partner opportunity to examine themselves, grow and transform into the kind of mate they desire to be. When a mate decides to cheat because they are not getting from their partner what they want and need, he or she cheats their mate out of the opportunity to improve the relationship. The cheating partner is not being faithful, meaning that they lack courage and are fearful. It takes courage and faith to speak to our mate and openly, honestly and non-judgmentally share with them what we are missing in the relationship, and communicate what our needs and desires are. It takes courage to look someone in the eye and say, "I am not getting what I need and want in our relationship. What I need and want is _____. I feel attracted to someone else who makes me feel good at the moment because our relationship is not where I'd like it to be. I want to stay faithful and keep my integrity, so I am speaking to you about my concerns now so that we can address them and grow together. This is what I am willing to do to improve our relationship."

The reason this approach takes so much courage and faith is because it requires each mate to do deep soul searching work on an ongoing basis.

Most of us have a tendency to blame others for our internal state of affairs. We love to say that others are responsible for our behavior, though it is impossible for someone else to be in charge of our internal feelings, emotions and reactions. You alone are the owner and architect of your internal feelings, thoughts and emotions. However, because such a strong tendency exists within us to look outwardly for the answers to our internal emotional hurt and pain, we choose blaming our mates as a first response. It is very easy to point a finger at our partner and say, "It's all his/her fault. If they didn't do _____, I could do _____." Or, "If they would just do _____, then I could be happy." What fills in the blanks is of little importance or consequence as the issue is not with what our mates will or won't do. The issue is what we ourselves will or won't do for our own internal peace of mind and well being. A vital and key element for living in a peaceful state is going within and learning ourselves as fully and completely as we are able to, given our level of spiritual development.

Most people do not engage in an ongoing examination of themselves to see what they need to weed out of their consciousness and what they need to keep, add or expand. This kind of ongoing self-examination is necessary in order for us to become a loving, kind, compassionate partner who is open, honest and willing to be vulnerable. If we are not willing to be vulnerable, we are not willing to have true love in our lives. Love equals vulnerability. Deep, abiding love says, "I know I'll be okay no matter what, because I have the God-voice within that directs, comforts and guides me at every turn. Therefore, I do not have to hide my true feelings, nor do I need to pretend to be something I am not. I can be who I really am, and it will be okay, even when I don't meet with the approval of others." Only deep soul searching and radical self examination will lead us to this enlightened level of thought and emotion.

Until we grow up—by becoming relentless personal soul searchers—we cannot invite and attract lasting love to ourselves. *You must first learn yourself, and love every aspect of your being, before you can fully love someone else.* When we know what we like, what we can live with and what we can't live with, we become more comfortable with our choices. We are mature in our approach, and don't expect more of others than they are willing, or able, to give. Because we have learned to love ourselves and have given ourselves permission to be human, we can more easily learn to love another and give them permission and forgiving space to be human as well.

Those who have the highest demands on others are usually people who place the highest demands on themselves. High demands are impossible to meet, and even if they are met, more demands will pop up to keep the vicious cycle in motion.

I seek to meet no one's demands or expectations. I arrived at this peaceful place in my life after I stopped putting so many demands on myself. Once I realized that I didn't have to jump through multiple hoops to be happy, I could step out of the three-ring-circus my life had become. I could rest from endless attempts to please. After all, the only one who had been putting up all the hoops for me to jump through was **me.** Paradoxically, less demands in my life equated to my relationships becoming better. They began to naturally conform to my soul's desires, which are different from the passing fancies of the ego-mind. Our soul's desires arise from our innate divinity. They are for our highest good and represent the best use of our life. Our ego-mind's desires are whatever is seductive, easy or convenient in the moment, and will likely cause us to feel comfortable, fearful, and stagnant or will land us in deep trouble as the ego-mind seeks only to keep us fearful, stifle our growth and, in the end, assassinate us.

Once I began to recognize the differences between my soul's desires and my ego-mind's fancies, I could better follow the path that was laid out for me by God. I could stop being a cheater and walk in integrity. I could stop speaking the lie and tell the truth. I could tune in to that quiet, still voice at the center of my soul and know that it would surely guide me home. This is the essence of love.

Love requires faith; faith in oneself and our innate ability to be divinely led and guided in any situation, and faith in others to the extent that we allow them to be human and grow in their own way, at their own pace, and know that they will surely get there. As my mother-in-law wisely says of relationships with others who may seem difficult: "You got to love them all the way there."

In the meantime, we will always know how to handle the people and relationships in our lives when we are tuned in to our inner voice of guidance because it will offer us caution, advice, direction and instruction on how to proceed with each person we come into contact with. We need only listen and act immediately, without reservation or hesitation.

Love also requires honesty and a willingness to be frank about what we want. Tell your mate how you want your loving, without assuming that they already know. Tell your mate how you desire to be loved, openly, honestly and compassionately. Once you know yourself down to the core, you will find that self-examination leads to clarity. When you are clear, you are better able to communicate to others what you want from a relationship and how you desire to receive it. Then you can allow them to decide if they can comply or not, just as you will have to decide if you can comply with what your partner needs and desires in a relationship.

It is easy to fall into the trap of not communicating our desires, then getting mad or frustrated with our mate because they didn't live up to an expectation that they were not even aware of. It is the path of love to tell others what we want, need and expect in a relationship, and then give them reasonable opportunity to decide if they can provide that or not. If they cannot, then this person may not be the one for you. If they say they can, a time period is needed to see if the person can actually live up to what they are promising. What a person says is one thing, what they are actually able to back up with action is another. Before becoming deeply involved with a person, allow adequate time to see if they can meet your needs, desires and expectations in a relationship. You will need time for observation. Observing a potential mate in all types of scenarios gives you a peek into their emotional and mental state. What do they do when someone provokes them? How do they respond when they are under pressure? What do they do when they are sad, or happy? How do they treat you in each of these situations? It is critical to your future with this person that you observe them in light of your communicated desires, needs and expectations. Only then do you begin to understand them on a deeper level, seeing all aspects of their persona.

It took me and my current husband over seven years of dating to finally decide to get married. In retrospect, there was not one wasted moment, as we were getting to know each other better and better all the while. By the time we got married, I knew exactly what I was getting; there were few surprises. I knew how he responded when he was angry, happy, sad, frustrated, concerned. I had spent sufficient time with him in different scenarios and had carefully observed his reactions and responses. I had also grown to an understanding of his love for me, and knew that he could (and how he would) meet my needs, expectations and desires in our relationship. Though all was not perfect, I knew conclusively that he was God's choice for me at the time.

Now, I thank God that I have chosen to walk in integrity rather than not, and I also thank God for, and bless, my journey, which included infidelity, as it has been a valuable part of my learning experience. I would not be who I am today had I not been a cheater previously. I certainly would not be able to teach on the topic of being a cheater from a cheater's standpoint had I not been through the experience. This is not to say that you have to have the experience of cheating in order to see how good it is not to cheat!

If you are in a relationship now and are violating your word and honor by being a cheater, ask yourself:

- *Since I don't have peace of mind, what do I hope to gain from cheating?*
- *When will it end?*
- *Who am I hurting, in addition to myself, by lying?*
- *Have I examined myself for my role and responsibility in the breakdown of my current love relationship?*
- *If I have, am I willing to grow up and take responsibility for my negative thoughts, attitudes,*

**emotions and actions that have hurt my relation-
ship without playing the victim and blaming my
mate?**
- **Have I given my mate the opportunity to help
make our relationship better by communicating
clearly, openly and honestly how I feel, based on
an assessment, examination and inventory of my
physical, mental, emotional and spiritual needs
and my soul's desires?**

If you have not answered these questions honestly,
you may believe that you are lying to, and cheating on,
someone else. In actuality, you are lying to, and cheating on yourself.

If you are in such a situation, either as the one who
is cheating or the one who is being cheated on (if you
are being cheated on, you probably know the truth,
though you may not want to admit it), determine today
to make a change. Determine today to work on yourself
spiritually by going inward, in moments of quiet contemplation and meditation, to determine what in you
feels the need to cheat or to stay with a cheater. More
than likely, you will find deep feelings of low self-
worth, fear, insecurity, guilt and shame; none of which
are productive to your being nor do they aid you in
spiritual growth and transformation. When you begin
to discover and uncover, in periods of quiet solitude,
reasons why you move about in the world as you do
(either as a cheater or as the one being cheated on), you
can then begin to see solutions and options that lead
you away from a life of dishonesty and into a life of
truth and the vulnerability that accompanies it. When
you begin to fix your own deep-seated feelings of low
self-worth and address your fears of what would happen to you if you didn't have your current mate, then

you will become the kind of person that would neither cheat nor settle for being cheated on.

This is not the path of least resistance, nor is it the path for wimps. The path of self-examination and discovery, truth, faith and love will exact a high toll from you. This path is expensive, for it requires your time, attention, energy and willingness to see clearly what ails you and be willing to surrender all of it for something better. In spite of the huge requirements of this path, you need not fear it, for it is the path to freedom. If you do not feel that you can head down this path today, eventually you will have suffered sufficiently to warrant a change. It is at that moment that you will be ready to leap head first onto the path of freedom!

I should know; I've walked the path, and continue to do so every day, with God's ever present hand, the Holy Spirit, the angels, and by careful attention and attunement to the divine voice of guidance from within. I can speak to you from experience: love is the path of freedom.

Godspeed to you as you embrace the path of love.

"And so faith, hope, love abide, these three; but the greatest of these is love."

1 Corinthians 13:13, AMP

God Speaks Through Money

"The rich man's wealth is his strong city; the poverty of the poor is their ruin."

Proverbs 10:15 AMP

My Story:—$1,269.38

I couldn't believe it—here it was, payday, and I was staring in disbelief at my paycheck. I was looking at what should have been a substantial commission check, except that the four figures to the left of the decimal point had a "minus" sign in front them. I had just received my first "negative" paycheck! After working for two whole weeks, over 50 hours per week, I owed money to the company I was working for. I sat in my office staring down at that wretched piece of paper, trying, and failing miserably, to squelch the panic that was forming a nasty knot in the pit of my stomach. Here I was, a single mother of two young children and not even able to pay my rent, much less the countless other bills that were due. I heard a voice inside my head yell, *"Valerie, this is pathetic. You don't even have enough money to buy groceries!"*

How had I arrived at this destination, financially battered and almost ready to give up? Powerful life lessons would reveal themselves in the answer.

I started my financial life, as most do, with perfect credit, and was quite adept at maintaining it for several years. I remember the day I received an American Express card in the mail. I ripped open the stiff envelope, my heart racing feverishly. I stood for a moment to soak in the words: my name printed in crisp black letters on a green background, VALERIE LOVE, with the prestigious word "Card member" next to it, all guarded by a steadfast Centurion in the center. The card spoke volumes. It was as if I was instantly a member of an elite, prestigious club. At just 19 years of age, I had *arrived*. After reveling in a moment of self-accomplished pride, I raced off to apprise Mom and Dad of the latest developments: their daughter was now a "Card member." Surely they'd be proud, ecstatic, barely able to contain themselves.

"Mom, Dad, look what I just got!"

I sprinted into the living room waving the green plastic in the air as if I'd just won a Nobel Prize. My parents, engrossed in the evening news, looked up to see what all the commotion was about. It took a few seconds for the idea to sink in, but when it did, their gaze turned from mild curiosity to near horror. They looked at me as if I were recklessly waving around the Polio virus in the middle of the living room! A few seconds passed, and once we all had an opportunity to settle down, my conservative, cash-paying, debt-free parents spoke. Considering their facial expressions, I was more than a little concerned about what was about to fall out of their mouths. They delivered a tag-team soliloquy reminding me, yet again, of the perils of credit. They wrapped it all up with a warning, "Just be careful, young lady. You could get yourself into serious trouble with that plastic."

Considering the "high" I'd been on just minutes earlier, I found their reply deflating. Little did I know how
prophetic their words would prove to be.

A few years later, I married my high school sweet-
heart when I was just 23 years old. Though I had managed my financial life splendidly as a single woman, I
started to encounter financial problems after I got married. My husband and I didn't work together to manage
our money, and a series of bad financial decisions
(founded upon the need for instant gratification) landed
us in monumental debt. After the joyous birth of our
first child, expenses and financial demands loomed
larger than ever. Like many American families, we were
drowning in debt and bills. Feeling as if we had no
way out, we filed for bankruptcy.

After the bankruptcy, we worked to rebuild our
credit, a painstaking, albeit worthy, ambition. We decided to relocate to the state of Maryland. After doing
so, we studied the real estate market and found that
buying a house in Maryland was much more affordable
than buying a home in New York. Though we wanted
to own a home for our growing family, we knew our
credit would bar us from qualifying for a mortgage.
When we were presented with the opportunity to purchase a home using "creative financing", we jumped at
the chance. We assumed an existing mortgage, and a
real estate investor loaned us the balance of the money
we needed to purchase our first home. The situation
was ideal. We were able to experience the pride of
homeownership despite our severely impaired credit.

The feeling that we were finally rebuilding our financial lives was starting to give us hope. That feeling
and sense of security was short-lived. My husband
didn't have steady employment, and our financial obli-

gations and family were growing—we were now blessed
with another child, a beautiful daughter. Considering
my husband's rocky employment history and my desire to stay home with our children, we both agreed
that starting a business would give us the financial
freedom we longed for. The prospect of owning and
operating a lucrative enterprise that could afford us financial independence and the time freedom to spend
with our family intrigued us. We embarked upon a
quest for the perfect home-based business. We looked
at every kind of business imaginable, from arts and
crafts to vending machines. After months of researching home-based businesses—including attending several "hot" business opportunity meetings—we decided
to become distributors of a large metropolitan newspaper. Yes, we bought a paper route.

Granted, buying a paper route would hardly seem
the beginnings of a great financial empire. However,
we were convinced that delivering newspapers could
be highly profitable. In a good month, we could gross
$25,000 or more, which was far in excess of the ex-
penses we would incur. And for the time, in the early
1990's, this was considered an excellent level of income. The opportunity seemed to contain all the elements we'd been searching so desperately for; so we
dug in our heels and started our new venture.

In the beginning, business was difficult. Our schedules were erratic and afforded little time for sufficient
sleep. We were required to be at the drop-off point to
pick up our newspapers at 1:00 a.m.. In the silence of
the night, we would drive on the wrong side of the
street to throw newspapers onto our customer's drive-
ways. Every day, we'd pick up approximately 1,500
newspapers for delivery during the week, and about
2,500 newspapers to be delivered on the weekends. If

any of our newspaper subscribers awoke in the morning without a dry, readable newspaper on their doorstep, they could call for us to come back and deliver a
newspaper up until 10:00 a.m. that morning. So, after
returning at about 8:00 a.m. from delivering newspapers all night, my husband or I would have to go
back out and deliver the "missed" papers. The other
parent had home duty: getting the children fed, dressed
and ready for school. After the missed papers were delivered by 10:30 a.m., there was but a brief respite to
grab a bite to eat, shower and, with any fortune, complete a tiny bit of paperwork before it was time for the
next round of papers: the evening paper, 800 of which
had to be delivered Monday through Friday by 5:00 p.m.
As with the morning paper, if a subscriber came home
from work and his or her doorstep was not adorned
with a copy of the evening news, you guessed it, they
could call for a missed paper up until 7:00 p.m.; and
off we would go to deliver those "misses." We would
grab snippets of sleep here and there between house-
work, caring for the children and doing paperwork for
the business.

At one point, things got so hectic that our dining
room table was covered with incoming mail. There
were stacks of unopened envelopes. My brother-in-
law, who was visiting at the time, asked, "What are all
those envelopes?"

"Oh, those are payments from our customers," I
replied nonchalantly.

"Why are they sitting on the dining room table?"

"I don't have the time to open them, catalog them
onto the computer and take the checks to the bank. I'll
get around to it over the weekend."

"How much money do you think is in that stack?" he
asked curiously.

"Probably several thousand dollars; but I don't have time for that right now."

With an attitude like that toward money, you can imagine that a downward spiral was in the making.

A hectic lifestyle, lack of sleep and general mayhem seemed to pervade our household. Life quickly became painful and arduous—an endless procession of newspapers, sleepless nights, unreliable employees, customer complaints, disheveled kids and migraine headaches. The time freedom we were seeking was impossible to achieve.

The grandest irony of all was that our financial woes persisted and worsened. Increased income does not make for financial stability if sound money management is non-existent in the first place. More money only magnified and multiplied the personal inadequacies and financial mismanagement that were ever present in our marriage. Far from providing the high net income and quality family time my husband and I had hoped for, our business had grown into a time-and-money-devouring monster of huge proportions.

In the middle of this saga, my husband paid a visit to the car dealership. There he spotted the car of his dreams: a Lincoln Continental. The lure of temporarily high income had erroneously convinced him of our ability to afford a new luxury car. Since his credit was still seriously impaired, he wasn't approved for the loan to buy his dream car. He came home and urged me to visit the dealership with him to see the beautiful new car he'd picked out for our family. He also informed me that he could not get the vehicle without my financial support. I reluctantly went to the Lincoln car dealership with him and agreed to allow the car salesman to pull my credit report. After doing so, the bank told us that we could purchase the car, but the loan had to be in my name in order for it to be approved. Apparently, my credit restoration efforts were progressing better than my husband's.

Nevertheless, I had huge reservations about buying a $40,000 luxury vehicle with a monthly car note of $636 (which was quite expensive in the early 1990's). Somewhere deep inside, I knew why my husband wanted this car so badly. My guess was that this luxury car was like a salve he could apply to the wounds he had incurred in the heat of battle with our war on money. Over the years, financial mismanagement had wreaked havoc on both of us and had eroded our sense of self-worth. He may have been thinking: *Even if we're not financially stable, we can at least look the part.* An understandable, and common reaction.

After I could deliberate no longer about signing for the vehicle, I finally acquiesced. After all, this was the car of his dreams, and it seemed we had the money (and I had the credit) to finally make the dream attainable. We went back to the car dealership where I signed the loan documents to purchase the car in my name. We left a post-dated check for $4,000, and drove the car home.

Meanwhile, we continued to struggle with the business, and it's little wonder that we eventually lost it due to mismanagement. When our business slipped out of our hands, a considerable amount of family and marital happiness went out the door with it. We were never the same.

We were now faced with a large car note, a mortgage, unpaid taxes (from our failed business enterprise) and several other bills we'd created when we thought we had high income. We couldn't keep up with the car note, and the bank constantly threatened me with repossession. Months went by and the situation only worsened. After haggling with the lender and completely worn out from stress, I voluntarily surrendered the Lincoln Continental. I was more elated on the day I left the car at the dealership than I was the day I picked it up. However, that move landed me back in trouble with my credit. A repossession now appeared on my credit report for a car I didn't even want in the first place! I was later informed by the lender that the car was sold at auction. But the auction proceeds didn't yield enough to satisfy my outstanding balance, so I still owed the bank several thousand dollars. I hadn't understood the concept of "negative equity" until then.

With the loss of our business and our temporarily inflated income, we weren't able to maintain our mortgage payments and other obligations. Our home fell into foreclosure. Three times. Each time I worked with the mortgage lender (and the investor who provided private financing) for a resolution. Each time, we barely managed to save our home.

I was emotionally worn out.

The unresolved issues and resulting stresses caused my husband and I to draw apart, he and I assuming separate sides on an ever-widening chasm that could not be bridged. Without a foundation of emotional and spiritual support, we eventually separated. After the separation, we sold the house to the investor who had provided the private financing. The investor agreed that I could continue to live in the house if I could afford and maintain the monthly rent payments. The idea was attractive because it would save me from having to uproot and move my children, which I dreaded doing. Nevertheless, I was reluctant because I didn't know how I would pay the rent on my own. Just then—as synchronicity would have it—a close friend of mine, who is really like a sister, called to inform me

that she and her husband were also separating. She
asked if she could stay with me until she decided
where she wanted to live. I quickly agreed—it would
be comforting to have my sister-friend around after the
nasty break-up of my own marriage. Besides, having a
roommate would help defray expenses. The house was
big enough for each of us to have our own space, so the
arrangement worked perfectly.

Now I could settle down in a moment of solitude to
think about my circumstances: a newly single mom of
two children with no money, bad credit, a mountain of
debt, unpaid back taxes (which had now turned into
tax liens on my credit report), and the bank still hound-
ing me for the unpaid balance on our repossessed luxury vehicle. Seeing no way out, I filed for and was
granted bankruptcy for the second time. However, the
bankruptcy couldn't erase the unpaid taxes, which
now amounted to thousands of dollars including
penalties and daily accruing interest. I was in financial
hot water, drowning in a sea of bills, debt and despair.

I decided that I needed to search for work that would
give me flexibility with my children, yet provide a siz-
able income. I was involved in network marketing at
the time, and it was then that I met a man who was to
become a great mentor and guide to me. He and I met
at a hotel where our network marketing companies
held meetings. His company held a weekly meeting in
a hotel room right next door to the hotel room where
my company met weekly. We would always greet each
other, until one day we decided to talk. We immediately clicked and formed a friendship. He saw in me
extremely high potential to do great things. Because I
was beat up at the time, I wasn't able to hold such a
high vision for myself. After all, my life had become a
failure in my eyes. He felt I could become a high pro-

ducing sales person, and he told me so. He also owned a company and he offered me the opportunity to work for his company in a sales position while he taught me the ropes. I told him there was no way I was ever going to be a salesperson. He insisted, and I eventually decided to accept his offer. After all, I needed money to take care of my kids, and a sales position seemed to be the perfect fit if it was indeed all he said it was.

I learned that I was a good salesperson, skills I had probably learned over the years without even knowing it. I was always at the top of the charts for the sales people, and things were going quite well. I was making very good money, and my sales position did not require me to work very hard, which afforded me time with my kids. In the summer, when my kids were away at their grandmother's homes in New York, I could even go to the beach with my girlfriends some afternoons.

Eventually, I was able to land a position working in the financial services industry with small business owners. My job, ironically, was to help them successfully manage their cash flow. Having been in the same boat—a small business owner with out-of-control cash flow issues—I could empathize well with them.

Shortly thereafter, I learned that American Express was seeking to hire several new financial advisors in my area. They were offering a presentation that would give an overview of what was required to become a financial advisor. Even though I held no licenses for the position, nor did I have the requisite training, my inner voice said to go to the presentation anyway. I'll never forget the thrill that rushed through my veins while listening to the speaker—a highly successful financial advisor. My brain picked up on several keywords: "flexible schedule," "high commissions," "prestige,"

"learn the financial services industry," "manage investments." I thought, *This is it! This is perfect for me!
Where do I sign!?* After a series of interviews, psycho-
logical exams and aptitude tests, I was offered the position.

That was the good news.

The bad news was that it would cost me a significant
amount of money upfront to get trained and licensed—
money I didn't have. It would cost my time as well. I'd
have to spend a considerable amount of time studying
for classes; so I wouldn't be able to work full time
while preparing myself for the formidable exams I'd
have to take. Without much thought, based almost entirely on gut feelings, I decided to risk it all. I resigned
my position. To make ends meet, I fought for and was
granted unemployment benefits, and prayed every
month that the child support checks would show up
on time.

I immersed myself in study, all day, every day, for
months. I took intensive classes that required me to
wake up brain cells that had fallen asleep back in high
school algebra. Finally, it was time for me to take the
exams. I felt ready, but it still didn't prevent me from
having the mother of all nightmares the night before
my first big exam! In the dream, my score popped up at
the end of the test and I was only one point shy of passing. I became so enraged that I picked up and hurled
every computer in the place through the window. In
the dream, I completely and single handedly destroyed
the entire office.

So much was riding on this one: if I was successful
in passing this all-day exam, I'd be a stockbroker. If I
failed, I'd lose valuable time and the money I'd paid to
take the test. I'd also have to shell out more money to
do a retake. I had neither luxury, time or money, so I

completely convinced myself that I had to pass this exam on the initial attempt. Despite the exam's steep failure rate, I passed it the first time I took it. I was ecstatic! But the excitement was soon replaced with anxiety. There were still several more exams to pass.

The remaining requisite exams proved difficult and expensive, but I passed each of them on the first take too, which is highly unusual. Several months and thousands of borrowed dollars later, I was ready to begin my new career as a financial advisor.

I began working at American Express Financial Advisors earning a small salary plus commissions. However, the meager salary was subject to multiple business expenses, which meant that there was always the possibility of receiving a "negative paycheck"; a paycheck in which business expenses exceeded salary as well as any commissions earned. I am thankful that I only experienced this dilemma on rare occasions and when I did, the loving financial support of family and friends (and a couple of payday loans here and there) got me through. The only way to resolve a negative paycheck scenario was to do as our managers urged, "write more business!" This was, on occasion, an enormous task; an advisor may have to submit thousands of dollars of commissionable business transactions to pay off the debt to the company and still receive a paycheck.

As I sat in my office on the inauspicious occasion of receiving my first negative paycheck (at the worst imaginable time), tears welled up in my eyes. Though it was only noon, I decided to go home for the day. When I reached the solitary safety of my home, I climbed the stairs, closed my bedroom door, sat down on a stepstool in my closet and wailed. I bawled for what seemed like hours. I cried out for God to rescue me from the financial death trap I felt caught up in. I cried so loud and long that, when I was done, my head pounded, my eyes had swollen to twice their normal size and my voice was nearly gone. I was emotionally spent from releasing what felt like years of anguish over money.

My financial woes and I had been having an ongoing wrestling match, but that day went down in infamy as the day the money woes triumphed—I was slammed down on my back with the wind knocked out of me. I had suffered setbacks before, but this latest financial fiasco was almost too painful and debilitating to bear. I sat there praying and privately wondering why every attempt at creating a financially abundant life for myself and my children had been met with abrupt and complete obliteration.

My story illustrates the self-made crucible I carried for nearly 20 years: poor money management. Paradoxically, what occupation did God draw me to? Being a financial advisor, managing money for the clients who trusted me. The irony is too obvious to miss. God put me in a position where I had to handle money on a daily basis so that I could learn to do for myself what I hadn't done in almost two decades: *take care of my money responsibly*. I was forced to face the same lesson each and every day until I mastered it—and master it I did.

After two years in my position as a financial advisor, I became a franchise owner at American Express Financial Advisors. I now owned my financial planning business! This was an enormous thrill for me as I'd always recognized the important role entrepreneurship played in becoming financially independent. My business grew and grew. I eventually acquired over two hundred clients, managing several million dollars for them. I was blessed by God to have built mutually en-

riching, life-changing relationships with hundreds of
clients, and to have been able to teach them how to be
wise stewards over what God was entrusting to them.
Though part of what I taught clients came from books,
much of what I taught them came from one of the most
effective classrooms of all: my own life experiences.

Over the next several years, my financial situation
continued to improve while I built a thriving financial
planning business supported almost entirely by refer-
rals from existing clients.

I spent seven years in the financial services industry
before I retired from financial planning to do the work
God created and called me to do: to teach a larger audience how to find and fulfill their Divine life's purpose
and use it to serve humanity in a way that supports
themselves, their families, their communities and their
most cherished charitable endeavors. I call it "living
on purpose." Living on purpose has allowed me to design and live my life each day based upon the creative
use of my skills, talents and abilities. It is a most joyful
way to live.

Because of God's grace and care and my prayerful
decision to live on purpose, as a conscious creator, *I've
been able to dramatically improve my financial condition.* My self-created financial *test* for almost 20 years
has now become my financial *testimony.*

Now that I've re-established my credit, pre-approved
credit cards, lines of credit and mortgage offers arrive
in my mailbox almost daily. I own real estate investment property. As a part-time real estate investor, and
as a result of my commitment to my ongoing financial
education, I've made more money on single transactions than many people earn in an entire year. I've paid
the IRS in full. I have savings and investments, as do

all three of my children. I receive thousands of dollars in monthly residual, recurring income. My children are also entrepreneurs and receive residual income also. Though I'm retired from building a successful financial planning practice, that business still provides me with income, years after leaving it. One of my greatest gifts from God is generosity and being able to give freely to those who need my help. I've been infinitely blessed. I now have a third child, a beautiful home and a loving husband. If I never received another blessing, I would still maintain that my life is infinitely blessed. Thankfully, my Creator and I have so much more to co-create!

You, too, may have been wrestling with an opponent just as imposing as the money monster I battled for years. Maybe it's your weight, low self-esteem, problems in your relationships or the unfulfilled desire for a mate. Or perhaps it's health crises, or disturbances in your family. If you have an unresolved nagging problem that continues to cause you discomfort and pain, no matter what it is, *there is hope.* There is a bright light at the end of your tunnel. God wants nothing less than your complete, unbridled, unmitigated joy and abundance. Surely, then, you would be provided with a way for you to achieve just that. If I can do it, you can too!

The lessons I learned from my painful 20 year bout with financial woes are detailed here for the purpose of bringing you healing and hope. Each of the gifts I received from God is a tool that you can use today to effect powerful, positive change in your life. I urge you to do the work of applying these principles, and thus experience for yourself, as I have, release from pain and worry, and freedom to experience limitless joy and unending abundance!

God Speaks

Sacred Lesson #1—God has a specific, magnificent plan for your life which reflects the purpose He had in mind when He formed you. Your job here is to discover what makes you happy and joyful and live it with reckless abandon.

"For I know the thoughts and plans that I have for you, says the Lord, thoughts and plans for welfare and peace and not for evil, to give you hope in your final outcome."

Jeremiah 29:11 (AMP)

So many of us walk trancelike through life, in a state of confusion, dismay, or dissatisfaction with wherever we are. Many of us take the role of spectator in our own lives. Rather then defining and designing the kind of life we want, we prefer to wait and "see what happens." The results of the reactive "see what happens" approach tend to keep us at the edge of survival rather than partaking in the bounteous and glorious life God destined for us.

God has a clearly defined purpose and plan for your life. It is a purpose that you are perfectly created and uniquely equipped for. Before you were born, you resided with God in the spirit world where you knew the magnificent impact you would make once you got to the earth plane. Whether you remember it or not, you agreed to come here and co-create a life of purpose and fulfillment, filled with spiritual growth, and you knew you could be a blessing to others as well.

God made you so uniquely different from everyone else because you are sent here on a special, peculiar mission that only you can accomplish. The specific contribution to God's plan and purpose that you were created for can only be made by you. No one else can do what God sent you here to do. You are that important and necessary. This should help you to understand that you were not born by accident, no matter what the circumstances of your "birthday" (or "earth day" as Bishop T.D. Jakes refers to it) and what led up to it might be. *You were summoned into and agreed to enter earthly existence to embark upon an elite and specialized purpose that only you can fulfill. You are equipped with everything you need to enjoy that happy and purposeful life right now.*

So what are you doing about it? If you're like most of the inhabitants of this planet, you're not sure what to do about it, if you fully believe and accept it in the first place. Second, if you do believe it, you don't know what your mission or purpose is, so you may be drifting about in an ocean of uncertainty. Third, if you do believe and accept it, and if you do know exactly what your purpose is, you may not have the courage required to boldly strike out and live it.

However, if you do believe in, accept, know and live your purpose each and every day, you've a reached a Nirvana on earth that most will only fantasize about.

Look at the lives of Christ, Moses, Abraham, and Buddha. Look at Leonardo Da Vinci, Florence Nightingale, Mother Teresa, Louis Pasteur, Sigmund Freud, Carl Jung, Albert Einstein and Benjamin Franklin. Look at Martin Luther King, Jr., Marcus Garvey, Malcolm X, Adam Clayton Powell, Langston Hughes, Zora Neale Hurston. Look at Muhammad Ali, Hilary Clinton, Oprah Winfrey, Sister Souljah, Suze Ormon. Look at Donald Trump, Bill Gates, Maya Angelou, Bill Cosby, Ernest Holmes and Charles Filmore. All of them stepped out boldly and made their unique and specialized contribution to the world—one that could only have been made by them. Look around you at the outstanding women and men you know who became mothers and fathers and decided to stay home and tackle earth's most important job: raising a child well. Look at any person you know who has the courage to live their purpose, and you'll be witnessing joy in motion.

If you live your life knowing and accepting God's purpose for you, and live it with reckless abandon, you will co-create a magnificent life that will be well spent. Your days will be joyfully tranquil and you will revel in the satisfaction that comes from doing what God specially made you for.

I realize that all of this may be a radical departure for some of us, considering our conditioning and what we may have been told about ourselves. Some of us were told, in one way or another, that we weren't worthy or deserving, or that we deserved punishment. Let me state right now *that you are worthy and deserving of every good thing.* That is why God made you, and God don't make junk!

Some of us were led to believe that we were "accidents", that our parents didn't "expect" us. We may have heard our parents refer to us as an unplanned pregnancy. For those who bought into this belief, let me ask you one question: Could anything have gone wrong in God's plan when you came here, such as the timing, or where you showed up, or who you showed up with? God's gift of life is bestowed upon each one of us at the perfect time. There are no "accidental" births. Whether human minds remember it or not, *everything in God's plan and purpose is perfect.*

Some of us were led to believe that we weren't enough;

not good enough, not skinny enough, not smart enough, not tall enough, not cool enough, not wealthy enough, not fast enough. The list drones on, but you get the picture. If any fiber of your being contains this belief, consider this: God is a master artist. Everything The Creator produces is a masterpiece, *including you*. You are perfect, whole, complete and magnificent, right now, just as you are. Understand your origins. You were imagined in the great mind of God before you were formed. When God thought about you and how wonderful you would be, God smiled with delight and couldn't wait to bring you into existence. You began as a spirit, and when you're done on the earth plane this time around, you'll end up as a spirit once again. You are truly immortal.

No expense was spared in creating the physical you— Your Creator thought of everything. God gave you the perfect physical appearance for what you're here to do. You came into the perfect family so that you could learn the lessons you needed to learn from them, both pleasant and painful. You have the perfect talents, abilities and gifts to complete the special mission you're here on. Your unfolding path here is one that will allow you to grow spiritually and evolve into a new and higher being.

To top it all off, the great artist added a little something extra before you came here: a spark of the Divine— the inner fire that makes us all like our Creator— creative powerful and magnificent. Yes, you are made in the image and likeness of God, and after you were made, God called you "GOOD."

That's what you are: GOOD. No matter what anyone else called you while you were growing up or what they call you now, no matter what people said about you, no matter what people tell you, God says you are

GOOD. And if you're GOOD enough for God, are you really concerned about what anyone else thinks?

One of the abiding principles I live by is encapsulated in this simple and clear statement: *What you think of me is none of my business.*

If you're not living your life purpose, or don't know what it is, I can empathize with you. For many years, I, too, didn't heed the clues God was sending me about what to do with my life. Even though I've always thought myself a spiritually aware person, I'd experienced periods when I felt directionless; wandering about in a desert of uncertainty and confusion.

I didn't begin to fully understand my divine life's purpose until I started a practice of getting silent and asking God what he wanted me to do. The answers were and continue to be astounding.

Are you aware of the spectacular plans—and they are nothing short of spectacular—that God has for your life? Are you aware of the magnitude of what you could accomplish? If you aren't, how will you ever live the life you were created for and so richly deserve? The universe is speaking to your heart right now, imbuing it with a passion to do something that only you can do. Are you listening? Are you taking action to live your life "on purpose"?

You may have the nagging feeling inside that there's something special you're commissioned to do. You're right! We all come here as artists: commissioned to do a magnificent work of art for the world in which we live. That work of art becomes the tapestry that forms our life's work and purpose. Whatever that magnificent creation looks like for you, it is all your choosing and by your design. God gave you the power to do it all!

If you have not yet discovered your divine life's purpose, the best way to do so is to ask God in prayer, then sit in silence and listen for answers. It's just that simple. One of the greatest and wisest men to ever walk the earth, Christ, taught his followers at Matthew 7:7-11, "If a child asks his father for bread, the father will not give him a stone, will he? Or if the child asks for a fish, his father will not give him a serpent, will he?" What is the point of these questions? If you, as a human parent, know how to give good gifts to your children, how much more so will God give good gifts to you if you ask?

One of the best questions you could ever ask of the Creator is, "What is my divine life's purpose? What do I need to learn while I am here? How can I best grow spiritually and serve the world around me?" God is Love. He will do nothing less than generously and lovingly supply you with the greatest gift of all: the answers you seek.

A word of caution: logic doesn't usually provide the answers about your life's purpose and your particular spiritual lessons. The challenge many people express to me is, "I've thought and thought about my life's purpose, but I haven't been able to find the answers." Just to let you in on a little secret, you'll discover far more answers through your intuition and feelings than you ever will trying to figure it out in your head. Get in contact with your intuitive side and use it well to guide you to your life's purpose and your spiritual lessons. As we've already seen, God speaks to us from within.

To aid you in continuing your journey toward your life's purpose and your specific spiritual lessons, develop a daily communion with The Creator that allows you to ask and receive answers about your particular life path, which is different from every other creation on this earth. Then listen carefully and vigilantly for the divine answers that will faithfully and unfailingly flow to you. The answers have been deposited in the center of your being. During the process, be assured that God's highest and best idea for you is identical to your own Soul's highest and best idea for you.

If you're unsure of how to build that kind of deep communion and constant connection with God, just remember one thing: *you are already connected to the Source of all light, you just have to fully realize it.* You can't be disconnected from God, for God is your origin, and the spark of the divine is your essential nature.

To help you more fully realize your divine nature and your inseparable connection to God, I have listed here practices that have helped me effect immense spiritual transformation:

- **Prayer—Out loud is always powerful whenever possible. It has been my experience that praying aloud imbues my words with more energy and power.**
- **Daily Meditation**
- **Reading holy books & writings, including The Bible, The Teachings of Buddha, A Course in Miracles, The Bhagavad Gita, works on Kabbalah, etc.**
- **Dream recall and recordation**
- **Journaling**
- **Research, workshops and classes to better understand how God communicates with us**

In my meditations and communion with God and the angels, I've learned that our Divine life's purpose is really two-fold. The primary aspect of why we are here is simply *spiritual transformation.* Spiritual transformation—which is really spiritual growth through experiential learning—is a process by which we become more like God. It is also the key to unleashing Divine power in our life and resolving ANY difficulty we have or ever will encounter. As His Holiness the Dalai Lama put it, "the purpose of life is to be happy." This perspective illustrates that your primary purpose for being here, in this life, at this time, in this moment, is spiritual transformation. The result is that you will remember who you really are: a divine, powerful creation of God who is endowed with the ability to manifest all that you desire. This revelation and enlightenment, and atonement (at-one-ment) with God, create true happiness. Yes, your reason for being is to be *happy on purpose.*

Remember that spiritual transformation and finding and fulfilling your divine life's purpose will be the most rewarding thing you could ever do with your life. Don't let anyone or anything stop you from living the life you were perfectly designed for, since nothing else will bring you total happiness. Living your life "on purpose" will ultimately become your only path to complete, blissful fulfillment because you will be doing what God wants you to do with your life; you will live your life being completely led by the voice of the divine within. There is no question that this path will bring unimaginable blessings.

The second aspect of your divine life's purpose has to do with your special and unique gifts, talents and abilities. These gifts can be used to sustain yourself and those you love, and profound joy only comes when you use them to serve others.

God made your Divine life's purpose **S.U.P.E.R.**:

- **S**pecialized
- **U**nique
- **P**assionate
- **E**nriching
- **R**ewarding

I've learned from many spiritual masters that—in addition to spiritual transformation—finding a way to serve others using our God-given, individual gifts is the second key to why we are here and finding lasting happiness. To discover and fulfill your Divine life's purpose and use it to serve others is to bring yourself immense and profound contentment and joy. Whatever you love doing, find a way to do more of it!

Consider the words of Frederick Buechner: "The place where God calls you is the place where your deep gladness and the world's deep hunger meet."

Your first reason for being here is to learn the lessons that will facilitate your spiritual growth, development and transformation. Your secondary reason for being here is to find a way to use your unique gifts, talents, skills and abilities to serve others in a way that brings excellence to your mission and joy to your heart. Accomplish that tall order and you will be irresistibly happy and attain everything you've ever wanted or dreamed of!

Sacred Lesson #2—You are not a victim. You are an infinite, creative and powerful being with the capability to design the life of your dreams.

For me, this lesson is akin to the first, but is still distinct enough to warrant its own discussion.

At one time, I thought I was a victim. I behaved like a victim. I blamed other people for the negative experiences I encountered. When I wasn't blaming someone else for my woes, I was busy entrenching myself in the belief that unpleasant and unwanted occurrences happened to me for no reason other than pure chance. I felt that nothing in life was destined: it was all arbitrary and random, leaving me no control over the things that befell me, good or bad.

Then a series of events completely reshaped my paradigm, or my way of looking at the world and my life.

Many years ago, when my first husband and I decided to relocate to Maryland from New York City, we went apartment shopping in the areas we wanted to move to. We saw many suitable places to live for our young family of three, but there was a particular garden apartment community I fell in love with—the location was perfect, the neighborhood seemed quite safe (a big plus moving from New York City), the apartment was beautiful, and the up-front money and income required to move in were affordable. Considering that our apartment in New York was in an old, but beautiful, building that had no air conditioning, central heating, or modern amenities such as dishwashers and garbage disposals, the new apartment in Maryland looked like the Taj Mahal. Another big plus was that unlike our apartment in New York, it had no roaches.

I didn't know if we would be able to qualify for the apartment because our credit wasn't the best at the time. However, I decided somewhere deep inside that that apartment was for me. I pictured myself in the small modern kitchen, stacking dishes in my brand new dishwasher, cleaning my shiny new stove, wiping down my new frost-free refrigerator (no more defrosting my freezer with an ice pick and pots of boiling water). I visualized myself doing everything in that apartment: eating, sleeping, playing with my son, waking up in the morning and looking out of the window, walking out onto the patio and seeking shade under the enormous weeping willow tree right outside our window. My visualizations were so vivid that I could smell the air around me. I could almost reach out and touch everything in the brand new apartment. I didn't know at the time that I was being prompted by Spirit to use visualization to bring into manifestation something I deeply desired.

We applied for the apartment, and, after some time, got the news that we were approved to move in. I was past delighted and elated! We moved in and life in the apartment was exactly as I'd imagined it would be.

After living in the apartment for a period of time, I found out that we were expecting another child. Soon, this two-bedroom-with-a-den unit would be too small for us—we'd need more room. I went out looking for a place for us and happened upon some rental town homes in the neighborhood that had three finished levels with three bedrooms. On the lower level was a finished basement with a laundry room and sliding glass doors that opened out to a back yard, which faced the woods. I thought to myself, *This is the perfect place for us to live!* Again, I wondered if we would qualify. I felt we didn't earn enough money to live there. Even if we did, the three bedroom units were hard to come by because no one ever seemed to move out of them, so the waiting list was quite long.

But, desire entered the picture again, and again, prompted by the Spirit, I went into visualization mode— I pictured myself moving in, fixing up my son's room and the nursery for the baby we were expecting, making dinner in the large eat-in kitchen, sitting in the backyard watching the kids play. I would drive by the town homes and just look at them, knowing that one day I'd live in one of them.

Sure enough, we applied for a three-bedroom-with-a-basement unit, and we quickly got it. Again I was elated! I started to really get the hang of visualization though I didn't completely understand it. One thing I became convinced of: it worked like magic. If I could see something in my mind, and hold that picture long enough to get excited about it, soon enough, it would show up in my life.

We enjoyed living there for three years. But after a while, I knew we couldn't keep renting forever and longed to own a home. I would drive through the neighborhood looking for suitable homes, when synchronism led me to a townhouse community not far from where we lived. The homes were spacious, affordable, in a great community, with an excellent school nearby.

As you can guess, the same creative process that I had practiced successfully before gave us that home too.

As I began to read success literature and study my life, I saw a pattern:

- *Things didn't just happen at random.*
- *There are no victims.*
- *There's no such thing as coincidence, as we commonly refer to it. There is only synchronicity.*
- *All things that appear in the physical world came into existence by a formula, or creative process.*
- *Everyone on earth is engaged in this creative process.*

I saw in my own life that I could will things that I wanted into existence, or even will certain things that I didn't want in my life out of existence. In a sense, I was co-creating my life and everything in it while simultaneously believing on some level that it couldn't be done. I was learning, through my own life experiences, that I was in charge of my life. There was nothing random about anything that had happened to me.

There is a statement made in a Buddhist holy book that is astoundingly true: *You are right now the result of all your past thoughts.*

That means that whatever you spent time dwelling on yesterday is in your life today or will appear tomorrow in some form or fashion. Whatever you told yourself you could or couldn't do yesterday is proving true for you today or will prove true for you tomorrow.

Therefore, it follows that you are an architect. And, as an architect, you are capable of designing your life and everything that you want in it.

Let me continue telling you my story.

Many, many years went by. I eventually divorced my first husband and subsequently spent a few years as a single mother. Some time after my separation from my husband, I met a man that I was instantly attracted to. We happily dated for many years, and five years into our relationship, had a baby girl. By that time, I knew I was the powerful co-creator of my life, but I still wasn't sure exactly how it all worked.

A couple of years after the baby was born, I made a conscious decision to eliminate certain things from my life, and get more of what I wanted into my life. Then it happened. Exactly as I desired it. It was that simple. Here's what happened.

I wanted to be married, with my new husband, myself and our baby girl under the same roof rather than toting her back and forth from my house to his. I wanted to engross myself in more spiritual transformative work. I wanted to fulfill my purpose, passion and mission of writing and public speaking. I wanted to live in a beautiful home. I wanted to have guaranteed income whether I went to work or not. I wanted to be able to travel to exotic locations around the world.

After I sat down and decided exactly what I wanted, I am joyful to state that the man I love and I got married in the exotic location of my dreams—Hawaii. He, our daughter and I live under the same roof, in a beautiful home; there's no more "Mommy's house" and "Daddy's house." I sold my financial planning practice, providing me with monthly income which allows me to spend my days writing and preparing for public speaking engagements. I have a guaranteed income from the sale of my business that will continue for several years. Since retiring from my financial planning practice, I've created yet another residual stream of income from a network marketing business venture. This business provides thousands of dollars of monthly residual, leveraged income.

It sounds as if everything I desired came true—and indeed it has. Was it easy? Absolutely not. At times, it was downright terrifying! I'll give you an example.

A few years into my relationship with my third child's father, I arrived at the place where I knew I wanted to be married to the man I loved. To me, our relationship had reached a plateau and had become convenient. In such an atmosphere, growth cannot take place. Stagnancy sets in. I wanted us to experience the challenges that I knew would push our growth and development to the next level, rather than sitting com-

fortably where we were. To me, this meant moving forward to the challenging and demanding realm of marriage. The decision was not entirely mine.

God spoke to me and said, "Get married or get out of
this relationship." My reply was, "What?" God said
clearly, over and over again, "Get married or get out of
this relationship. What you're doing right now doesn't
feed either of you anymore."

That was the terrifying part. I thought to myself, *I
love this man. He is the father of my child. I don't want
to give him an ultimatum! Besides, if he doesn't want
to get married, how will I have the strength to leave
him? It'll rip my heart out!*

Spirit was insistent, and I wasn't getting any inner
peace.

This is where the difficulty comes in with following
our inner voice of guidance. The voice appears suddenly, seemingly out of nowhere, and simply speaks
the truth. It doesn't explain, or give extensive detail. It
doesn't make an argument for itself, nor does it attempt
to list all the reasons why a certain course of action
should be taken. It just speaks the truth: simply, plainly,
and clearly.

Finally, I told the love of my life that God said we
have to get married or I have to move on.

"God told you that?" He asked.

"Uh-huh," I responded.

"How did He say it?"

"Just like I'm saying it to you right now; get married,
or move on."

I didn't know what the response would be. At that
point, I had to do what was right for me, whether or
not he agreed. God gave me the strength to say what I
needed to say to him and mean it. If we hadn't gotten
married, God had infused me with enough courage to

walk away, if it had to come to that. Regardless of my heart being ripped out.

Perhaps that was just the push we both needed. We were married shortly thereafter.

This was yet another milestone for me in learning how life works. You see, I had the desire to be married, but I hesitated because I wasn't sure that's what my lover wanted too. God gave me the push I needed to be the proactive creator in my life, not the spectator.

And in the process, I learned the creative process, or the formula, for creating anything I desired. I learned to create my world by using the same step-by-step formula God used to create the manifest world.

This formula works perfectly every time. It was created by God and is fool-proof. Here is the creative process:

Thought + Visualization + Intense emotions + Time = Words, Actions & Physical Manifestation

Let's consider this formula step by step.

First, before anything can happen on the physical plane of existence, it must first happen in the mind. This is true of all physical manifestations, whether wanted or unwanted. Mind is the master, and God is the great mind. We all began in the mind of God. God had a creative idea, and that idea was to bring us into existence along with a world that would support us. Whatever we experience in our lives on the physical level has been delivered to us via this exact process. The first step is that we spent time _thinking_ about something. Our thoughts, which are things, have immense magnetic power. The longer you thought about something you wanted (or didn't want) the closer you were to actually experiencing it. All matter began with a thought. When we speak of thoughts, we are referring to ideas, intentions, beliefs, convictions, opinions, perceptions and any other aspect of thought that is held in the mind. Sometimes our thoughts are conscious and we know exactly what we are thinking about. Most of the time, however, what is really running the show is our subconscious mind; that vast ocean of consciousness that is hidden from our every day awareness (We do get a nightly glimpse into the sub-conscious mind during the dream state.).

The subconscious mind in each and every individual has been programmed, or conditioned, by others and by the environment. Some of the people and institutions who usually have a hand in conditioning us from birth are:

- Parents/Grandparents
- Custodians/Guardians
- Religion
- School/Teachers
- Family
- Friends

So the thoughts in your conscious mind and the thoughts in your sub-conscious mind are acting as a magnet all day every day, drawing you closer and closer to what you are thinking about. This is where the creation process begins, in the mind, whether conscious or subconscious.

Next, we naturally start to visualize what we are thinking about. While our conscious mind thinks in terms of words, concepts and ideas, our subconscious mind prefers to work with pictures and symbols. While I was thinking about getting the homes I wanted, I created mental pictures to go along with my dominant thoughts. I visualized myself in the homes I wanted until the mental pictures were laser sharp. The power of internal visualization adds another layer of magnetic power to our thoughts. Now that the conscious mind and subconscious mind are working together—the conscious mind through the idea and concept of what you want and the subconscious through the mental pictures you are creating—you are that much closer to experiencing what you are thinking about, and now seeing, in your mind.

Usually, seeing a clearly focused mental image will begin to evoke emotions within us. Powerful mental pictures trigger us in such a way that intense emotions begin to flow. You've probably had the experience of just picturing something you consider to be terrifying and feeling your heart jump. Or you might have pictured something extremely pleasurable and found that your feelings and body responded instantly. At this stage of creation, in addition to our conscious and subconscious minds being involved, our emotions and body are now involved in the creative process, which adds yet another boost of powerful magnetic energy to whatever we are focusing on.

If you continue repeating the above systematically over time, you will have a result in the physical world. You will speak in accord with what you have been focusing on, and you will begin to act on your original thoughts also. Next, you will begin to see physical manifestation of your thoughts, mental pictures and intense emotions.

Notice that there has been no reference to whether the creation is wanted or unwanted. This is because the creative process works exactly the same whether we want something or not.

What does that mean?

Let's first examine how this foolproof creative process unfolds when you really don't want something to happen, or when there is something in your life that you really don't want.

I'll give you an actual example from my own life. When I had extreme financial difficulties, I remember being frustrated, fed up, and stressed out. During this time in my life, I had a lot of bills, and it seemed that they just kept multiplying. No matter how strongly I protested that I didn't want any more bills, I just couldn't stop the flood of bills from coming.

Since I was raised as a Christian, and taught to pray, I would pray to God saying "God, help me to get rid of these bills. God, I don't want any more bills. If I see one more bill, I think I will lose my mind. God, please help me to be in debt-free heaven!"

I couldn't figure out why I wasn't getting the answer to my prayers that I wanted. I wanted the bills gone, but more kept coming.

During this painful process, I discovered that although I didn't want any more bills, most of my time and attention was focused on bills. I also observed within myself that I had mental pictures of bills. I went to bed with pictures of bills floating around in my head with envelopes of all colors to go along with them— some pink, some green, some blue. I was also feeling the intense emotion of fear of getting more bills. Whenever I would go to the mailbox, my body would physically revolt because I knew I would find more bills. When I opened the bills, I felt sick at the pit of my stomach. I was talking about how much I didn't want bills, and I was acting on it too by not opening the pile of bills that were in the corner. However, every time I went past the pile, I felt it mentally, emotionally and physically.

I had all the components in play for the foolproof formula. The creative process was working full speed at this point, bringing me more of what I didn't want!

Then I learned another piece of valuable information about my own mind. I discovered that my sub-conscious mind didn't understand words like "rid of", "any", "no", "don't" or "debt-free". The subconscious mind, which is an enormous part of the creative pro-cess, doesn't understand negative pronouns and conjunctions. So, to my sub-conscious mind, my prayer sounded like this:

"God, help me to get _____ these bills. God, I _____ want _____ more bills. If I see one more bill, I think I will _____ my mind. God, please help me to be in debt_____ heaven!"

As you can see, the message I was giving myself was that I wanted bills. Bills were what I was focused on, and more and more bills were what I was getting.

This example shows that the creative process is working regardless of whether you want the things you are focused on or you do not. I didn't want more bills. But my focus and thoughts were still on bills.

Instead of my previous prayers, I began to offer a different kind of prayer, which got results. The following prayer never mentions bills. It focuses solely on creating wealth and abundance:

Dear God, Loving Lord of all, I acknowledge You as my Maker, my Provider and my Sustainer. I am your precious child, and the heir to a fortune. God, thank You that You richly supply all that I need, physically, mentally, emotionally and spiritually. Great Creator, I now ask for Your guidance in cre-ating more sources and streams of income to en-rich myself and my family. All abundance comes from You and I thank You that Your abundant hand is open to me now as I go forward to create more money and wealth for myself than I ever have before. Help me this day to use my talents and gifts from You in ways that bless others and provide me with greatly increased compensation. Help me today, Oh God, to bring value to the lives of others and to be highly compensated for doing so. I thank You, Jehovah-Jireh, Great Provider, for the abundance that I am now experiencing as more income and wealth than I have ever had before. Thank You that You have shown me how to be generous and to give away at least 10% of all I receive, so as to plant a seed that will take root, sprout and grow and feed many. I am rich! Hallelujah and thank You God!

As you've probably noticed, the latter prayer even made me feel better than the first prayer.

The first prayer held me somewhat captive to my situation, and confirmed and solidified the presence of bills. It also didn't call upon me to do much of anything, I wanted and expected God to do all the work and miraculously remove all my bills. That simply wasn't going to happen.

The latter prayer contains critical components that must be present to get results in the creative process:

- The prayer affirms that I am God's child who has access to a fortune. Therefore, abundance is already here, I just need to access it.
- The prayer states that I am willing to use what God has already given me—my talents and gifts— to create more wealth and abundance for myself than I've ever had before.

- The prayer asks for guidance and help rather than just for money, which is reminiscent of Solomon's plea for wisdom rather than riches.
- The prayer is stated in the present tense, rather than referring to a distant time in the future.
- The prayer states that I have a desire to enrich other's lives as well, not just my own. I understand the spiritual principle of tithing and am willing to practice it faithfully.
- The prayer uses one of the many names for God, specifically referring to God's capacity as a Provider.
- This prayer has the energy of joy and praise and gives thanks several times.

I cannot explain to you in words how well this prayer has worked. You are encouraged to use it often.

Knowing and understanding how this creative process works, even with unwanted events and happenings in our lives, causes us to become more aware of what we are thinking about, what we are focusing our attention on and what we are feeling.

You cannot experience anything in your physical world that you did not first create with this exact same process in your mental and emotional world. This is how creation works, and it works the same way every time.

I would challenge you to examine your life thoroughly and completely. Are there any unwanted people, situations or circumstances present? Next, monitor your thoughts closely regarding each of these unwanted aspects of your life. You may find that you are giving more mental time and attention to these parts of your life than you may realize.

The antidote would be to focus on the solution, or

what you do want. The latter prayer above doesn't focus on, nor does it even mentions bills. It focuses only on the opposite, which is what I truly desired: enough wealth and abundance for me, my kids and for gifting to others.

It's clear to see why the process worked so well to bring to me the homes I desired. I had clear thoughts and intentions, with powerful mental images, amplified by intense emotions. A brief time elapsed, during which I spoke about what I wanted as if I already had it, and I performed a few minor actions to get what I wanted. The next thing I knew, I had what I wanted!

I have used this process over and over and over again to create all manner of positive experiences for myself. God has revealed to us exactly how creation works in order for us to take charge of our lives and understand that we too, being created in the image and likeness of God, are powerful creators.

These successes do not signal the end of the designing road for me. There's much more in my life that I desire to design and accomplish. Just like our Creator, we are creative beings, always eager to bring new and better things into manifestation. The moment we reach several desired outcomes, we are now presented with a new vantage point from which to bring even more into existence.

I share this with you today because I'm no longer steeped in the untrue belief that what manifests in my life is random. Far from it, my entire life is designed by two forces: first, God, because I ask for my every step to be divinely guided; and second, by my own thoughts, feelings, decisions words and actions. Though God has the power to create a magnificent life for me, it wouldn't materialize in the natural world if my thoughts, feelings, decisions, words and actions were not harmoniously co-creating the same thing. I would be fighting

God, and hurting myself. Instead, I now know to the core of my being that I create Karma every day by what I think, intend, decide, feel, say and do.

Karma is like a boomerang.

Karma is like a mirror.

Karma is like a yo-yo.

You cannot have in your material life what you did not design and co-create in the world of potentiality. As a student of Kabbalah, I know that there is a spiritual realm called the 99% world, and there is a physical plane of existence, called the 1% world. In order to have anything show up in the 1% physical world, it must first be created in the 99% spiritual world of thought, feelings, intentions and desires. To have every good thing in your physical world, it must first be co-created with God in the spiritual world.

You'll have in your life exactly what you choose to think about all day, wanted or unwanted.

Remember the foolproof formula:

Thought + Visualization + Intense emotions + Time = Words, Actions & Physical Manifestation

Use this immense and limitless creative power wisely—don't settle for just living your life, choose to design and create your life exactly as it would please you.

After all, you are the creator of your own reality.

Sacred Lesson #3—Learn to create and develop new and different intentions, thoughts, speech patterns and actions.

My recurring money problems persisted for almost 20 years until I decided to do something different than what I had been doing. *I created new intentions. Entertained new thoughts. Spoke a new language. And conducted myself in a new fashion.* Only then could I learn the lessons lack was trying for so long to teach me. The lessons of abundance, generosity, sensibleness, wisdom, careful adherence to a well thought out financial plan and complete and total reliance upon the Universe's unfailing ability to provide everything I need or want.

Think about it, if you keep doing the same things you're doing now, what will change your future results? If you continue repeating the same negative patterns of behavior, you're destined to land right back in the same messes over and over again.

Alternatively, if you choose to adopt (and it is a choice) new intentions, thoughts, speech patterns and habits, you will be radically and permanently transformed.

As a public speaker on the topics of spirituality, personal development and wealth building, my financial situation is now far removed from the chaotic mess it once was. I learned to intend prosperity for myself. To think abundant thoughts. To speak the language of wealth and to act in a manner that invites wealth and abundance in and closes the door forever on lack and insufficiency.

By God's grace, I conquered my tribulation and *you can conquer yours, too.* It's not too late for you to become the victor in the wrestling match you've been fighting and losing for years. Your life is waiting for you to create new intentions and welcome new outcomes.

How? Consider the following 6-step process that graduated me right out of the tumultuous mess I kept re-creating:

Step 1: Humbly remember that you don't have to conquer your major adversities on your own, nor can you. Left to my own devices, I would fail miserably at improving difficult situations completely alone. Conversely, we need to call upon God, the angels, spirit guides, the Holy Spirit and all other supernatural powers God has put at our disposal to rid ourselves of whatever plagues us and draws us away from God's love. There are many spiritual tools that are available for your use to conquer or cope with any difficulty, and one of the greatest of these is prayer. In the midst of all the difficulties, you'll learn exactly what your trial is there to teach you if you pray for wisdom and listen to your inner divinely guided voice.

Using the spiritual tools that God has put at your disposal is only possible if *you know what the spiritual tools are and understand how to use them for your greatest benefit.* I learned, understood and appreciated more about these tools by reading and studying spiritual and inspirational literature that helped to effect my ongoing spiritual transformation. Read, study, learn and grow.

After you've graduated from the lesson you're now facing, your worst problems and the pain they cause will be erased. The book *A Course in Miracles* offers to us the truth that in the face of faith, problems disappear.

In addition, you will emerge a stronger and wiser soul—a soul that could never again be shackled. Trust me.

Step 2: Next, ask for Divine aid to fill your mind with intentions that reflect the answers you receive about your life's purpose and spiritual path. Dwell on these intentions every day, and intermittently throughout the day. Once an intention is introduced into the universe, it will take form and manifest into your existence. This is true whether the intention is negative or favorable. Whatever you intend, you will create in your world. Therefore, why not intend for yourself the life that reflects God's S.U.P.E.R. purpose for you? Why not intend vibrant, radiant health; loving, nurturing relationships; overflowing, enduring wealth and deeply satisfying and fulfilling work? Why not?

Step 3: After creating new intentions with help from God and your inner voice of wisdom, you must then begin to change your thought patterns. Ask yourself, "What do I think about most of the time?" Whatever it is, be assured that it will continue to show up on your doorstep. Why? Because thoughts are things. Whatever you focus on expands. In the words of Ralph Waldo Emerson, "A man is what he thinks about all day long." Remember, "So a man thinketh, so shall he be." Your thoughts and intentions manifest in the physical realm.

When I was suffering financially, I began to read success literature that I felt deep within could help me. I was struck by the idea of monitoring my thoughts. When I began to really pay attention to the chatter that was constantly playing in my head, I was horrified! I would spend tremendous time and massive energy thinking about how broke I was. What bills I couldn't pay. How much money I didn't have. What things I couldn't afford. Being so focused on lack only served to invite more lack into my daily existence, the very thing I was so desperately trying to avoid.

What are you thinking about right now? What are you focused on? If you're not sure, let me suggest that you monitor your thoughts over the next seven days. This is not for the purpose of challenging or judging your thoughts as they arise. This exercise simply calls upon you to be a silent observer in the vast world of your own mind. You will likely be surprised at how much time you spend thinking about your problems and difficulties. Each time you expend precious time and energy worrying about some problem you have, you actually open the door and invite the problem to come into your house, sit down and stay for as long as it pleases. The longer and stronger you focus on the problem, you will see that other related problems will also begin to show up. This is how the Universe works.

One of my mentors says that you can't fix a problem with the same sick mind that created the problem in the first place!

Here's a powerful process that turned my "sick" mind around into being a healthy, well-adjusted, consciously creative machine.

During my tumultuous years, I read a book that outlined how to keep a gratitude journal—a journal in which I had to make at least three to five entries each day of all the things I was thankful for. After taking up the habit, I noticed that more of my attention started to become focused on the bounty in my life. I began to draw focus away from the poverty that I had previously (and subconsciously) been inviting in. As I began to shift my thoughts to concentrating on how richly blessed I was, and how many things I had to be thankful for, a critical shift in my life took place: no longer was my problem expanding. Instead, the realm of possibilities was expanding. I was gradually able to invite more bounty in and allow lack to quietly slip away.

The point is this: problems need time, attention and energy focused on them in order to persist and grow. If you remove all anxious and worried focus from your problems, they cannot survive. If you will consistently and consciously focus on the opposite which is the solution to your problems, then that is what will soon show up in your world. Cutting off the energy flow to your problems is like cutting off the blood supply to a leech. Eventually, it will detach and die. So will your most stubborn difficulties. Force yourself to focus on the blessed aspects of your life, the things that are going particularly well, the happenings that bring you the most joy, and all the things for which you are so grateful. If you feel you don't have anything good in your life to focus on, make something up. Your subconscious mind doesn't know the difference between what's real and what's imagined anyway. Before long, the blessings in your life will mushroom and multiply under the nourishment that your focused attention and energy bring to them.

Step 4: Next, check in with your emotions. Connect to how you are feeling. How do you feel at this very instant? Happy? Joyful? Tranquil? Thankful?

What is the range of emotions you go through in a day? Do you swing wildly from one emotion to the next, or do you remain even tempered most of the time?

Emotions are powerful. They amplify your thoughts and intentions to levels that may be surprising. Since emotions are so powerful and have the capacity to draw to us what we desire, what emotions support us? The most powerful emotions in creating a life you love are:

- Love
- Sincere, deep and heartfelt gratitude
- Bliss
- Joy/Elation
- Enthusiasm/Passion/Excitement
- Happiness
- Hope/Expectation/Eager & Confident Anticipation

- High self-worth and self-value
- Curiosity/Eagerness to learn, grow and transform
- Courage/Boldness/Faith
- Peace/Inner Calm

These emotions are most helpful when creating a life of your dreams. These emotions support and encourage your forward progress toward physical manifestation of what you want. They act as wood in the fire to keep the flames of your soul's desires burning.

Step 5: Next, examine what is coming out of your mouth. What are you talking about? If you're not completely sure, monitor everything you say over the next seven days. Once again, there's no need to judge what you're saying, just observe.

When I was a financial advisor, I would warn my financial planning clients of words that I never wanted to hear them mention. Words like:

"I am broke."

"I am so poor."

"I am busted this week until next payday."

I became more aware of the creative power of words, so anytime a person uttered "I'm broke!" I would respond by saying, "You certainly are, and what else would happen now that you've told the Universe what you expect it to give you?"

The term "I AM" is the most powerfully creative statement in the universe. Whatever you put behind the words "I AM", will be more fully brought into your life, so be careful! Only put words behind "I AM" that you truly desire to embody.

Before you open your mouth, determine if what you are going to say is healing or debilitating to your current situation. Your words betray your thinking, so what falls out of your mouth is never by accident.

If thoughts are things, words are boomerangs. I'm sure you've curiously witnessed a boomerang, perhaps as a child, and thought briefly about its uncanny, unfailing ability to return to the person who tossed it. Words are as precise as boomerangs in returning to you the fulfillment of whatever you spoke. I used to speak of my money woes in a self-defeating manner, saying that I couldn't afford this or that, and that one day I might have enough money to get the things I really wanted. Naturally, my words always reverberated; it was as if they were bouncing off an invisible wall in front of me and heading straight back to the source with lightning speed! I was never going to create wealth while articulating words of poverty. It goes against all the rules of the Universe, especially the powerful law of cause and effect.

As my understanding of how to become wealthy continued to grow, I saw and read that truly wealthy people rarely say what they can't afford, although I'm sure there are some things that even the richest people can't afford. If there is something that they desire, instead of saying "I can't afford that," they ask themselves, "How can I afford that?" Asking and subsequently answering that question opens your mind to endless possibilities for creating wealth. Whereas merely stating the word "can't" immediately shuts down your brain and all the imagination and creativity that could lead to increased wealth.

What are you saying about your problems? Do you talk about how unbearable your situation is, how defeated you feel and how long you've had the problem? After monitoring your words, you may be surprised to discover how much doom and gloom you vocalize. Ask people around you if you complain. They'll tell you the truth. Do not become upset when they tell you the truth. This is simply information. Don't shoot the messenger.

What helped me change my speech patterns was daily repetition of affirmations that were life-enhancing. There was one particular affirmation that I liked: "I am now making all the money I could possibly desire through my skill and expertise as a Financial Advisor." This affirmation was useful in helping me secure higher commissions which equated to higher income. Surprisingly, it happened without me doing much more physical work. This is because the work I was doing was in the 99% world, which actually requires less physical work on my part in the 1% world.

You see, words, like thoughts and intentions, are determined to manifest and return in-kind results to you. What else could they do?

Harness the power of your words by speaking thanks for the dynamic blessings that are right now present in your life. Speak radiant health and overwhelming abundance into your life. Speak a loving, caring, compassionate and passionate mate into your life. Speak beautiful, well-adjusted children into your life. Speak serenity, tranquility and peaceful joy beyond measure into your life.

Say it like you mean it! Say it with aplomb and with full knowledge that the blessing you are speaking is already happening for you right now, for that is truth.

If the exact affirmations do not come easily to you, try some of my favorites:

Overall Positive Affirmations:

- *"God loves me unconditionally, therefore I am unconditionally lovable. I love myself unconditionally."*

- *"There is a supernatural power in my life for well-being, prosperity and joy!"*
- *"I am rich in mind, body and spirit!"*
- *"I am a co-creator with God in designing a magnificent life for myself!"*
- *"All things work together for my benefit and for my soul's highest purpose."*

Abundance Affirmations:

- *"I am a divine creation of God, summoned into the light to receive unlimited abundance."*
- *"The Source of all treasure is now granting me the abundance I deserve!"*
- *"Manna falls from heaven into my life every day!"*
- *"I am open to receiving all the bounty of the universe!"*

Good Health Affirmations:

- *"I believe in and now possess perfect, vibrant, radiant, enduring health because that is from God; therefore it is real."*
- *"I support my body with a healthy diet, exercise and extreme care!"*
- *"I love my body for its wonder and splendor!"*

Monitor what is coming out of your mouth, and then make the necessary changes in your language to mirror the changes you desire in your life. Many Native American chiefs take a considerable amount of time to formulate an answer in words to questions they are asked. This is because they believe that the words we speak are eternal, and will have an undeniable effect. In light of this ancient wisdom, we do well to carefully consider what comes out of our mouths.

For you to remember the power of words, simply reflect on the wonder of the creation story in the Bible book of Genesis and God's supernatural ability to bring everything into existence through the Word. The entire universe was created by God's spoken word.

Being a child of God, you can create the life you desire with the power of your words as well.

Try it. Remember that words have an enduring and encompassing power, therefore they should be dispensed and handled with the greatest of care. Use your words wisely, never wasting them, and send them forth with the intention that they will bring good to yourself as well as to your hearers. Use them to create what you want for yourself and for others. Speak goodness, love, success, prosperity and abundance into your life and the lives of your spouse, children, parents, friends and others. Use your thoughtful words today to create whatever you desire.

Tell your spouse or partner how much you love and respect them, and how much they live up to your expectations. If you do, they will.

Speak into your children's lives telling them how much you love and admire them, how much hope you have for their future, how valuable you count them, how beautiful they are, how strong and determined they are and how far you know they'll fly. If you do, they will.

You have an enormous potential for doing good and an incredibly powerful gift from God in the form of communication. What we say, and how we say it, helps to create and shape our world. Use your gift of speech wisely!

Step 6: Act differently than how you've been acting. The definition of insane is doing the same thing over and over again and expecting different results. If you're stuck in a problematic situation, it's because you haven't changed your behavior and habits. According to studies of human behavior, a habit is formed after repeating an action for at least 21 consecutive times. Following this amount of repetition, a new pattern is developed in the brain, thus making it easier to continue repeating the same action over and over. In essence, a habit is born. When a habit is born, it creates an internal pathway in the brain, almost like a flowing river. This internal process can be used to your advantage.

Stephen Covey, in his world-renowned book, *The 7 Habits of Highly Effective People,* explains that a habit exists where there is an overlapping of knowledge (what to do), skill (how to do) and attitude (desire to do).

Let's examine this concept from the aspect of a cigarette smoker. The cigarette smoker's habit persists because he or she:

1) Knows what to do (knowledge)
2) Knows how to smoke a cigarette (skill)
3) Wants to smoke a cigarette (attitude or desire)

A pathway has been created in the physical brain. The longer the smoker keeps smoking, and reinforcing the behavior, the deeper the grooves in the brain become (this doesn't include the numerous physiological responses that are affected as well). The brain pathway's "riverbed" deepens and widens.

According to Mr. Covey, in the absence of any one of the above three aspects, a habit can not develop or persist.

For instance, at any time that the smoker decides to quit smoking, three elements must be included in the cessation process:

1) Knowing what to do to quit smoking (knowledge)
2) Practicing the steps daily that lead to quitting cigarettes (skill)
3) Desire to quit smoking (attitude)

Now that you know a little bit about how your brain establishes new habits, it would be helpful to use this process to create beneficial habits, rather than the destructive ones we usually create. Developing habits or patterns of behavior that are beneficial and restorative is not difficult to do. In order to make a change, you must first examine what it is that you're doing now that's producing undesirable results. Your careful attention to your current habits and actions will help you to become *aware.* Awareness is a necessary first step in effecting any change. If you are not aware of what you're doing to create negative results, how can you stop doing it?

After becoming aware of where your difficulties lie, you'll possess a certain clarity that's necessary for lasting change. Armed with this new clarity, you must *decide,* make a conscious determination that you need and want to change. Nothing happens unless you *decide* that it will. Conversely, anything you decide to do, you accomplish.

Remember this:

There's nothing more powerful and unstoppable than a person who has made a steadfast, unwavering and unshakable decision.

Once you *decide* to change and begin to act on that decision, elements in the Universe will start to come together to support you in your new decision. You will have help in systematically replacing your old, debilitating, crippling habits with new, restorative habits that will support your continued spiritual transformation. It will be amazing how much help will show up to keep you on track.

Let me tell you a story to clarify my point.

While building my financial planning practice, a prospective client came into my office for an initial consultation. He was referred by another client of mine, who was a good friend of his. An intelligent and articulate young man with aggressive financial goals, he was definitely not moving in the direction he desired or dreamed of. When he presented his financial situation to me, he was agitated and perplexed. Though he earned a good salary, he complained of not knowing where his money went. He was in debt, had bad credit, and owed back taxes. None of which made sense to him considering how much he earned. In addition, he was often without cash, and would frequently borrow money from family members. His sister, he said, would often berate him, "You live at home with Mom. You have no bills to pay. I'm a single mother of two children and I earn less than you do, but I always seem to have money whenever you need to borrow some. Where's all your money going?"

She was right. If he could answer her question, he knew he would be much better off financially than he was. It was gnawing at him that he didn't have the answer to what was siphoning away most of his hard earned cash.

After I gathered all the pertinent financial information that I needed to assess his situation, we set a date to meet again within the next few days to review my findings and map out a financial strategy.

In the meantime, I went to work analyzing the numbers he provided to me in order to flesh out the deficit. As part of the analysis, I added all the expenses he incurred on a monthly basis. After subtracting his expenses from his income, there was a difference of over $1,500.00; which meant that, theoretically, he should have had $1,500.00 per month left over after paying all of his obligations. The results surprised me, based on the discussion I had had with him in our initial meeting. I prepared for our next meeting.

When we met again, I informed him of my findings. He was shocked. As he stated previously, he had no idea where his money was going. He certainly didn't think he had an extra $1,500.00 lying around at the end of every month. This wasn't the first time I'd heard this complaint from clients and potential clients. In fact, it's rather common, but not quite to this extent. Most people can't account for $200.00 to $300.00 per month, which is usually acceptable to them. However, not being able to account for $1,500.00 per month, considering his income, was highly objectionable to him.

He wanted to find a solution. He desired a change.

I proceeded how I normally did when clients were not able to account for money that my calculations say they should have had. I started asking him a series of "lifestyle" questions, such as:

"What do you do and where do you go on a typical payday?"

"Do you buy breakfast and lunch every day?"

"Where do you go on the weekends?"

"Do you normally pay for dates or take other people along with you?"

"When you go out, what kind of establishments do you frequent?"

"How much would you spend on an average Friday or Saturday night?"

"What about expenditures you may not remember or keep track of, like CD's, DVD's, books, magazines, birthday gifts, and holiday spending?"

After asking these questions and many more, we discovered a pattern of behavior that was producing negative results. He would frequently go out on Friday nights, spending money on drinks for himself and friends. On occasion, he would spring for dinner for he and his friends also, especially on paydays. Including drinks and dinner, he could easily spend $80.00 or more in one evening. Often he would go out on Saturdays with his girlfriend to a mall and to lunch, and perhaps to dinner. He would spend an additional $100.00 or more on a typical Saturday with his girlfriend. If he decided to go to Sunday brunch after church, he would sometimes pick up the tab for his mom and other family members, which could cost $80.00 or more. He bought breakfast and lunch on most days during the week. And if he didn't like what his mom fixed for dinner, he'd order dinner from a carryout restaurant. After adding up all the money he might spend in a typical week, the total came to well *over* $350.00. If he spent $350.00 to $400.00 each week, it wasn't hard to see where the extra $1,500.00 per month had been disappearing to!

Careful examination of his patterns of behavior illuminated clearly what he needed to change. If he wanted to become financially stable, he would have to stop most of his frivolous and impulsive spending. He would also have to establish a savings and investment plan, as well as a strategy to get out of debt. He agreed to implement all of the above—he *decided* that he wanted and needed to make a change. He had met with significant pain and distress over his financial situation, so he determined that he would commit to building his wealth rather than systematically destroying it. He experienced a mental shift, which then shifted his actions.

I recommended that he save $1,000.00 per month in a combination of savings and investment vehicles, or $500.00 from each semi-monthly paycheck. Initially, he bristled at the level of savings I was recommending for him. After discussing the advantages, he agreed to cut back on his dining out and trips to the mall to save $400.00 from each paycheck, or $800.00 per month. Just three months after that decision, he had saved $2,400.00. He was incredulous. "I've never had this much money in one place before without touching it— I can't believe I can actually save money!" A few short months later, he had several thousand dollars in a combination of cash and investments. If he continues on his current wealth-building path, there's no doubt that he will become financially independent in a few short years.

What was the key to transforming his fiasco into a fortune? Several factors, with the foremost being that he was disgusted and fed up enough that he truly desired to do something different than what he had been doing. He identified the cause of his financial hardship through observation of his current habits. When he saw which habits didn't serve his desire to become wealthy, he made a choice to dispose of those weakening habits and form new wealth-building habits. In other words, he *decided*. And he was determined to stick to his new decision every day.

To assist him in creating new habits, I implemented a "forced" savings plan for him that would automatically withdraw $400.00 from his bank account each time a payroll direct deposit was made. Through the "forced" savings plan, he was able to change his behavior. He no longer had plenty of money lying around in his checking account, therefore he had to *pay attention* to what he was spending. Two new important habits were formed. The first habit was saving money, replacing his old habit of spending every dime he got his hands on. The second habit was paying attention to how much he was spending at any given time. Practicing his two new habits produced a desirable outcome for him, much different than what he had been experiencing. He was now aware of where his money was going, and his actions were now consistent with his stated goals. Consequently, he became wealthier with each successive payday.

How does this example help you in your resolve to change negative habits? Remember that becoming *aware* of your undesirable habits is paramount in creating transformation. After you've become aware of what you're doing, it won't be difficult to see what new habits you must initiate to replace negative patterns of behavior. Thus, observation leads to awareness. Awareness leads to identification of what you need to eliminate. A decision to take action follows. Eventually, the new action, if repeated sufficiently, will become a habit. In this way you can systematically release your old negative habits and replace them with new, productive, supportive habits. Once you've created a new habit that sustains your growth and development, fortunately, it will be difficult to eradicate your new positive pattern of behavior. The riverbed will be in place, and as you continue practicing positive behaviors, the riverbed will widen and deepen in new and positive ways.

To discriminate between which actions lead to results you desire and which ones don't, ask yourself:

- **Is this action rooted in fear or in love?** Unfortunately, fear is a huge motivator for most people. However, if your actions and habits are fear-based, they will yield negative results.
- **If I fully understood God's ineffable love for me, would I take this action?** If you answered in the affirmative, you will know beyond any doubt that you should move forward.
- **If I knew that everything in the Universe fully supports me at all times, what would I do?** This question is tantamount to: **If it were impossible for me to fail, what would I do?**

Nancy Reagan had a point. Her motto *"JUST SAY NO"* may not have worked to stop the spread and use of illegal drugs, but I believe it does have a useful application. The essence of *JUST SAY NO* is this: If you *decide,* your actions will flow from the decision. Expressing NO is a spoken manifestation of your decision not to do a certain thing. In like manner, you can create a new habit and drop the old habit if you just *decide. JUST SAY NO* to what you've been doing, and *JUST SAY YES* to a new course of action that will produce positive results.

An excellent example of this is my grandmother, who at 70 years of age, after having been a smoker for 50 years, one day just *decided* to quit. She quit smoking because her doctor warned her that if she didn't, she would be dead inside of a year. She walked out of the doctor's office that day and never picked up another cigarette ever again. Just like that. She simply *de-*

cided, and after she did, a fifty year old habit was erased in an instant! She lived to be 95 years of age and never went back to smoking again.

I share this with you to illustrate that it's not very difficult to decide to change your habits if enough desire is present.

When we fully realize and manifest our divine, creative nature, we automatically cease creating what we *don't* want, and start manifesting more of what we *do* want.

Ask yourself:

- *What new habits should I cultivate, and what old habits do I need to lay aside?*
- *What would my life be like if I rid myself of all the debilitating habits I've developed and replace them with positive habits that support me?*

I've used all of the steps listed above—with great success—to create different outcomes for myself; outcomes that bring me joy and happiness rather than stress and pain. If you will pray for divine guidance, create new and different intentions, thoughts, speech patterns and habits, you will transform your present undesirable reality into a new reality that reflects your desires and dreams. It's not as difficult as you might think and any effort that goes into remaking yourself is well worth the time and energy spent!

Sacred Lesson #4—The Universe is abundant—God didn't create lack.

There is no lack anywhere in this awesome Universe.

The Creator didn't make one hummingbird, but hun-

dreds of thousands. The Creator didn't make one petu-
nia, but millions. The Creator didn't make one star, but
billions. The Creator didn't make one blade of grass,
but trillions. Every single thing God created overflows
with abundance and every single thing God made understands and functions in abundance.

As divinely created expressions of God, we naturally
desire an abundant lifestyle. It's the way we are made,
the way God formed us: to be abundant, to enjoy what
is here and to live a life full of everything we could
ever hope for, dream of or imagine. That is God's will
for us, and it is innate and natural for us to desire the
good things life has to offer.

Most of us vocalize a belief that is in harmony with
God's will for us; we want an abundant life, full of
prosperity and overflowing with plenty. We want to
have enough resources to cover our needs and our
wants. We want to have enough resources to be able to
give away some of our bounty to those in need.

These considerations beg the question: if God created us to live abundantly, and if we truly desire the
same thing, why are so many people not abundant?

The sad truth is, most people live in lack, just scrap-
ing by. The average American family would be in serious
financial difficulty—maybe even near bankruptcy—if
they missed just three paychecks. Those who do have
cash reserves that would hold them over in the event
of an emergency probably would run out of funds
within six months to a year if they were not receiving a
regular paycheck. What has gone wrong? How have we
gotten off the abundance path God set us on when we
were created? How can we begin to receive an overflow
of abundance in our lives, as is manifest in all of God's
creations?

The solution lies in our understanding two powerful concepts:

1. God has an enormous storehouse filled with everything we could possibly desire: financial prosperity, vibrant health, a beautiful and safe home for our family, loyal and encouraging friends, a mate, and anything else we naturally desire.
2. God gave you the key to the storehouse—you just need to use it.

If we're experiencing any type of lack, it's not because there really is lack. Lack is an evil state of mind we create with our consciousness, and it is rooted in fear.

God doesn't know lack. God doesn't know insufficiency. There is only abundance in everything God created. God only knows and operates in plenty. God only works in the realm of wealth and abundance, and has put the same abundance feature into everything that has ever been created, including you. If you don't possess all the overwhelming abundance you desire and deserve, it's because you're not allowing it in.

Once I learned this valuable lesson, my life began to transform in amazing ways. I began to understand *that I am abundance, I am prosperity, I am plenty.* Once I internalized that belief, everything started to turn around. I no longer believed that I didn't have enough. I came to believe that "enough" already exists; I just had to learn to attract it into my life on an ongoing basis.

As I mentioned earlier, at the root of not having enough is fear. Deep inside, I had a very real fear that if I got a lot of money, I wouldn't know what to do with it anyway, so therefore I must not be deserving of actually having it. After all, if I did deserve wealth, wouldn't I already have it? Therefore, because I didn't have it, I looked in the mirror and laid blame. I believed that one day, in the future, when I became deserving enough, I would have the money I needed and wanted.

This is a common thought pattern. We look at our present state of affairs, and because it doesn't look good, we assume that there's a reason it's not good. Which would be true, because there is a reason that any situation shows up, especially negative situations. Where things go wrong is (according to what I've learned from most people I've talked to, including myself) that we feel that *something is inherently wrong with us.* We don't see our bad financial predicament as a learning lesson, but as a means to punish ourselves. We continue punishing ourselves, because, somewhere inside, we believe we deserve punishing. We feel unworthy of receiving unlimited blessings. This whole charade becomes a self-fulfilling prophecy which continually sucks us into a downward spiral.

I noticed this pattern with myself and went into discovery mode to determine where this belief and thought pattern about money first originated in my psyche. If I could get to the source of the belief, I could purge it. After some time, I realized that there was an event in my childhood that profoundly shaped how I felt about money. This realization only came after much prayer, meditation and contemplation on what was driving me when it came to money. Here's the story.

When I was about nine years old, my class was going on a field trip to Coney Island, an amusement park in Brooklyn, New York. I was so thrilled about the field trip that I hounded my parents to sign the permission slip. I returned the signed permission slip to my teacher and anxiously awaited the day we would go to the amusement park. My imagination took me on wild rides in anticipation of the big day. I visualized over and over a day full of fun, riding the Cyclone, gobbling down cotton candy, eating franks from the world famous Nathan's restaurant on the boardwalk, and having a ball with my classmates. Far in advance, I asked my parents for spending money to take on the approaching field trip. Mom told me to ask my dad since she was a stay-at-home mom at the time, and Dad supplied all the income. I asked and asked and asked Dad for the money. I was used to the process: Dad didn't let go of his money quickly or easily. You had to start asking far in advance, and you had to ask over and over and over again in order to get anything. Finally, the night before the big day arrived. I reminded Dad, yet again, that I needed spending money for the trip the next day. He agreed and said he would give me money in the morning.

After barely being able to sleep the night before, I popped out of bed early in the morning to catch up with my dad before he left for work. I didn't want to take a chance that he may forget to leave money for me, so I caught him in the hallway of our apartment and asked for the money, yet again. By now, in my little child mind, I had come to deduce that money is hard to come by, and will only come after repeatedly begging for it to show up.

What happened next was indelibly imprinted on my psyche, though I had no idea then of the power of the moment I was about to experience. My dad reached into his pocket, and pulled out $2.00 and gave it to me.

He followed it with the comment, "Don't go over there riding all the rides."

I was stunned.

Crushed.

Mortified.

How was I supposed to enjoy a full day of rides and excitement on two dollars? How was I even supposed to buy lunch with two dollars? Even back then in the 70's, $2.00 wasn't a lot of money. Two dollars was miniscule compared to what I was expecting: at least fifteen or twenty dollars.

No matter what I said, I couldn't get any more money out of my dad. He didn't feel that a class trip to Coney Island warranted more than two dollars. After all, I didn't have to buy lunch there, he said. He suggested I go into the kitchen and make my lunch and bring it with me.

Needless to say, the fun and excitement was sucked out of my day at Coney Island before it even started. I convinced myself that I wouldn't be able to have fun at the amusement park on just two dollars. And since thoughts create our reality, I proved myself right.

In the days following the incident, I was so angry with my dad that I didn't want to speak to him. In the months and years following the incident, a twinge of pain accompanied the replaying of that painfully disappointing moment. Eventually, I consciously forgot about it; though the residual effects stuck with me, hanging around just beneath the surface.

One of the biggest issues that arose from this incident was my feeling that I didn't deserve to get what I wanted, that I didn't deserve, for some reason, to have a good time and enjoy myself.

Certainly, that was not my father's aim. His aim was the same as most parent's: to keep within a specified family budget and to make ends meet.

As a child, not being able to see from the vantage point of our parents, we can draw immature, unwise and possibly incorrect conclusions from certain events in childhood. I realized much later, as an adult woman, that for years I carried subliminal beliefs based on that incident, none of which were correct:

- I believed I wouldn't get what I asked for or wanted.
- I believed I had to beg incessantly and be forced to wait for long periods of time before I would be given what I wanted.
- I believed that when I did receive anything, it would always fall far short of my expectations, and, worse yet, there would be nothing I could do about it.

Clearly, these beliefs are all based on fear and are completely false. They are also incredibly debilitating, because, for a very long time, they robbed me of a measure of my personal power and ability to create what I wanted.

I don't mean to imply here that our parents are to blame if our lives are not going as well as we would like. This simply isn't true. I don't care what kind of family a person comes from, there is a point where we must make a conscious, personal decision to move forward in spite of an ugly past, even in spite of a hideously ugly past. We must decide that we are no longer going to be bound by yesterday, and whatever ugliness transpired there, real or imagined. In the present moment is where we decide and create our tomorrows. In the present moment we decide that we are going to move forward to be the best person we can be, despite yesterday, last week, last month or last year.

Today.

Right now.

In this very moment.

That was a huge "light bulb" moment for me, when I realized all the baggage I'd been carrying around for decades; based, in part, on a brief conversation in the hallway one morning with my dad. It wasn't what he did that caused my self-destructive beliefs, it's how I translated and internalized the events that caused me to create and harbor those beliefs. Just as I was the one who created them, I had to be the one to go in and dismantle them. Once I submitted to the process, painful as it was, I experienced relief and freedom from an old movie I was playing over and over again inside my head. That old movie never had a happy ending.

I submit that the same will be true for you. When you journey inward—to the darkest depths of your psyche—you will find old, debilitating ideas, beliefs and thought patterns that must be yielded if you are to experience prosperity.

You'll have to believe deep inside that you are worthy and deserving of wealth, prosperity and abundance and all that it brings. Your entire being must resonate with that truth for it to become a reality. The more you do experience the truth of this new unfolding reality, the more it will be solidified and repeated.

It worked for me.

Remember, *lack only exists in our minds and springs from fear.*

Never forget God's generous and caring nature and your powerfully, creative nature. The Universe simply doesn't know lack.

This is the starting point for eliminating all insufficiency you may be currently suffering through, and attaining the life you deserve: a life full of abundance and every imaginable good thing!

Sacred Lesson #5—The more you give away, the more God will give you—YOU CAN'T BEAT GOD'S GIVING.

The lyrics to a favorite little song of mine that we frequently sing in worship service remind us that we can't beat God's giving. No matter how much we give, *we will never be able to out-give God.*

A critical lesson I learned from my financial debacle was simply this: to have wealth and prosperity flow to me, I had to be willing to give it away.

This becomes a tall order for some of us, because humans can be stingy, which is a fear-based, lack mindset.

However, if we remember that we're made in the image and likeness of God, then we know that we are natural givers. When we can give freely and enjoy it, we will come to have more than we ever dreamed possible or even probable. God knows who the givers are, and they are richly blessed. They have so much because they have given so much.

Like everything else, money is energy and moves in a cycle. Money is not static and staid, but is a dynamic force; always changing, shifting, flowing, moving. Money has a flow all its own, and once you master the flow, you can cause more of it to flow to you. One way to create the flow of money into your life is to keep a flow of money going away from you. Picture yourself as an enormous keg that is continually being filled from the top. The keg also has a tap near the bottom. Since the keg is continually being filled with blessings from above, you can open your tap at any time and let blessings flow out to others whose cups need filling. You become a life-sustaining (and maybe even life-saving) force for good in the Universe. As a result, more will flow into your keg; and you'll have enough room to receive infinitely because you regularly open your tap to release a steady stream of some (10% is a good start) of the blessings you've received.

Paradoxical as it seems, it is a fact that the more generous you are, the more you will receive. This is in direct opposition to what most people think. We think, "to have more, I have to hold on tightly to what I have." This is an inaccurate and mistaken belief. To have more, we have to give away more. I've witnessed this dynamic principle in my own life. Formerly, I never tithed. I felt like I couldn't afford to give away 10% of everything I made. I told myself that I wanted to, and that as soon as I felt more financially "comfortable", I would immediately start tithing. What I didn't realize at the time was that tithing would be a catalyst in making me more financially "comfortable."

In the meantime, I hadn't taken the leap of faith required to tithe and stick with it through the rough times. I always gave $25 here or $15 there. Never a large commitment. And my results were in direct proportion to my giving: there was never a large bountiful harvest. Always need, always lack.

No farmer in his right mind would go out to harvest if he hadn't spent a considerable amount of months before preparing the soil, planting seed, pruning, feeding, watering and carefully watching for any threat to the produce. How and why was I expecting to reap where I had not sown? Strange as it may seem, I've met a lot of people who've fallen into this exact trap of false reasoning that I had.

That all changed when I decided to become a dedicated tither. I didn't decide this on my own, God helped me to see that in order to set my own finances in proper order, I had to give away more than I had been. I had to give out of my need, not out of my surplus, just as the widow did in Christ's story of the Widow's Mite. I was waiting for a surplus that was never going to materialize on the path of stinginess I was on. I would never have begun giving 10% by waiting to have 10% left over after I paid all my bills. It simply would never have happened. I had to give away 10% first (stepping out completely on faith), and then live on what was left.

Almost instantly, I had more bounty in my life. More money came. My financial life eased. I no longer stressed over money because deep inside I had a comfort that comes from doing what God says will bring me wealth. I had complete faith that He would supply all my needs and desires as well. I didn't have that knowledge and assuredness until I did the right thing with my money.

One of my favorite tithing stories, among many, is that of Kevin. He's a good friend of mine and a generous and dedicated tither. He tithed even when he didn't have much money, and was strapped with credit card debt. Some would call his level of giving strange, considering that his tithe checks were substantial, and he could well have used that money to pay his bills. But he never wavered; regardless of what financial pressure he was under, he just kept on tithing.

One day, a piece of important information made its way across his desk at work; he found out that there were other people at the company where he was employed who were doing the same job he was doing, but who were making considerably more money than he was. He decided to approach his manager and lay the facts on the table, and respectfully ask for a substantial raise. When he came out of the meeting, not only did his manager agree to give him a raise, but the amount was astonishing: he secured a raise of $24,000 per year! Some people don't even earn $24,000 per year, so imagine his excitement at securing an *additional* $24,000 in annual income to his salary.

Both he and I believe that he was so tremendously blessed with this raise because he was (and still is) a dedicated tither, through thick and thin, through financial good times and bad.

The essence of this principle is having the faith to step out and give more than you've been giving before. If you're a tither, can you be a double-tither, giving away 20%? If you give away 20%, can you become a triple-tither and give away 30%? Wherever we are with our giving should not be the last and final stop on the train. We can always find a way to give more, even if we feel we're giving enough already. One of my dreams was to have enough money to leave outrageously large tips for waitstaff in restaurants and others who help me. I've been able to do that and it feels so good.

Maybe you don't belong to a church. Maybe you don't know who to give to. Ask God to open your eyes. Scales will fall and you will see all the people around you that need your help and your money. I don't mean cousin Johnny who wants to start yet another business and use your hard-earned money as seed capital; even though not one of his many businesses has ever turned a profit.

There are countless people in the world that God wants us to help; people who are in desperate and dire straits. Children who are hungry, elders who barely eke out an existence, single moms who work hard for their families, AIDS/HIV babies, crack babies. Do I need to continue? Just look around, it's not hard to figure out who needs your help.

The universe provides you with a steady and unlimited supply of resources every day, with the express intent that you'll give some of it away. Be a giver, and you'll be amazed at what you get. I was!

After hearing God speak to me regarding money and financial issues, I've been able to go out and help many others learn how to create a life of abundance for themselves. We learn our lessons not only for ourselves, but for the benefit of the world.

God Speaks Through Home Goings

"To everything there is a season, a time for every
purpose under heaven:
A time to be born, and a time to die."
Ecclesiastes 3:1, 2 (Gideon Bible)

Death is part of life. It is not an end;
but merely a transition.

Louann, Vaness, Algie & Grandpa

I guess you could say the first tragedy Frieda Taylor ever witnessed was the burning of her sister.

The next series of tragic events would be the accidental deaths of two of her three sons, including one who opened her womb.

When a child is born, also born are the parent's hopes, dreams, wishes and plans for that child. With each new baby there enters a set of hopeful expectations, one of which is that the child will outlive the parents.

When parents have to bury their own children, the balance of nature has been upset, causing a despair that is absent when events proceed in the reverse. Yes, children do mourn their parents, many times quite deeply, but the sorrow of a mother over a child lost is indescribable.

Frieda Taylor was born to Pinky & Ballard Clark in May of 1911; one of their 12 children. The family lived on a farm in New Jersey, where the children, without

the distractions of television, the Internet or comput-
ers, could let their imaginations run wild. This they
did daily, completion of chores allowing. Working and
living on a farm brought and kept them in close contact
with the earth and nature, which would later equate to
good health and long life for many of them.

Farm people wake up early; roosters and other creatures see to that. With so much to be done, there's no
time for sleeping late. When Pinky, Frieda's mom, would
arise at 5:00 a.m., one of the first tasks she would
undertake was starting a fire in the large pot belly stove
in the kitchen. Soon the cooperative fire would heat
water for bathing and cook food for eating. Nine-year-
old Louann, eager to help her mother with the endless
chores the family's upkeep required, would lend a hand
every morning.

One morning, Louann, being the early riser that she
was, got up just a little before 5:00 a.m. She decided it
would be a good idea to start the fire by herself before
the family woke up. *Mama will be so proud of me,* she
thought merrily as she quietly set about gathering all
she needed to start the fire. She carefully poured kerosene on the bark that was kept nearby for the fire, just
as she had seen her mother do. Then she struck a
match and dropped it onto the kerosene soaked bark.

Fire is an interesting phenomenon. On one hand, it
is friendly and willing to serve when under the control
of a wise and knowing hand. But when left to its own
devices, knowing no boundaries, it can rage disas-
trously out of control.

The flames erupted spontaneously and roared larger
than the little girl expected. In an instant, she was en-
gulfed in a blanket of blaze. The rest of the family awoke
to her blood-curdling screams.

Fire is swift and efficient. By the time they put out

the flames, surprisingly, her charred body still carried the breath of life. Hopeful, distraught and desperate, Pinky and Ballard rushed their daughter to the hospital. Louann clung tenaciously to life. Some in the family say that she sung all the way to the hospital.

Later that day, she stopped singing.

From them on, Frieda understood death.

I know this family and its stories well. Frieda Taylor was my maternal grandmother.

Years later, Frieda Clark would leave the family farm and venture to New York, where she would meet a dashing young man by the name of Jack Taylor, agree to marry him and together they would produce four children; Vaness, Algernon, Gary and the couple's only girl, Jacqueline, who would become my mother.

It's not surprising that Grandma and Grandpa were attracted to each other, considering they were quite similar in many respects, not the least of which was how they thought one should comport oneself. Jack Taylor was jovial, but refined; he believed that a man was never fully and properly dressed without a Fedora. It was no small matter when Jack Taylor got dressed; it was a ritual, a proceeding. First he would slip one leg at a time into carefully creased and cuffed trousers; then don the coordinating socks, shoes, tie and shirt. Lastly, he would carefully ease into the matching suit coat. He would check the mirror several times in the process to be sure that all was proceeding well and according to plan. When the body had been sharply and satisfactorily adorned from neck to feet, there was only one thing left to do. Grandpa would reach for his Fedora and place it confidently onto his head. The back straightening and elevated chest added two inches to his height. The hat added another six. Now he was ready for the world.

The whole proceeding usually took well over two hours.

Grandma was just as meticulous in her grooming and appearance, believing that no well-dressed woman would dare set out on the streets without her hat and gloves. Together, they maintained a formality about their presentation that spoke much to people before they did.

They and their four children lived in a small apartment in Harlem, New York. As one would expect, with each child came high hopes and dreams. Little did Grandma know that the Angel of Death would visit her twice in this apartment, each time carrying off one of her sons.

Algie was the driver in the first tragic car accident that killed his older brother Vaness. From that day on, according to Grandma, Algie was tormented by the tragedy, feeling responsible for the death of his brother. He struggled with the heavy burden every day, all day. Guilt and shame were his constant companions.

Algie, ironically, was also the driver in the second tragic car accident. This time, the Angel of Death came for him.

To quote Grandma: "There's nothing like getting a phone call that your son has been killed in a car accident. It never leaves you."

Grandma twice endured what no parent should ever have to contend with even once. She received that phone call twice.

After all of Grandma and Grandpa's children were grown and gone, they decided to move to a better neighborhood and building in New York City. They packed up and left a decaying, decrepit building on Manhattan's upper west side and moved to the East side of Harlem, on 110th Street and First Avenue. It was a good move, especially since the building they formerly lived in caught fire and burned to the ground shortly after they moved out.

Grandma and Grandpa enjoyed their new home for many years. In time, Grandpa, cognizant of the fact that all his friends had passed on, grew ill. His physical health deteriorated, spurred on by his loss of interest in going outside and overall weariness with life. On a summer day in 1995, the Angel of Death visited our family again. This time, Grandpa willingly walked away with him.

As of this writing, Grandma's sister Marvel (91 years young) and her brother Dick (88 years young) are the only remaining children of Pinky and Ballard Clark. Grandma has two living children, my mom, Jackie, and Uncle Gary; and many grandchildren and great-grandchildren, the youngest of which is my daughter Varonika.

Another reason Grandma is my hero is because she was diagnosed with lung cancer at the age of 93. For most, this would have been a death sentence. For Grandma, it was a challenge. The doctors had thrown down the gauntlet: "You've got lung cancer, and you may not be around much longer." For years prior to the diagnosis, she had been reading about natural remedies and supplements and their impact on health, which explains why she lived independently, preparing her meals, getting dressed and doing almost everything for herself up until the age of 94. Once in a while, she even traveled to Atlantic City, New Jersey to see if the slot machines would yield more quarters than she invested.

Living a vibrant, active life at an advanced age and with a cancer diagnosis would be quite remarkable for anyone except Grandma. She expected that she should be in good health and active and independent and lucid for as long as possible, and she pushed herself daily to make that goal a reality. She lived a fuller life at the age of 94 than others who are much younger. She was never bed-ridden, until shortly before she crossed over. In the summer of 2005, at 94 years of age, she traveled with my mom and I to my 18-year-old son, Cory's, high school graduation. The attendees commented that she was the oldest person there, and marveled at four generations of an irrepressible family of which Grandma was the matriarch.

For her brave determination and grit in the face of tragedy, she's my hero.

For all the sorrow she's withstood over the tragic and unexpected loss of two of her sons—including one who opened her womb—and the pain of losing a mate of almost 60 years, Grandma never lost her zest, enthusiasm and passion for living an extraordinary life. Just before she passed on, as she approached her 95th birthday, she was determined to live strong and leave an indelible mark on the world: the mark of a fighting spirit, a loving heart, a generous nature, and a powerful mind overflowing with wisdom.

"What's the secret to living so long?" I asked her one day.

"You have to have a good belly laugh every day. And, oh yeah, you have to stop and smell the roses."

Thank you, Grandma, for showing us the Great Spirit you are, and showing us all we could be.

God Speaks

Sacred Lesson #1—

> "To everything there is a season, and a time for
> every matter or purpose under heaven: A time to be
> born and a time to die."
> Ecclesiastes 3:1, 2 (AMP)

Death is part of life. It is not an end; but merely a transition. In every culture, and even in the animal kingdom, rites of passage accompany the home going of a loved one. Death of the physical body is to be understood as an inevitable part of the purpose for which we were sent here. Death played a prominent role in the Divine Purpose for Christ's life.

The actual timing of a loved one leaving this earth is not for us to determine or change. Although we may be grief-stricken with the timing of the event—particularly if the person leaving is a person we birthed into the world—there is nothing we can do about it, try as we might. That is between that Soul and God.

Accepting physical death as a natural occurrence is a spiritually mature stance. Our society has conditioned us to dread death, and to avoid any contemplation or discussion of its ramifications on the living. If we removed the shroud of fear that encompasses death, all that would remain would be a very natural, Divine and necessary transformation from one form into the next. There's not one thing inherently scary about that. The whole process is part of our spiritual growth and development, the next rung on the evolutionary ladder toward complete oneness with God. Viewed thus, our passing should be honored, expected (at some point in time) and accepted, but never feared. In the Tibetan culture, death is cooperated with. *The Tibetan Book of the Dead* actually prepares one for the eventuality.

However, accepting that a physical death will one day visit upon each one of us does not mean a fatalistic attitude is in order. While we are here, life must be lived to the full: with zeal, enthusiasm, joy and unbounded hope for the future, just as Grandma lived. We can fully embrace each new day and determine to live a joyful, productive, purposeful life while simultaneously understanding and honoring that one day our work here will be done. Then, it will be time for us to move on; just like moving from one house to another. It has been reported that many highly developed spiritual masters actually sensed when their time here was completed, and without dying of sickness or old age, just surrendered their spirit and left the earthly plane. This is the essence of living fully and dying well.

Grandma exemplifies a working knowledge of both principles: the eventuality of death and the necessity of living a full and purposeful life. Although tragic, she did not allow the physical deaths of her sons to completely consume her and rob her spirit of its will and determination to live abundantly.

When we are met with the unexpected death of a loved one, there may be a need to wail and cry out in unimaginable pain and suffering, *but we must vow to retain a heart full of hope.* We have a need to grieve fully and completely, *but we must vow increased faith in God and our unlimited ability to heal.*

This is the hallmark of a great spiritual person: to find the perfect balance between grieving and releasing sorrow, and accepting that the living must keep pressing forward, clinging to God, who is the boulder in the middle of a raging ocean.

Grandma endured it all and never gave up hope, never lost faith. God is the reason she still triumphs.

Sacred Lesson # 2—A good name is precious.

Since each of us will meet the end of our own earthly life at the appointed time, it would be wise to give consideration to King Solomon's words:

"A good name is better than precious perfume, and
the day

of death better than the day of one's birth. It is
better to go
to the house of mourning than to go to the house of
feasting,
for that is the end of all men; and the living will lay
it to heart."
Ecclesiastes 7:1, 2

This sage advice is powerful. Use your life to build a good name or reputation. That is the most worthy pursuit of all. Over the course of 95 years, Grandma built a legacy and reputation for being kind, generous and compassionate. She's also known for being quite humorous; never passing up an opportunity to lovingly needle her younger brother or sister. She's known for being witty and intelligent; crossword puzzles and the game of Scrabble sharpened her proficiency as a master of words. She has a reputation as a keeper of the family, as she was devoted to the preservation of our family's history, and was the storyteller of important events to the younger members of our "Clark Clan."
She has built an outstanding name.

As mentioned earlier, at the age of 93, she was diagnosed with lung cancer. The diagnosis made little difference in how she proceeded with the business of living; this in spite of having fought through two strokes over the preceding few years. When being released from the hospital following a stroke (in 2002 at the age of 92), Grandma suggested to my father, who picked her up from the hospital, "Let's walk home." They walked 13 city blocks to her home. She obviously needed and wanted the exercise.

The diagnosis had not convinced her to resign herself to and quietly accept cancer. To improve her health, she became almost a complete vegetarian, because, she stated, "Meat isn't always good for your health." She also embarked on taking several natural remedies for the overall health of her body, including vitamins, herbs and natural foods. She told me that she was adding more mushrooms to her diet, since they have powerful anti-cancer and disease fighting properties. She also had regular chelation therapy. As you might imagine, she declined all three of the doctor's recommendations for treating her cancer: the knife, chemicals, or radiation. I'm certain that she believed that if she had taken either of these options, she would not have gone on to live for over two years after being diagnosed with a disease that the doctors said would end her life within 60-90 days.

Whether she knows it or not, Grandma is still building an outstanding name for herself. When I think of Frieda Taylor, I think of unsinkable faith, persistence, endurance, strength, determination, enthusiasm, humor, hope, wisdom, an endless appetite for learning and unbounded pure joy in living.

What name are you building for yourself? What will people say about you when you're gone? What are they saying about you now? As long as there is life in our bodies, we have an opportunity to build a good reputation. You may not be able to walk, or run, or speak, or reach out and touch others. But your attitude and words and thoughts can still build a powerful reputation for good and bring blessings to others.

The reason King Solomon gave such import to building a good name is because everything else we have will be of no consequence when we are gone. We won't take earthly treasures with us, nor would we want to. What we leave behind—which is of eternal importance—are the thoughts and feelings we engendered in the people who knew us, or had heard of us. That, I believe, is the purpose of life, to leave this place in better condition than we found it. I concur with King Solomon; if we've built an outstanding reputation, our day of death will be better than our day of birth.

Grandma's was.

The Matriarch

When my husband was just 15 years old, his father went to work one morning, suffered a heart attack and never came home.

When Moses Ware passed, he left behind his wife, Magnolia Ware, who was now charged with the monumental task of caring for the family's eight children. Though not all of the children were living at home, they still relied on her for nurturing and maternal support.

She assumed the roles and responsibilities of two parents and has done a superb job. Why? Because God is her partner.

She's been a faithful member of the same church in the same neighborhood for over 50 years. She volunteers her time, energy, expertise and money without hesitation. And she's successfully taught her children, grandchildren and great-grandchildren to do the same.

She is a shining example of what it means to walk with God. Only her walk with God would have navigated her so well through the loss of her husband, and years later, through the loss of two of her five beautiful daughters. Each of the home goings was potentially devastating, except for the fact that, in each of her grieving moments, God was there.

Anyone who knows Magnolia Ware can attest to her exemplary and outstanding name. One of her gifts, among many, is the gift of being able to work with children. When she gave birth to my husband, the sixth child of eight, she decided not to return to work outside the home. She decided to stay home, take care of her own children while taking care of other children in a home daycare. That was over 40 years ago. At almost 80 years of age, she still maintains the daycare in her neighborhood, and is renowned for her love of children. Her specialty is being able to take in even the most unruly children and turn them into little people that others would want to be around. It's been said that when a parent has a child so undisciplined that no other daycare will accept them, they know they can call on Mrs. Ware for help. With a special blend of kindness, patience, discipline and love, she's able to handle any child. When others come to her complaining about their children, or about a spouse whom they are displeased with, Mrs. Ware has a saying, "You got to love them all the way there."

Mrs. Ware wakes up every morning, Monday through Friday, at about 5:00 a.m. By the time the clock displays 6:00 a.m., she's ready to get in her van and make the rounds, picking up her children. Some of them she will drop off at school. Others she will bring back to the daycare for the day. She carries on this routine day after day, month after month, year in and year out. Other than the vacation time she schedules during the year, she is never absent from the daycare and her children. Her eyes light up at the arrival of a new baby in the daycare.

Mrs. Ware's walk with God has paid off handsomely. She has six children living in the flesh, a multitude of grandchildren and great-grandchildren who all love, cherish and honor her.

God Speaks

Sacred Lesson #1—Walk with God.

Without a walk with God, humans can become hopeless, despondent, cynical and materialistic, believing only in what can be seen with the eyes and felt with the hands. Without the acknowledgement of God's presence in our lives, the 1% physical world (that is ruled by the five senses) has the potential to lock God firmly out of our life, as God cannot always be perceived on the physical level. Without a walk with God, it is quite possible to become so deeply enmeshed in the 1% world of form, and thinking it to be the only world, lose way to fear.

When we walk with God every day, as Mrs. Ware does, miracles happen. The beauty of miracles is we never know when, why or how they're going to happen. They just show up on time, because the universe always seeks to support us and give us all we need for our eternal good. Therefore, the best outlook to have is an outlook of expectancy. When we walk with God, we wake up in the morning and we expect that all will turn out well. We expect that all our challenges will present us with golden learning opportunities, and that we will grow stronger even when we are in pain. We expect that all things will work together for our good. We expect miracles, therefore we experience them every day.

Some might have thought, when looking at Mrs. Ware and her eight children at her husband's funeral, *How in the world is that woman going to make it?*

Mrs. Ware was obviously thinking, *Father, it's just You and me now.*

Sacred Lesson #2—Complaining is useless and destructive. Try praise instead.

Though she's had cause to, I've never heard Mrs. Ware complain.

When I was growing up, whenever we would complain, Mom would say, "Complainers are always heard, but they're never respected."

The point was lost on small children, but the lesson is not lost on me now—complaining is useless, counterproductive and can even destroy. That's probably why those who truly work to listen to God every day, all day, are not complainers.

Why? Because complaining is debilitating and siphons our energy. After a bout of whining, we are too depleted to take action to change the situation. Complaining produces a negative energy that infects those who are in hearing distance. Not listening distance, hearing distance. We don't listen to complainers, we hear them. And we'd prefer not to even hear them.

Complaining never improves any hardship; it only serves to make the complainer painfully aware of how distant they feel from God in that very moment, which only intensifies the pain.

The opposite of complaint is praise. Praise has an amazing expansive energy. Praise forces you to notice the countless wonders in your life for which thanks is due. It boosts your energy and is infectious; it gives others around you a reason to praise too. Praise is powerful, and power inducing!

The next time you feel the impulse to complain, think about Mrs. Ware. Then *stop and immediately give thanks for everything you have right now.* Be as unabashed about giving praise as was King David! (2 Samuel 6:14, 15)

Giving thanks and praise in this manner will change the focus of your attention from what you are complaining about to all that you have in your life to rejoice over. If you consistently turn your urge to complain into outright praise and thanks, the result will be an increase in the blessings you attract to yourself, and a decrease in anything to complain about. With no focused energy and words of complaint to sustain them, your problems will inevitably wither and die. After developing the "praise and thanks" habit, you'll look around and discover the truth: that you have nothing to complain about!

Ask yourself:

- *What will I immediately cease complaining about?*
- *What causes for praise and thanks do I have right now?*

Sacred Lesson #3—Proverbs 31:10-31 (AMP) Be a person of high value.

King Lemuel's mother wanted to give her son guidance on what kind of woman she thought would be ideal for him to marry. The woman King Lemuel's mother described in the passage of scripture at Proverbs chapter 31 has been nicknamed the "Virtuous Woman" and has become the ideal for millions of Godly women desiring to be excellent wives.

I include this passage of scripture here because Mrs. Ware has been able to embody the ideal of the virtuous woman. Through her hard work in her family, church and community, she has shown her vast capability, deep wisdom and high intelligence. She's proven that her value is far more precious than jewels (verse 10).

She earned the trust of her husband by maintaining

her household. Therefore, he came to trust her and have confidence in her abilities (verse 11).

She buys fabric and sews drapes and other beautiful items for the home. She goes to the market and keeps a storehouse of food. She regularly prepares a large Sunday dinner; feeding many of her children, grandchildren and great-grandchildren (verses 13 & 14).

She rises early in the morning to prepare herself and her household for the day by seeing God's face in prayer (verse 15).

She plants fruitful vines by sowing seeds of kindness, love and respect in the heart of each child in her care (verse 16).

"She girds herself with strength [spiritual, mental and physical fitness for her God-given task] and makes her arms strong and firm (verse 17)."

"She tastes and sees that her gain from work [with and for God] is good; and her lamp goes not out, but it burns on continually through the night [of trouble, privation, or sorrow, warning away fear, doubt, and distrust] (verse 18)."

"She opens her hands to the poor, yes, she reaches out her filled hands to the needy [whether in body, mind, or spirit] (verse 20)." Mrs. Ware takes care of children and does not discriminate based on the parent's ability to pay on time.

"Strength and dignity are her clothing and her position is strong and secure; she rejoices over the future [the latter day or time to come, knowing that she and her family are in readiness for it] (verse 25)!"

"She opens her mouth in skillful and godly wisdom, and on her tongue is the law of kindness [giving counsel and instruction] (verse 26)."

"She looks well to how things go in her household, and the bread of idleness (gossip, discontent, and self-pity) she will not eat (verse 27)." Mrs. Ware never has time for idle talk (and rarely stays on the telephone for very long).

"Her children rise up and call her blessed" (verse 28). Her family loves, appreciates and honors her. And rightly so, because she has done a phenomenal job of filling their hearts with love for God. Her youngest son is now heeding the call to become a minister, as is her son-in-law.

The undeniable truth that we can state about Mrs. Ware is that she is

". . . a woman who reverently and worshipfully fears the Lord, she shall be praised (Verse 30)!"

Thank you, Mrs. Ware, for showing us how powerful we become when we walk with God.

God Speaks Through Religion

"Every man for himself and God for us all."
Spanish Proverb

The Griot, My Mom and a Woman Named Kitty

As God's grace and synchronicity would have it, while planning my wedding reception, I came to find out about a certain griot, who came highly recommended for her outstanding gift of storytelling.

Griots are highly regarded in Africa, as they hold the history of the village and its ancestors in their memories and on their tongues, and like makers of fine silk, weave the history into stories. Enthralling stories. Stories that move and dance. Stories that, in the midst of the telling, evoke tears and laughter, and when the story's said and done, thoughtful reflection.

The first time I spoke with the griot was over the telephone. I sensed her wise and knowing presence, and her ability to tell an enrapturing story. We talked on the phone for over an hour in a very natural conversation that never dragged or lulled. *Instant kindred spirits, she and I,* I remember thinking when I hung up the phone.

A few weeks after speaking with her on the telephone, my husband and I arranged to meet her in person at our home. She wanted to come over to interview us to get the details that she would weave into a story to present at our wedding reception. The story she was to tell would be of how my husband and I met, fell in love and subsequently married.

When she arrived on our doorstep, my husband and I knew that this woman was extraordinary. She was statuesque—standing six feet two inches tall. As we greeted her and invited her in, we marveled at the resonating bellow of her voice and how perfectly suited for storytelling it was. There was little doubt in our minds that her presentation would be a fascinating and unforgettable part of our wedding reception.

During our conversation, she and I both recognized that there was much more to our meeting than her being hired as a storyteller for our wedding reception. Our meeting was providential, and we both felt it. The more she talked, the more I knew God crossed our paths like sticks. He sent her to me, and I to her. I can't tell you why He sent me to her, but I can tell you why He sent her to me.

Let me tell you a story about me, my mom, and a woman named Kitty.

I was born first of my mother's four children in 1961 when she was 20 years of age and single. Which explains why, from the very beginning of my life, my mom and I were closer than the typical mother and daughter. I was the object of her affection and the statement to my grandmother that my mom could raise a child better than she could.

Four years after I was born, my mother was walking home from the grocery store one day through the streets of New York City with me and a shopping cart loaded down with groceries in tow. She met a man on the corner, an older gentleman, with kind eyes and gray hair, wearing a dapper suit topped with a Fedora. He held religious pamphlets in his hand and approached my mom to strike up a conversation. His message? How to get saved from a wicked, dying system of things; this world which would soon be wiped clean of all sin and iniquity by God's almighty hand at the war of Armageddon, followed by a remaking of the earth into a paradise for the righteous ones where they will reside forever in peace.

The message so enraptured her, she engaged in a mesmerizing question and answer session with him right there on the corner where, four hours and a melted carton of Breyers later, he invited her to the Kingdom Hall of Jehovah's Witnesses.

That's how it all began.

As a result of that meeting, my mom, my two-year-old brother and I began to regularly attend the Kingdom Hall. My mom was so eager and enthusiastic about her new religious studies, that within a few months she dedicated her life to Jehovah God and was baptized as one of Jehovah's Witnesses. Two years later, she met a butcher at the corner store whom she was instantly attracted to and was later delighted to discover that he too was one of Jehovah's Witnesses. They married after being engaged in an appropriate courtship, and, years later, had two more children. My three siblings and I were raised in a loving but strict household of Jehovah's Witnesses.

My mom and I grew closer and closer over the years as I matured from young girl to adolescent to young woman. We were more than mother and daughter. We were comrades, confidants, friends.

I was deeply entrenched in my religious beliefs as one of Jehovah's Witnesses, and she was so proud of my progress in the Jehovah's Witness organization. Just as she expected, I fell in love with and married a fellow Jehovah's Witness, and continued the tradition by immersing our two children in the teachings of Jehovah's Witnesses also. There was even a period of time when I volunteered to do missionary work full time, which meant that I would spend at least 90 hours per month proselytizing by knocking on doors to reach the unsaved with the hope-filled message of salvation.

As a Witness, I'd always been taught that only those who belonged to our organization would be saved, everyone else (all non-Jehovah's Witnesses) would suffer an everlasting death at God's hand at the end of the world—the great battle of Armageddon—if they didn't repent, turn around and become Witnesses before the "end" came. I was told that all unbelievers (those who were not Jehovah's Witnesses) were wicked, or at best, ignorant, no matter how sincere in their worship they may be. Even churchgoers were in jeopardy of losing their lives if they didn't leave "Babylon the Great, the world empire of false religion." It was impressed upon us as Witnesses that the ignorant and the wicked people of the world are urgently in need of salvation through Jesus Christ's shed blood, and it was our job to go out and make disciples of them.

I lived my life like a sponge completely immersed in the ocean of Witness culture and beliefs, never surfacing to take a breath.

My mom was so proud.

Neither she nor I foresaw the drastic change that was looming on the horizon.

One day, in a business meeting, I met a woman named Kitty. Kitty, from the Witness perspective, was "worldly" (a term used to describe non-Witnesses) and therefore doomed to destruction if she didn't leave her "false religion," learn the Witness doctrines, get bap-

tized as a Witness, regularly attend the Kingdom Hall,
and go out making new disciples. Case closed. For me,
it would've proceeded that way, except this time,
something was strangely different. Kitty was different.
Though she had no way of knowing it, God was about
to use Kitty to change the course of my life forever.

Kitty was a middle-aged woman with a beautiful
home who cared for her sickly husband tirelessly. She
was kind, loving and compassionate, a genuinely joyful Christian, who regularly worshipped at her Church
and had a profound love for God and family. Kitty's
deep spirituality and reliance on God was like a thick
blanket that completely enveloped her, keeping her in-
sulated from the cold winds that swept over her life.
After years of being in close fellowship with others
who read their Bibles daily, as I did, and stayed in constant prayer, as I did, I developed the ability to discern
when I was in the presence of spirit-filled beings, and
when I wasn't. My experience with spirit-filled beings,
up until that point, was with Witnesses exclusively,
and I had noted that not all of them were spirit-filled.
In some respects, my eyes were like Saul's of the New
Testament: blinded to all the spirit-filled beings I'd
come into contact with all my life outside of my own
religious affiliation. For me that meant anyone outside
the Witness organization, whether they be Baptist,
Buddhist, Catholic, whatever.

But Kitty's radiant aura, among other signs, showed
the telltale markings of being undeniably blessed—an
aura reflected in a deeply joyful and serene counte-
nance that comes only from God. She seemed to glide
into the room on a cloud. She displayed so much compassion and kindness toward every person she touched.
There was no mistaking it. When I looked at Kitty for
who she really was, it was as if scales fell from my eyes

and I could clearly see that I was in the presence of a spirit-filled being—*a blessed spirit-filled being who was not one of Jehovah's Witnesses*. Up until then, I'd firmly held that being spirit-filled and being a Jehovah's Witness were synonymous. To go even further, I'd held the opinion that being spirit-filled and being of any religion or denomination other than Jehovah's Witnesses, was mutually exclusive.

According to my belief system, Kitty didn't exist, nor could she have.

How could a person be this spiritually grounded, this connected to God, this loving, this kind, this compassionate, this blessed and not be a Jehovah's Witness? How could that be possible?

Allow me to digress for a moment to give consideration to what may be running through your mind now. You may marvel at the ignorance of a thirty-something year old woman who is naive enough to believe that only her and her religious comrades are on the correct path to God. You may be incensed at the amount of bigotry one person could harbor, and the amount of judgmental egotism that could support that level of bigotry. You may even be outraged at a religion that would propagate such tenets.

I am not ashamed to bare my past feelings of bigotry and judgmental egotism in the hopes of thwarting them at every turn, whenever and wherever they may rear their ugly heads. If we declare that we dislike or even hate a certain group because of their bigotry, then we are no better than they are as any display of hatred and judgment is also a reflection of bigotry.

Over the next few months—after the initial idea of the existence of Kitty sank in—a nagging question began to peck at me like a pigeon pecking at a crumb, *Kitty exists, which means there could be others like*

*her. Other non-Witnesses who actually had God's favor
and lived just as blessed a life as I did.* I decided to put
my opinions and beliefs to the test. If they're right, I'd
label Kitty an aberration, the proverbial exception to
the rule. I could close the case in a neat, tidy, little
package that would make me feel comfortable again.
Then I'd proceed with my proselytizing, business as
usual, doing the same things I did before and holding
the same beliefs I had for years. No need to change. I
could live with being 99% right.

On the other hand, if more Kitty's did exist, I'd be
forced to face that what I'd held as sacred truth so fer-
vently for so long might not be the bedrock for me that
I'd thought it was. That would be uncomfortable. No,
that would be a painful quaking of the foundation of
my religious belief system. Such a discovery would
have monumental repercussions, some of which I
couldn't imagine. If there were more Kitty's, I'd have to
undertake a spiritual quest—one that I'd never under-
taken before—since I'd always maintained that I needn't
look anywhere else. I was told and always believed
that I had the truth right where I was, from the time I
was four years old.

The feeling that came over me was like being in the
desert, sitting at an oasis, happily lapping up what appeared to be a never-ending supply of refreshing water,
only to find one morning that the water source had
gone dry. There are but two choices: stay and die of thirst,
or venture out into the desert on a quest for water.

As you might imagine, Kitty wasn't the only one.
There were more, lots more. Now, everywhere I looked,
I saw people who genuinely loved God, lived spiritu-
ally full and fulfilling lives, who were loving and com-
passionate, and who also were not Jehovah's Witnesses.
God allowed them to constantly parade into my life so

I could understand where I was and why I couldn't stay there. While millions of Jehovah's Witnesses are quite happy in that organization and receive God's blessing there, it's not God's plan for every person on earth, and it wasn't God's plan for me. The discovery of Kitty and others like her compelled me to get up, pack my bags, leave my gone-dry oasis and venture into the desert on a search for water.

When I talked to my mom about the reasons behind the upheaval in what I'd held as truth previously, she replied that I shouldn't be so easily misled into thinking Kitty was blessed by God,

"You do know, Valerie," she told me "that the Devil will give lots of things to people to keep them satisfied and content enough that they don't seek God. Those people never find Him."

She was disappointed by my reply. "Mom, I know what Kitty has isn't from the Devil, it's from God. Besides, the devil can't bless people! *Only God can.*"

That interchange between me and my mom marked the beginning of a years-long division between us. We've been on separate spiritual paths ever since.

My Mom and Dad remain staunch Jehovah's Witnesses to this day, a fact I'm proud of. They're the quintessential example of making an unwavering decision to worship God in a prescribed fashion, and sticking to it for almost 40 years. God has blessed them for their faithfulness. My Mom has remained steadfast in her religious belief since that synchronistic meeting with the kind, elderly gentleman on the Harlem street corner in 1965, which as of this writing, was over 40 years ago.

One of my favorite quotes is by Dr. Martin Luther King, Jr.: "The man who doesn't have something he's willing to die for, isn't fit for living." Few people in this life have beliefs they're willing to die for. My parents do. They'd die on a hospital bed before accepting a blood transfusion. They'd go to jail or die before serving in any branch of the military, or bearing a firearm of any kind.

While I admire my parent's steadfast faithfulness to a spiritual path that suits them, my spiritual quest has revealed that being a Witness is not the path God paved for me. My spiritual evolution has revealed to me that the religion of my rearing is not the religion of my choosing. I'm no longer one of Jehovah's Witnesses, having long ago been disfellowshipped, the Witness equivalent to excommunication.

I'll characterize, but not classify, myself as an eclectic Christian. I've recently completed *reading The Teachings of Buddha.* And while I've always held a deep interest in Eastern religions and philosophy, I've not decided to become a Buddhist. However, I have seen that learning Buddhist teachings has made me better understand Christ—a paradox, but true. I don't think Jesus and Buddha would have argued each other on key spiritual issues. I've also learned and incorporated many metaphysical teachings into my daily life, including teachings on Kabbalah, which have added immensely and richly to my spiritual growth and development. I've been led down the perfect spiritual path for me.

Now, thank God, because of my trek, I'm equally at home in a Baptist Church with gospel music thundering, as I am in a Catholic Church listening to the melodic songs of a choir, as I am in the presence of a Muslim bowing face to the earth communing with Allah, as I am reflecting on the teachings of His Holiness the Dalai Lama.

I am at home and blessed in all these places because God is in all these places. God has become manifest to me everywhere, in every being. The presence of God is much too grand and magnificent to reside exclusively in any one church or religion. Much too grand and magnificent.

Yes, my spiritual quest in the desert has served me well. I've now arrived at a true never-ending oasis of truth, acceptance, love and compassion for all, regardless of race, religion, creed, color or any other meaningless characteristic. I love whom God loves, and that is everyone.

As a result of the changes I've made, my mom has chosen to have limited contact with me, in keeping with the Jehovah's Witness views on disfellowshipped individuals. She sat me down one day and tearfully explained that, according to Witness rules, which we both knew well, she could only discuss business or family issues with me from that point on. Staying true to their beliefs, she and my Dad did not attend my wedding or wedding reception.

In the midst of the change in my relationship with my mother, God gave me two gifts. The first gift was knowing that though the relationship between my mom and me has changed, the degree of love between us is as strong as it has ever been. She ends every conversation with me by saying, "I love you," and has done so for many years. That's a powerful statement. To me it means, *I can love and cherish you even though I don't agree with you. Our hearts can meet even if our minds don't.*

The second gift was the Griot.

As she was leaving, the Griot turned to our daughter, who was three years old at the time, and said, "You can call me Mama Shindana."

When her words fell upon my ears, it was as if a lightning bolt shot straight through me. I knew instantly

why God had put her in my life. She's the literal manifestation of God's answer to my prayer. I've asked God
to send me older women; mother figures who can and
will speak wisdom into my life. No one could ever replace my mom, nor is it necessary. Instead, I've asked
God for more relationships with older women that
would encourage me, and which would be instrumen-
tal in God's plan for me to become the fullest expression of the woman I was created to become. Just as a
baby elephant relies on wise matriarchs to find food,
water, rest and everything else she needs, having wise
matriarchs in my life is exactly what I need.

Thankfully, God was happy to oblige.

God Speaks

Sacred Lesson #1—God knows just who to send into your life, and when.

God knew exactly who to send into my life after the severing of certain ties with my mother. Though having that conversation with my mother about limited contact was a painful and tearful experience, God has surrounded me with so much love and guidance that I can no longer be sad or tearful.

Have you experienced the severing of a relationship that you didn't anticipate or didn't agree with? Do you find yourself aching to be with that person again? Don't despair. If you will look to God to lovingly supply your every need, you will be provided with loving relationships that nurture your spirit, your mind and your emotions. The new relationships will not be replacements for what you think you may have lost. We don't need to replace anything because nothing *real* is truly lost. The new relationships, however, can bring an added dimension to our lives, and communion with someone who is there to encourage and support us on our life's path.

Instead of lamenting and mourning the passing away or diminishing of a relationship that has served its important purpose, get busy connecting with the people God is bringing into your life for your mutual pleasure and fulfillment.

Sacred Lesson #2—Psalm 27:10—We are God's children, regardless of our earth parents.

This scripture has been my constant comfort. Long ago, I read this verse and it touched me so. I was a young girl, and I was touched to my core at the astounding depth of God's love for each of us. Here, God has promised to take in any orphan child, foster child, neglected child, abandoned child, run away child, left behind or left back child, disowned child, abused child, and any other child. Notice that our Father placed no conditions or stipulations on the agreement to take us in—there are no standards we have to meet, no bar we must jump.

This is an absolute and complete promise that we are God's children and remain so forever. God will never disown us.

I love reading this verse in different variations. Here are a few:

"Though my father and mother forsake me, the Lord
will receive me."
Psalm 27:10 (Message Bible)

"Even if my father and mother abandon me, the
Lord will hold me close."
Psalm 27:10 (NLT)

"My father and mother may abandon me, but the
Lord will take care of me."
Psalm 27:10 (Good News Bible)

"Although my father and my mother have forsaken
me, yet the Lord will take me up [adopt me as his
child]."
Psalm 27:10 (Amplified Bible)

The last variation is particularly reassuring because it says, in essence, that God adopts us. David, the writer of this particular Psalm, presents us with a glimpse into how deep and profound his faith was in the Most High God. David was absolutely certain that if everyone—even his father and mother—abandoned him, God would adopt him. No questions asked.

This is such a rewarding concept: God loves us so deeply, and cares for us so fully, that He becomes our surrogate Father, and indeed our surrogate Mother, if our earth parents are not, for whatever reason, filling those roles.

God is our Father and our Mother. God is everything we need, and all we will ever need.

Thank you, God, for adopting me.

Thank you, God, for being the most awesome parent a girl could ever ask for.

Sacred Lesson #3—We are not from here.

I am not from here.

Neither are you.

We may hold citizenship in a certain country, but in actuality, we came from a place far away from here. We came from pure spirit. We issued forth from God, as a magnificent, divine and totally new creation. Before we came here, we resided in spirit with our wondrous Parent. Then, God desired to give us human life and we were sent here to learn, grow, teach and give. Primarily, God desired for us to go forth and bring great things into creation that work in harmony with God's overall purpose and plan for humans and the cosmos.

Hence, we are not citizens of the country we think we are. We are citizens of the spirit world, for that is our true home (*Philippians 3:20*). It is where we issued forth from, and it is where we will return when we leave this plane of existence. God made us from dust, and to dust our earthly temple returns. Our eternal soul lives infinitely and is entrusted back to God when we take leave of our earthly temple. It is a beautiful process: from spirit world to human and back to God again.

The mix up that occurs with our citizenship is that we get here and we forget where we came from. We get here and we come to believe that we are American, or African or Asian or European. We think we are different from the others who are here. We think we are from the place where we were born.

Our true citizenship lies in spirit, and our true home is in God's bosom.

Since we all issued forth from the same parent, we are all brothers and sisters. We are much more alike, you and I, than we are different. There is little distinction between you and me, in many respects. I am your sister, and you are my sister or brother.

My son, Cory, is three years older than my daughter, Alana. Cory used to enjoy telling his younger sister a fib when they were growing up. He used to tell her that she was adopted and that we were not her real parents. He always ended the conversation with some statement that implied that we loved him more than we loved his sister. The lie used to enrage Alana and fill her with the worst kind of doubt, which is why Cory found delight in telling it to her so often. It was a rather cruel and unsettling practice.

The reason such a lie cuts so deeply is because some of us believe that an adopted child somehow does not merit or receive the same loving attention as the natural children do. Some of us believe, to an extent, that only natural children can be showered with true love and affection from the parents because those children share the parents' blood and DNA. While some may hold this idea in the physical world, it does not work the same way in the world of spirit.

The beauty of God being our parent is that there are no children who are not natural to God. All of us are God's natural children, sharing our Creator's traits and attributes. We are made in the image and likeness of our Father.

We are all chips off the old block.

We are all apples who haven't fallen far from the tree.

When we realize, understand and walk in this truth, we see every other human being as our brother and sister, regardless of the earth clothes they are wearing. Earth clothing is what we put on when we are born: skin, eyes, hair, etc.

We grow up and we come to believe that our earth clothing somehow means something. We think our earth clothing somehow defines who we really are. We believe that the brown skin we may be wearing as part of our earth suit is meaningful, and we probably learned this because we were born to parents who had brown skin. As we are growing up, our earth parents probably hung around a lot of other brown people, and we learned the stories of the brown people. We learned how and what brown people ate, how they slept, how they interacted with other brown people, and how that particular set of brown people interacted with God. We learned the language of the brown people and we learned to sing the songs of the brown people. We learned what the brown people found acceptable, and what they didn't.

Meanwhile, as the little brown baby is getting indoctrinated into the world of the brown people, the same thing is happening to the little red, white, black and yellow babies. They are each being indoctrinated into their particular tribe's customs, habits, attitudes, ideals, truths, behaviors, rituals, and so on.

One of the most detrimental things that happens is that each of these sets of people thinks that they are much different from the others. Some of these tribes tend to think that they are worse off than the others, and some of the tribes tend to think that they are better off than the others, largely depending upon what part of the earth the tribe happens to inhabit.

Not only do the tribes focus on what makes them different from the other tribes, there are sub-sets of the tribes. These sub-sets also focus on differences. For instance, there are some sub-sets of brown people that believe they are very much different from other subsets of brown people.

All in all, the tribes' constant focus on what makes them all different has caused considerable division, strife, war, turmoil and destruction on the planet the tribes came to visit.

There is only one solution: to simply remember that *I am not from here, and neither are you.*

We are all from another world, the world of spirit, the domain and kingdom ruled by Jah. We come into this human form for a short time. We put on these earth clothes for a few years. When we are done here, we go back home. We return to God's bosom.

When we come here for a short visit of 80 or so years, we have a challenge of huge proportions on our hands: *to remember who we really are and where we came from.* Our challenge is to look through the eyes of the Holy Spirit, which see no color, no race, no difference nor differences. The eyes of the Holy Spirit are God's eyes, and God's eyes see only a vast array of beautiful and varied children. Just as a proud parent looks upon his or her children, God looks upon us, with no differentiation. Not one of us is any better looking to God than the other, though we have done quite the outstanding job of convincing ourselves otherwise.

Remember often, as you work to do each day, that you are God's beloved child.

Remember that you are not from here, your citizenship is in another world. You are merely visiting this place, and you are merely sporting a particular brand and type of earth clothes for the short time that you are here. Do not give these earth clothes much import, and do not believe that these earth clothes hold meaning about your true identity.

Remember that you are God's child, and so is every other person who is on a temporary visit to this planet, no matter what tribe they belong to.

I am not from here, and neither are you.

God Speaks Through A Destitute Widow

"If God did not exist, it would be necessary to invent him."
Voltaire

The Elisha Treasure

I undertake the reading of spiritual literature every morning with few exceptions. One morning, as is often the case, I felt a profound sense of meaning while reading a particular passage. The passage is found at 2 Kings 4:1-7. I was so moved by its content, I read it over and over that morning; at least a dozen times. And I've read it at least a few dozen times since. It's still as striking to me now as it was that morning.

The reason this passage spoke to me is because it is at once amazingly simplistic and powerfully poignant. Truth is never complicated. The essence and nature of truth is simplicity.

The tale is of one of the many miracles performed by the prophet Elisha, and in comparison to some of his others, such as raising the dead, could easily pale. It is the story of an impoverished widow, left deep in debt by her late husband. The widow's distressing situation becomes even more desperate when her creditors threaten to take her sons and force them into slavery to pay off the family's debt.

Elisha's solution for the widow's misery is not only miraculous; it spawned at least eight sacred lessons, all of which I've detailed herein. I invite you to read the following pages with full presence, understanding that the key to unlocking your tremendous power lies within a simple but poignant account of a miracle performed by the holy man Elisha on behalf of a destitute widow.

Though you may have read the passage at 2 Kings 4:1-7 numerous times, I invite you to examine it in a new and different light. Allow yourself to visualize how Elisha's simple commands to a poor widow provided her and her sons with the following:

A) A family business
B) A debt elimination plan
C) A retirement plan

You may not have realized the powerhouse that is encapsulated in this tiny passage of just seven verses. Yet, understanding and practicing the principles involved will provide you with relief from any type of financial hardship, and allow you to grow your wealth in ways you never imagined. Please be aware that what is stated here is my understanding of this passage. I am a layperson, not a theologian.

The identical solution Elisha applied to the poor widow's financial crises still applies today, thousands of years later, and can effect powerful change in your financial picture. You'll discover the mindset necessary to manifest your desires, including being empowered to start your own business, rid yourself of consumer debt, or build generational wealth—all based on the simple ideas that follow.

Dissecting this passage of scripture will change your

paradigm about everything you own and give you the understanding and the tools to acquire your God pre-scribed inheritance. If you'll absorb and live this trea-sure, a life of abundance, joy and profound fulfillment will not elude you!

To begin the journey toward understanding these powerful spiritual principles, we must first read the passage of Holy Scripture found at 2 Kings 4:1-7. For your convenience, the following three quotations are from the King James Version, the Amplified Bible and the New Living Translation.

2 Kings 4:1-7:
Authorized King James Version

Now there cried a certain woman of the wives of the sons of the prophets unto Elisha, saying. Thy servant my husband is dead; and thou knowest that thy servant did fear the Lord: and the creditor is come to take unto him my two sons to be bondmen.

2 And Elisha said unto her, What shall I do for thee? Tell me, what hast thou in the house? And she said, Thine handmaid hath not any thing in the house, save a pot of oil.

3 Then he said, Go, borrow thee vessels abroad of all thy neighbors, even empty vessels; borrow not a few.

4 And when thou art come in, thou shalt shut the door upon thee and upon thy sons, and shalt pour out into all those vessels, and thou shalt set aside that which is full.

5 So she went from him, and shut the door upon her and upon her sons, who brought *the vessels* to her; and she poured out.

6 And it came to pass, when the vessels were full, that she said unto her son, Bring me yet a vessel. And he said unto her, *There is* not a vessel more. And the oil stayed.

7 Then she came and told the man of God, and he said, Go, sell the oil, and pay thy debt, and live thou and thy children of the rest.

2 Kings 4:1-7
Amplified Bible

Now the wife of a son of the prophets cried to Elisha, Your servant my husband is dead, and you know that your servant feared the Lord. But the creditor has come to take my two sons to be his slaves.

2 Elisha said to her, What shall I do for you? Tell me, what have you [of sale value] in the house? She said, Your handmaid has nothing in the house except a jar of oil.

3 Then he said, Go around and borrow vessels from all your neighbors, empty vessels—and not a few.

4 And when you come in, shut the door upon you and your sons. Then pour out [the oil you have] into all those vessels, setting aside each one when it is full.

5 So she went from him and shut the door upon herself and her sons, who brought to her the vessels as she poured the oil.

6 When the vessels were all full, she said to her son, Bring me another vessel. And he said to her, There is not a one left. Then the oil stopped multiplying.

7 Then she came and told the man of God. He said, Go, sell the oil and pay your debt, and you and your sons live on the rest.

2 Kings 4:1-7
New Living Translation:

One day the widow of a member of the group of prophets came to Elisha and cried out, "My husband who served you is dead, and you know how he feared the Lord. But now a creditor has come, threatening to take my two sons as slaves."

2 "What can I do to help you?" Elisha asked. "Tell me, what do you have in the house?" "Nothing at all, except a flask of olive oil," she replied.

3 And Elisha said, "Borrow as many empty jars as you can from your friends and neighbors. 4 Then go into your house with your sons and shut the door behind you. Pour olive oil from your flask into the jars, setting each one aside when it is filled."

5 So she did as she was told. Her sons kept bringing jars to her, and she filled one after another. 6 Soon every container was full to the brim!

"Bring me another jar," she said to one of her sons.

"There aren't any more!" he told her. And then the olive oil stopped flowing.

7 When she told the man of God what had happened, he said to her, "Now sell the olive oil and pay your debts, and you and your sons can live on what is left over."

This story begins ominously. A recently widowed woman is left penniless and deep in debt. Her situation deteriorates—knowing that the widow has no income or means to repay the outstanding debt, her creditors have come to confiscate her sons and force them into slavery so that they might work off the debt of their parents.

This story is written for you if you find yourself in any type of crisis right now. What the specific crisis is really doesn't matter, you will receive benefit. Though your current crisis may not be tantamount to the financial, emotional and mental crisis of this poor widow, your situation may still be quite dire and stress-inducing. Let's examine what the widow decides to do about her devastation.

Verse 1 says she came to the man of God and cried out. *She immediately goes to someone who has the power to help. She went to Elisha and "cried out".*

God Speaks

Sacred Lesson #1—Humility vs. Super Heroism

When you find yourself in a dire predicament, the first thing you need to acknowledge is—*I need help.* In any crisis, be humble enough to recognize the need for human or superhuman help. God never expects us to solve our major problems, or even the smallest ones, completely alone. Allow humility to teach you that you can't do it alone, and that you need to, as the poor widow did, "cry out" for assistance.

There is exquisite beauty and enduring peace in the knowledge that you don't have to solve every problem alone. You always have an army in your corner—God and the messengers He employs for your eternal benefit. Our Creator and powerful spirit beings are always standing right there, ready to help, even when we're completely ignoring them.

Recognizing her need for divine assistance, the widow sought the man of God for help.

Do not allow pride to force you into trying to solve your worst problems by yourself. Pride is rooted in fear. It is a dam that blocks the powerful rush of supernatural energy and assistance that flows from the Creator of the universe.

Learn to surrender and let God guide you. Allow God to show you how to proceed with your monumental and your miniscule problems. Learn to "cry out" to God.

God can, and will, provide just the help you need, when you need it. Remember that the widow sought a highly regarded prophet to help her, a man of God who was known as a miracle worker and a mighty prophet.

He had been trained by Elijah, who also was a great prophet.

If you are in a bind, it would be wise to go to a spiritual giant whom you respect rather than going to one of your peers for help. We can't ask just anyone for help. We need to be quite discriminating about who we approach when we need spiritual guidance and direction. A man or woman of God will give us spiritual guidance, support and direction that are from God, and not from their own ego mind. Such a spiritually advanced and mature person will not solve our problems for us, nor will they tell us what to do. They will simply support us in reaching our own God given answers to what ails us. They are conduits and channels for God's wisdom during times when we may not be fully attuned to our own internal voice of wisdom from God.

When you approach such a person for help, don't ask them to tell you what to do. Don't ask them what they would do if they were you. If they were you, they would be doing the same thing you are doing.

Instead, ask the spiritual giant what you might not be looking at in this situation, and what Godly qualities might be able to help you through it. Ask them what spiritual tools you can use that would help you, and what spiritual resources you could draw from. Ask them to pray for you and with you, and more important, you pray for yourself.

There is no denying that many times we may find ourselves in situations that we believe are beyond our ability to handle, even though they never truly are. When we are not be able to see all aspects of the situation clearly—we know we need help. It is at these times that a counselor, therapist, spiritual teacher, guide or coach can be of immense benefit.

Ask your Self the following questions:

- ***What problems have I tried to handle on my own without success?***
- ***Is there a "man or woman of God" who can offer guidance which will help me solve my own problem?***
- ***What is preventing me from getting the help I need?***

Search yourself for answers. If you need help, never be ashamed to ask for it. Do not allow the internal prideful demon of "what will people think of me" stop you from getting the help you know you need.

Sacred Lesson #2—Expect miracles, every day.

The woman in the story came to Elisha with an expectation. The scripture does not say exactly what she expected, but she obviously expected something, otherwise, she would not have gone to him. Being formerly married to a prophet, and knowing Elisha and the work of the prophets, it may not be inappropriate to state that the widow expected something supernatural to happen—she may have expected a miracle.

I've always found that whenever the circumstances in my life appeared the most bleak, I was on the cusp of a miracle. Just when I thought I was going to crash and burn, something absolutely amazing happened. Often not due to my own conscious efforts.

One of my favorite movie characters, Forest Gump, was the embodiment of this concept. He led a life of serendipity. He didn't harbor a single negative expectation. He lived life with innocence and purity, taking everything that occurred at face value. He expected everything to work out well; and in his world, it always did. As a result, he lived an extraordinary life. Not bad for a person whom most labeled stupid.

Like both Forest and the widow, I've come to expect miracles. As a result, I notice them happening several times each day. They were unfolding before in my life as well, I just didn't have the eyes to see them. The book *A Course in Miracles* states miracles arise from a miraculous state of mind, or, as I like to refer to it, a state of miracle-readiness. A miracle is simply a shift in our perception.

Do you expect miracles every day? Are you miracle-ready? Whether you are aware and expectant or not, miracles happen quite frequently. Do you notice? Or are you caught up in a whirlwind of negative expectations that blinds you? The miracles that occur for you each day are magical doors of opportunity that could propel you forward in your divine life's purpose; but only if you live with enough presence to realize each miracle for what it is while it's happening. Most don't, and therefore miss out on priceless opportunities the universe lays before them.

Akin to this concept is the Kabbalah teaching of Bat Kol. Bat Kol can be said to mean the voice from above, and kabbalists teach that it "is a gentle inner whisper that calls upon us to draw closer to God." (*The Way* by Michael Berg) It sweeps over each of us once daily and when it does, it calls upon us to take some specific action that would bring us closer to God. The positive action—that day's Bat Kol—could manifest as the sudden urge to call your grandmother or a close friend. Each time we heed the directive and take the action we are being called upon to take, we grow spiritually and become closer to God. For us to benefit from Bat Kol, we need only be aware of its existence and expect a daily visit.

How many Bat Kol's have you missed? How many miracles have you allowed to pass by unnoticed? Before I became conscious of the presence of daily miracles (or Bat Kol), I probably missed thousands of opportunities to grow, develop, transform and just be bigger and better than I was before—in every aspect.

Some mislabel miracles as "coincidence" or happenstance. If you know the Creator of the universe, you know that there are no coincidences. Nothing happens by accident, nor do we live in a random universe. Everything that happens to and for us lies within the larger context of being for our eternal benefit. Therefore, if we know and believe that there are no coincidences, we have no alternative but to view the spectacularly beneficial and fortunate events that unfurl for us every day as nothing short of miracles.

If that be the case, then it follows that a spirit of expectancy would prevent us from missing our miracles. When they do actualize, recognize them for what they are: a powerful but brief window of opportunity that if seized, speeds us forward in realizing our life's mission. If we don't have the presence of mind and spirit to recognize our daily miracles and take the leap of faith they require, poof, the opportunity of that moment is gone!

Ask yourself:

- *What miracles occurred for me today?*
- *Did I notice them while they were unfolding, or only in hindsight?*
- *Did I take advantage of the miracles I noticed? If not, why not*?

Decide right here and right now that you will open your eyes and heart, and live with full presence so that you can observe and act on the miracles the universe presents to you on a daily basis. Commit to a miracle-expectancy and miracle-readiness mindset, and your life will be transformed in ways that will astonish you!

Sacred Lesson #3—Tell the truth. Be honest with yourself and others.

Next, notice how bluntly the woman tells Elisha about her situation, from start to finish, with no shame, leaving nothing out. She says that her husband is now dead, but while he was alive, he held God in high regard and awe. She goes on to state that the creditor is coming to take her sons away for conscripted labor until her debt is repaid.

The widow held no denial, delusions, or illusions. Her situation was grave, and she faced it with full awareness. She didn't mince words with Elisha nor did she sugarcoat—*she told the whole ugly truth.*

Are you honest with yourself, or do you lie to yourself (which is the worst lie we can tell)? If you can't remember ever lying to yourself, think about whether you've ever said:

"I'll do it later."

"I don't really have that much debt."

"I'll start saving money soon."

"I'm not that fat."

"I'll start my diet on Monday."

"I can change him/her."

"He really does love me, he just has a strange way of showing it."

"I'll quit smoking soon."

In ancient China, young girls were subjected to having their feet tightly and painfully bound with cloths. The bandages prevented their feet from growing to the length nature intended, which, in some cases, would have been considered too large. It was highly desirable for a woman to have petite feet and take small halting steps.

Denial and lies are like bandages that tightly and painfully bind us, constricting our growth. Only truth can cut through bonds that seek to choke and prevent us from growing to the full potential God intended.

Accept and embrace the whole truth about yourself and your current situation. Speak, think and act with full truth about yourself, without delusions or illusions. Remember, healing and love abide with truth.

Ask yourself:

- ***What truth about myself that may be considered ugly do I need to admit, accept, acknowledge and therefore be able to change?***

Sacred Lesson #4—Abandon fear. Embrace love.

How much nerve do you think it took for this woman to go find Elisha and lay bare her soul and personal business to him? She could have weakly and fearfully stood by helplessly while the creditors took her sons, acting like a victim. But she didn't. She displayed enough courage and personal power to get up, find someone who could help, and speak up! In essence, she told Elisha, "You know as well as I do that my husband was a God-loving man, and I'm here because I expect you to do something, and do it fast. We don't have much time!'

When you want or need anything, whatever it is, speak up. Be courageous. There's a quote in the Bible that contains an excellent question: "so I will have no fear. What can mere people do to me?" (Hebrews 13:6b—NLT)

Are you courageous, taking decisive action and speaking up for yourself when necessary? Or are you fearful and hesitant?

If you don't always feel fearless, you're not alone. Most of us fight an ongoing battle with fear on a daily basis; losing more battles than we win. Though the battle may be lost, the war is not if we continue to abandon fear and embrace love at every turn. How?

The only remedy for fear is to immerse yourself in whatever it is you fear most. Fear is an unsustainable emotion—it cannot persist once you've faced and exposed it. A child may be fearful that a monster is hiding under the bed, but after looking under the bed and finding no monster, the fear can be alleviated. Our worst fears are just as unsustainable as a child's fear of a monster lurking under the bed.

The phantom nature of fear can be more closely scrutinized as it relates to public speaking. When a survey was conducted of thousands of adults in the United States concerning what they feared most, the fear of public speaking ranked number one. The fear of death ranked sixth. One might draw the conclusion that most Americans are more afraid of speaking in front of a group of people than they are of dying. While we know this may not be completely accurate, dread of public speaking is undeniably widespread. Why? Because at the root of the fear of speaking in public are many other related fears: the fear of not being liked, the fear of looking foolish in front of others, the concern about one's personal appearance in front of others, the fear of making a mistake in front of others, the fear of not being good enough.

However, if we put each of these fears under the microscope of God's immutable love, they quickly vanish.

For instance, if we have a fear of not being liked, does it really matter anyway?

If no one liked us, which is unlikely in itself, doesn't God always love us unconditionally?

Therefore, could we not assume that if God likes and loves us, that we are likable and lovable?

Would you care as much about who didn't like you if you always held a deep-rooted belief that God loved you unconditionally and nothing you could do could ever separate you from that love?

And would that feeling of knowing how much God loved you cause you to have an inner confidence?

And might that inner confidence be reflected on the outside when you interact with other people?

And might others sense how deeply you love yourself and therefore how unconcerned you must be as to whether or not they love you?

And might that help to alleviate some of the fear of public speaking if you had to stand up and speak in front of a group?

I can state all of the above to you with confidence because I lived it. I was *terrified* of speaking in front of groups. At the time, I was part of a religious order that required its members to speak publicly in front of the congregation on a regular basis. The practice forced me to confront the fear of speaking over and over again, until I began to master it. Eventually, I felt at home addressing large groups of people. Some years later, I joined Toastmasters International, an organization that trains public speakers in a supportive environment. I became so gifted at public speaking that, with powerful coaching, I went on to win many speech contests! If I had not been forced to confront this monumental fear, I may still be living in a cocoon of fear.

The same is true for you and all your fears, since not one of them is sustainable. If you doubt the validity of my suggestion, please suspend your disbelief long enough to consider what would happen if you confronted all your dreads.

Might they just vanish into thin air?

Remember, fear contracts, while love expands. The presence of fearful thoughts creates negative reactions in the body—muscle tension, rapid heartbeat, shortness of breath. If left unchecked, your fears will completely paralyze you, rendering you unable to move forward. Do not allow fear to debilitate you and decimate your hopes and dreams.

Contrarily, love is expanding. Thoughts and feelings of love promote good health, lessen stress, and produce a sense of calm and tranquility. Love moves you to action and convinces you that you can do all things with God's power, including accomplishing superhuman feats.

Your life is waiting for you to manifest the polar opposite of fear—*limitless love.* Make a habit of doing so and you will experience a transformation you had not dreamed possible!

Ask yourself:

- *What situation have I been enduring because I am riddled with fear?*
- *If I imagined two enormous angels that accompanied me everywhere I went, one on my right and one on my left, how would that change the level of fear I experience?*

- **If I didn't have any fears, what would I be doing, who would I be speaking up to, and what would I be saying?**
- **Since fear is not my natural state, am I willing to move toward living in my natural state, which is love?**

Lesson #5—You are perfect, complete and whole. Right here. Right now.

Consider the powerful question Elisha next asks the widow:

"Tell me, what do you have in the house?"

or

"What do you already have? Because whatever it is, you are going to use it to create a way out of this mess."

How profound and enlightening.

Herein lies the crux of this entire Elisha treasure:

You already have all you need to be all you were created to be, to do all you were created to do, and to have all that you were created to have. You are perfect. You are complete—right here and right now. You do not need anything that you do not currently possess and you currently possess all that you need. You are able to gain everything that you desire with what you already have.

Please understand this and never forget it. Commit it to memory. Write it down if you have to.

When faced with a challenge or difficulty, so often we look outside of ourselves for answers or reasons. We accuse or we excuse. We look for scapegoats to pin blame on. We've all forgotten, at one time or another (or perhaps never realized), that we are complete, right here, right now. So let these words serve as a reminder to you:

You are perfect.

That's the "Elisha treasure".

You may be looking at Elisha's question from another perspective: wasn't Elisha one of the greatest miracle workers in the Holy Scriptures? Didn't he go on to raise the dead? Wasn't he a mighty prophet? Didn't he have the mighty power of God undeniably resting within him?

Then why on earth did he ask this woman what *she* had? Wasn't what *she* had considerably less than what *he* had? Couldn't he have just given her what she needed? Couldn't he have just pulled the solution to all of her woes out of thin air, miraculously?

Yes he could have, but he didn't.

He asked her the critical question: "Tell me, what do *you* have in the house?"

How many times have you said to yourself, "I could do so much more, if only I had _____." That is a lie. You can do so much more with what you have *right now.* Can you unequivocally state that you are doing *everything you possibly can* with all the talents, gifts, skills, abilities, health, money, position, influence, expertise, qualities, and attributes that you have in your possession right now? Probably not. If you're like most people, you haven't even explored the smallest iota of what you can do with what you already have.

We tend to think we need something else to get what we want. We often tell ourselves, *"When* I get _____, *then* I'll be so much better off than I am now." What fills in the blank is really inconsequential, because if you are immersed in this mode of thinking, you'll always feel that you need something else in order to get what you want.

The truth is, you won't be any better off in the future than you are in this very moment. In fact, you will never be better off until you realize your utter and complete perfection in this very moment. How liberating!

Considering again Elisha's query, the widow replies that she has nothing in the house except a flask of olive oil. I don't know if Elisha knew what the woman was going to say before she said it. Her answer could have been, "I have only some flour for making bread." Or, "I have only some hay for the animals". Or, "I have only an extra garment."

The oil in the story is really symbolic. Of one thing I'm certain: the instrument of transformation for this widow was going to be something she already had possession of. In her case, an ordinary, everyday flask of olive oil.

If you had asked the widow that morning when she woke up how important her flask of olive oil was to her, do you think she would have responded by saying:

> "This oil is critically important, it will become the instrument that will enable me and my sons to have a family business, it will save my sons from slavery, and the proceeds from the sale of it will become a retirement plan that will take care of me and my family for the rest of our natural days."

To the contrary, she probably had no idea that a simple flask of olive oil would so powerfully transform her life.

Understanding that you are perfect and right now possess everything you need to gain everything you desire, ask yourelf:

- **What do I have right now in my possession that could be a powerful force for transformation and bring me everything that my Soul desires? in other words,**
- **What do I have in my house?**

To further illustrate this point, consider the story of a young man who passed to the other side due to AIDS.

The other day I was talking to a relative who told me the astounding story of a young man she saw on television. He was from Africa where the AIDS virus had decimated his village. He'd lost his mother and father, and he himself was now smitten with the deadly virus. He had lived for many years with the virus before he eventually succumbed.

Before he left his physical body, he uttered these words to an audience assembled for the purpose of listening to the extent of the devastation of AIDS in Africa: "I implore you to do everything you can with what you have, in the time you have, in the place you are."

Astounding words, considering they were uttered by a 10 year old. After telling me his story, my husband's cousin, Wendy, and I sat for a moment, silently pondering his words, and wondering why most people don't live by this simple, yet life-empowering principle.

I've been guilty of it on so many occasions; not giving my all. But the implications of doing ALL we can with what we have are too huge to ignore. There are a bevy of blessings to be derived from living at your peak and giving all of yourself in any given situation. Consider some of the benefits:

1. Doing everything you can with what you have removes dependency upon others, therefore cre-

ating self-sufficiency, which leads to increased confidence. Increased confidence creates the ability to conquer even bigger tasks in the future. It is the ultimate expression of our inherent personal power.

2. Doing everything you can with what you have initiates an energy flow that travels through the universe summoning divine aid. If you start a worthy ambition that you know you can't finish on your own, but proceed anyway by doing ALL you can, you will begin to attract all the assistance and resources you require to complete the undertaking. Remember, the aid will appear only **after** you've done what you can with what you already have. It requires the proverbial leap of faith.

3. Doing all you can with what you have fixates your mind and attentions *on what you have, rather than on what you don't have.* A critical mindset for building wealth and abundance in every arena of your life is to develop an "Abundance Mentality." When you don't take action because of all the things you lack, such as money, resources, or expertise, you are focused on what you don't have. Focusing on what you don't have will only invite more lack into your life. Doing all you can with what you already have forces you to focus on all that you do have, which creates and invites even more abundance.

God's actions in our lives are always efficient—exactly what is needed for the moment for us, not less, not more. True to His modus operandi, the content and timing of the conversation was perfectly formulated for me, as I got the opportunity to practice this principle shortly after my conversation with Wendy.

This is what happened.

I had a piece of investment real estate that I was planning to sell, but the former tenants had left the house in deplorable condition. Though it wasn't structurally damaged, it was foul: dirt and debris were everywhere, and dog manure littered the entire basement. The stench arrested you at the front door. Being near Christmas time, it was nearly impossible for me to get the help I needed to quickly clear the unit of all dirt and debris in preparation to be shown to potential buyers. I was frustrated, and a little furious at the former tenants who I felt had put me in this predicament. Here I was with a filthy, uninhabitable house that I was obliged to prepare for human habitation. In addition, I had to continue paying mortgage payments on an empty house—an expensive proposition that could lead to an undesirable outcome.

While I was smack dab in the middle of ruminating on all the resources I didn't have to get this job done—namely the manpower, the money and the time I thought I needed—God recalled the 10-year-old's words to me. That little boy's haunting plea was being whispered from within: "Do all that you can with what you have in the time you have in the place you are."

I asked myself if I'd done ALL I could with what I did have in this undesirable situation. The answer was a resounding "NO"! I hadn't done everything in my power to prepare this unit for sale, and I was the only one being hurt by it: if I didn't take action, there'd be no profits, and I would have to continue maintenance and payments on a despicable house.

God helped me change my focus, and I got to work. I

went over to the house and starting bagging the trash that met me at the front door. I worked all day until I had the entire first floor of the house cleared of debris. There were at least a dozen huge trash bags at the curb when I was finished that day.

The next day my husband, seeing how hard I'd worked the previous day, and knowing that I was back on my way over to attack the house again, called a friend who knew some workers who could come over that day and quickly get rid of all the rest of the debris in and around the house. He called them, and for an inexpensive fee, they cleared the house and the outside of the remaining trash and furniture. They moved it all outside. A day or two later, my husband's friend was able to haul it all away for me.

With all the debris cleared away, next came the repulsive job of cleaning the house—no easy task as the laziness of the former tenants allowed them to live with dog feces everywhere.

I told my adolescent children that I needed their help and was prepared to hire them for some dirty work. The three of us rolled up our sleeves, covered ourselves in protective gear, and went inside the house. Within two days we had the house looking and smelling as if people could live in it. It was one of the worst experiences I've ever been confronted with, but I managed to get through it. A bonus lesson was spoken to me in the process: "Valerie, you're never above doing menial labor—always be humble".

Consequently, the house sold quickly, and I received a large profit, more money than what a large portion of the population would earn in an entire year. However, the monetary reward from this experience was secondary to the paramount lesson from God—*do all that you can with what you already have.* God has given you everything you need to get everything you desire. Are you fully utilizing all the gifts and resources you possess?

Remember:

You are perfect, complete and whole. Right here. Right now.

Sacred Lesson #6—NEVER put limits on God. (They don't belong on you either.)

Elisha next gives the widow instructions:

"Go, borrow thee vessels abroad of all thy neighbors, even empty vessels; *borrow not a few.*" (KJV)

or,

Then he said, "Go around and borrow vessels from all your neighbors, empty vessels—*and not a few.*" (AMP)

or,

"Borrow *as many empty jars as you can* from your friends and neighbors . . ." (NLT)

Notice Elisha setting the stage for something BIG to happen. When Elisha tells her to borrow empty vessels, he specifically instructs her to:

"*. . . borrow not a few . . .*"

or

"*Borrow as many empty jars as you can . . .*"
What was Elisha *really* saying?

"Don't limit God in what is about to happen for you and your sons."

or

"Don't think small."

or

"Don't think *just enough.*"

or, more fully,

> "Don't think about how your life was before, while your husband was alive. Don't limit yourself to just having enough, as you're accustomed to. Be open to the idea that you will soon have more than you've ever had before. Understand that your life is about to change in a radical and unimaginable way. God is preparing to do something spectacular—hold onto your socks!"

Before the miracle even takes place, Elisha is preparing the widow for what is most certainly going to happen. He's showing her how to make room for prosperity in her life where debt, lack and insufficiency had taken up residency. He's stretching her by getting her to think BIG.

There is a valuable lesson here for every one of us: *don't ever limit God!*

When God is preparing you for something BIG, do you respond with a willingness to grow, even when you're apprehensive about what the new growth will mean for you and everyone around you? You may feel God preparing your mind and heart right now for something much bigger than you've ever experienced. How are you responding? Whatever you do, *do not limit God. Do as the widow did and gather as many empty vessels as you can!* What do I mean by gathering as many empty vessels as you can?

In this story, the empty vessels symbolize to me *the intention followed by the act of making room for growth—intentionally creating space in your life for everything that you desire but currently lack, and for everything that God desires to give you. The empty vessels represent expectancy for what you do not currently have, but for what you know you will surely soon receive. Gathering vessels is symbolic of doing the work that supports your new intention.*

We all practice this principle of "gathering empty vessels" on some level right now. An expectant mother buys a crib or bassinet, along with clothing, diapers and other necessities for the baby. She may start doing this early in pregnancy because she *expects* a baby. The empty vessels she gathers—a crib, bassinet and clothing—will soon be filled with a new baby.

The host of a dinner party arranges seating and place settings for his guests before they arrive. He *expects* that they will attend, enjoy dinner and that the evening will proceed beautifully, just as he planned.

A congregation may plan to build a bigger church than they actually need. Building a church larger than what is actually needed to accommodate the current congregation is a form of "gathering empty vessels": extra seats that the congregation expects will one day soon be filled with worshippers.

In every instance of "gathering empty vessels", we are expecting growth and expansion, perhaps much more than we had before, and consciously preparing a space for the new increase. Remember that the widow didn't have enough empty vessels herself, she had to go abroad to all her neighbors to borrow enough vessels to house what she was going to receive! She did as Elisha instructed, even though she may have had little idea of the outcome.

A personal example of this principle is illustrated in my experience of losing over 60 pounds after the birth of my third child. I wanted an entirely new wardrobe for my trimmer figure, even though I knew I would not be able to go out and buy all new clothes at once, at least not the clothes I wanted. That would have been a very expensive proposition, and I was not in a position to spend that much money on a whole new wardrobe at once. I remember going into my closet and clearing out the clothes that were too big for me. I gave them all away, which made room in my closet for new clothes. Then, I created a large empty space in my closet where several dresses, suits, skirts, pants and blouses could hang. I looked at the empty space and said to myself, *"This is where all my new clothes will soon hang."* I didn't know at the time how it was going to happen, and I certainly didn't have the excess money just floating around to make it happen, but I *expected* that it would. As you can probably guess, I had the empty space filled with new clothes in short order.

So too with you—the size of your miracles is directly linked to your expectations, and the capacity you create to receive them. You get *exactly* what you expect to get and not a bit more. If you don't like the results of your current expectations, change what you expect, and you will quickly change what you receive. Having low expectations gives you poor or marginal results.

By expecting huge increase and acting in harmony with that expectation by creating space for the increase, it will soon be realized. It can't not be!

Ask yourself:

- *If I examined my life right now, have I been gathering as many empty vessels as I can by intending to receive much more and acting in accord with that intention, or have I been satisfied to settle for much less?*
- *Have I expected and cleared space for absolutely grand, magnificent things to happen for me and to come into my life, or am I in some way limiting God and myself?*
- *What increase would I like to see but have not been truly expecting?*
- *Along with expecting that increase, how can I create a space for it or "gather empty vessels"?*

Set an intention for what you expect to receive, no matter how grand and lofty it may seem, no matter how astonishingly greater it is than anything else you've had. Then, act in accord with your intention by doing the work necessary to increase your capacity and ability to receive great things, which sets in motion powerful forces that will act to bring increased good to you.

Sacred Lesson #7—Everything in the universe is in infinite supply. It is a law.

Back to our story: the widow is now inside her home along with her two sons and the empty jars she has borrowed from neighbors. As Elisha has instructed, she has closed the door and begins to pour olive oil from her flask into each of the vessels. She pours and pours, filling jar after jar. After unknowingly filling the last jar, she says to her son, "Bring me another jar." Her son replies, "There are no more jars, you have filled them all!" With that, the olive oil instantly stops multiplying!

Notice that as long as the widow keeps pouring, the oil keeps flowing. When she has no more empty vessels, the oil stops.

Whether she had 10, 20 or 100 vessels didn't matter. Regardless of the number, all of the empty vessels would have been filled. The amount of multiplying olive oil depended upon her pre-work of gathering as many empty vessels as she could, not limiting herself or God, as we have already discussed. Had she been too timid or reluctant to ask all of her neighbors for empty jars, she would have had fewer jars. Had she been aggressive and gone to all of her neighbors, she would have had more jars.

The only limitation on the size of the widow's miracle was her self-created capacity for it. The same is true in your life.

The only thing that limits you is you!

In order to fully grasp this concept, we must first remember that the Universe and everything in it is in *infinite supply*. As Dr. Wayne Dyer masterfully points out, "It doesn't matter if you go to the ocean to fill up a thimble or a bucket, the ocean doesn't care." This means that the ocean is a limitless body of water. If you need water and you go to the ocean to fill up a thimble, the ocean will not miss what you've taken. The same is true if you go to the ocean and fill up a bucket. The exact same is true if you go to the ocean and fill up a huge barrel. It's all the same to the ocean because the ocean doesn't know scarcity, and it's not going to miss whatever you've taken. The ocean is set up to re-create itself, endlessly. So, if you're in need of water, what kind of vessel would you take to the ocean?

As ridiculous as it would be to go to the ocean and fill only a thimble, it is equally absurd to settle for lack. It means, on some level, you believe in a limited supply—a limited supply of money, a limited supply of opportunities, or of any other resource. Just as the ocean is an enormous, powerful, replenishing body of water, God has made everything else to be in infinite supply, including your thoughts, ideas and creations. If you find the "infinite supply" idea difficult to assimilate, consider this:

- *How many leaves are on a full grown oak tree in the middle of summer?*
- *How many fish swim in a healthy body of water?*
- *When the skies above darken with birds, how many wings are overhead?*
- *How many grapes can grow on a well-cultivated, disease-free grapevine over the course of many hundreds of years?*
- *If your eyes looked heavenward, how many stars could you count?*
- *How many galaxies exist beyond our own Milky Way?*
- *How many blades of grass are in just one square foot patch of earth?*
- *How many ants invaded your last picnic?*

As you can see, there are *endless* examples that illustrate the infinite nature of every facet of the universe. God made such a rich and bountiful universe that we could never, ever, ever postulate nor prove lack with regard to God and what God has created.

If the universe exhibits infinite supply so magnificently, what makes your situation any different? Why wouldn't any and everything you need be in infinite supply? God is anxious to give you a life rich in every arena: spiritually, emotionally, mentally, physically, romantically, financially. There is no lack in the universe because God doesn't create lack, we do. Any lack we experience comes from not fully recognizing that we are the creators of our own life experience. Therefore, if we are experiencing lack, somehow, we had a hand in creating it. To create something different, we must access and harness all the powers that God has put at our disposal, including recognizing and working in harmony with the law of *infinite supply*.

Ask yourself:

- *Do I really believe that everything I need and want is in infinite supply, or do I believe that there's not enough of what I want?*
- *If I did believe that everything I need and want is in infinite supply, how would that knowingness change my intentions, thoughts, words and actions?*
- *In turn, how would that change the outcome of what I am now experiencing in my world?*

Allow the law of infinite supply to work for you. To gain full benefit of this law, go out in nature and spend as much time as is feasible in God's creations. You will soon witness—and begin to know firsthand—the infinite nature of everything our Creator has brought into existence.

Sacred Lesson #8: You are a co-creator with God.

When the olive oil ceases to flow, the widow returns to Elisha to tell him all that has transpired. She then receives a plan of action by Elisha:

"Go, sell the oil and pay your debt, and you and your sons live on the rest."

or

"Now sell the olive oil and pay your debts, and you and your sons can live on what is left over."

How elated she must be to know that she and her sons will soon be debt-free and stress-free! They now have the inventory to start a business enterprise selling olive oil. An appropriate name for the widow's new business venture could have been: "Widow & Sons Miraculous Olive Oil, Inc."

Elisha also assures her that she'll be so successful in her business endeavor that she will have sufficient monies to pay off her creditors, becoming completely debt-free! After her debts have been paid, she will have enough money left over for her and her sons to live on *for the rest of their natural days!*

Not only does the widow gain an overflowing supply of an in-demand staple, but she will be able to sell it and walk away with enough profits that she will never have to work or worry again!

This, to me, is the most marvelous aspect of the story—the widow is empowered to become a co-creator with God to manifest a comfortable life for herself and her sons. Nowhere in this story is the proverbial "magic wand" waved, removing every vestige of the widow's trouble. Though she was assisted every step of the way, the widow was expected to and empowered to play a critical role in *solving her own dilemma.*

In this most exciting part of the story, the widow becomes a co-creator of her future because the fullness and breadth of her prosperity will depend, as it did previously, on how well she executes the instructions she's given. Once again, the onus is on her: she must go to the market, sell all the olive oil that has miraculously appeared and then pay off her creditors. She must complete certain critical tasks herself. Upon successful completion of her duties, she will reap enormous rewards.

This same truth applies to any situation where you may feel hopeless or victimized. Perhaps you think you have no way out. When you're feeling this way, I implore you to remember your status as a co-creator with God. What does that mean? It means that God endowed and imbued you with the same creative energy He used to bring every single thing into existence. You are made in God's image and likeness. Though your power may not be to the extent and degree of God's power, you have the exact same *kind* of creative energy coursing through you. You are, as God is also, *constantly creating.* You are capable of creating everything your soul desires. And your soul desires only that which is good for you because your soul is always in attuned with God.

Each and every day, you create your life situation, moment by moment, day by day, year by year. Your life is an amalgam and manifestation of your prior creations. The question becomes: are you happy with what you've created?

Elisha *revealed to the widow the power and ability*

she possessed to co-create with God. The results were
phenomenal, since we must assume that she did nothing other than exactly what she was told. There is no
reason to believe otherwise, as she had faithfully con-
summated each assignment she'd received up to that
point. Doubtless, she sold the olive oil, paid her debts,
and lived well and debt-free for the rest of her life—
full of faith and quite joyful. Thus, the widow was able
to co-create a magnificent result.

If you're unhappy with or feeling dismay or disap-
proval over what you've created thus far, *begin today
to create anew.* You have the power and ability to do
so; you received it from God. You are not a helpless
victim, you are a powerful co-creator!

Even if you desire or intend to create something that
is much bigger than you know how, ask God for the assistance that is promised and always available to you,
just for the asking. Indeed, co-creating with God means
seeking God's guidance and being open to acting upon
what the Holy Spirit tells you to do through your voice
of wisdom from within. By following divine guidance,
you will begin to co-create a magnificent life that reflects our Creator's perfect will for you.

Ask yourself:

- *What different results would I like to create in
  my life?*
- *What could I begin co-creating with God right
  now?*

ONE FINAL WORD

"Finish!"

I am a writer. If I don't write, I feel a blockage that manifests itself mentally, emotionally and even physically. I write every day of my life.

Therefore, I was a little taken aback by the lesson I learned recently from God through a close and trusted friend, who is also a writer.

One day, he and I were discussing the writing world and the conversation turned to what I was currently working on. I admitted to him that I was writing three books at the same time. He laughed. When I asked what was so funny, he responded that he too was writing more than one project simultaneously, and thought it humorous that I was having the exact same challenge he was: not finishing any of them.

I suffer from a condition that frequently attacks the highly creative souls among us. I can be a notorious "non-finisher." I start new projects with zeal and a determined, focused enthusiasm. While working on the project that I'm so excited about, I get another creative idea which gets me even more excited. So I start the new topic with just as much zeal and enthusiasm. You can guess what happens next, yet another project excites me, and I find myself, once again, at the starting line hearing a gun shot. I have great starts. I am learning to have great finishes.

This internal process occurs because my mind is highly creative; it wants to create lots of exciting things. It is highly artistic and moves incredibly fast. You too may have this challenge. Perhaps you've gotten a creative idea about a new business opportunity or a project that you become so excited about you can barely sleep. However, when you roll up your sleeves and are confronted with the work that invariably goes along with bringing your idea to fruition, you may slow down. Delayed gratification doesn't help, and the shiny newness of your opportunity quickly fades. Soon, another exciting door opens, and you zestfully and enthusiastically jump through that door too.

The problem that is inherent in jumping at all these exciting opportunities is this: you may never finish anything.

My friend gave me excellent advice that day; advice I knew came from God. He said one word. It was simply:

"Finish."

"Valerie, no one can read your books if you don't finish at least one. You don't have one completed project, which means if you met an agent or made a valuable contact with someone who could publish your work today, you'd have nothing to give them because you haven't finished anything."

His words held an astounding truth. If I didn't finish my writing projects, it didn't matter how beautiful and heartfelt my writing was. It didn't matter if I could move a reader to change his or her life. It didn't matter that my book could sell millions of copies. None of it mattered because it wasn't *finished.*

The exhilaration we all experience when embarking on something new wears off somewhere between finding out how much work is involved in bringing the project to fruition and actually beginning the associated work. When we discover how much work is actually involved in bringing our creative idea to full fruition, the former thrill can easily be replaced with a mixture of disdain, frustration, loss of interest and procrastination. The full rush of excitement may not return until we have successfully completed the task to our own satisfaction. Then, and only then, do we feel the surge of excitement that springs from the beauty of a completed project.

What I learned from God today was simply: *finish.*

I obeyed.

The result is the book you've just read.

Let me now return the favor that I was given in that one word: *finish.*

I want to take this opportunity to remind you of Mr. Ware, Uncle Algie, Uncle Vaness and Aunt Louann, who all share a commonality: *they woke up one morning and thought it was going to be just another day. They didn't realize that that day would be their last.*

Life is transient and fleeting. But most of all, life is a gift; to be treated with the utmost care, appreciation, reverence and respect. While we are here, with every breath we take, we should be giving thanks and co-creating the life our Maker had in mind when we were fashioned.

Now I'd like to give you a nudge.

Is there a book you've been wanting to write? If there is, do it *NOW.*

Is there a poem floating around in your head that you've not committed to paper? If so, do it *NOW.*

Is there a song you want to share? Share it *NOW.*

Are there words you want to express to someone you love? Muster the courage to tell them how you feel about them *NOW.*

Is there a business you'd like to start? Begin researching how to do it *NOW.*

Is there an idea you have that the world is waiting for? Start working to give it to the world *NOW.*

Is there an invention you've been thinking about for years? Start figuring out how to get your invention created NOW.

Remember, you may not be here tomorrow. Allow me to illustrate.

Many years ago, before the great discoveries of modern science, if a person fell into a coma, it was presumed that they were dead. The usual death rituals would be performed, and the person would be buried. This was most unfortunate, because quite a few people who were presumed dead, in actuality, weren't. They were buried alive, only to wake up and find that they were trapped six feet under.

Later, when bodies were exhumed for various reasons, there would be a horrific discovery: scratch marks on the inside lids of several coffins informed the people of the time that they had buried many of their fellow humans alive.

Humans are an ingenious race, so the people of that time came up with a solution. They decided that whenever a person died a questionable death, they would tie a rope around the person's hand. Then a hole would be bored into the lid of the coffin the person was placed in for burial. The rope that was tied to the resting person's hand would be drawn up through the hole in the coffin before the lid was closed. While the coffin was lowered, the folks who buried the resting person would hold on to the rope, and after the coffin was covered with dirt, they would tie the rope to a stake in the ground next to the grave. They would then attach a bell to the rope. If the resting person woke up in the coffin, the panicked movement of their hand would ring the bell. Those who were in the graveyard watching for such occurrences (back then referred to as working the graveyard shift), would rush over and dig up the person who had been buried alive. The person who was dug up would thereafter be referred to as a "dead ringer".

My definition of a dead ringer is a person who is buried with all or most of their unexpressed God-gifts, talents and abilities in the coffin with them. To me, a dead ringer is the person who never got around to expressing their fullest potential before the angel of death came knocking.

You may know someone who is an excellent artist, but whose half-finished artwork is tossed in a corner somewhere in their home; or a writer whose pile of half-done works are abandoned in the corner of a dark closet, or taking up space on a computer hard drive.

There is a very sad fact of life that I've observed: most people, in a lifetime of 70, 80 or more years, never reach their fullest potential, nor do they accomplish even a fraction of what they are capable of.

I read an interesting Kaballah story about a Rabbi who was highly and widely esteemed for being a great spiritual teacher. He had written many books, and had taught many students the Holy Scriptures and how to use them to create a better life. He was well regarded long after his death.

However, he had not always realized his fathomless potential to transform himself and others through the power of God's word.

When he was a little boy, he spent his time in school as if he were on the playground and never took his studies seriously. He would frequently misbehave in class, which earned him poor grades and the disdain of his teachers. His parents were distressed at his misconduct and unwillingness to learn. His parents and teachers knew he was on the wrong path, and if he didn't turn himself around, would certainly make a pure mess of his life.

One night, the young boy happened past his parents' bedroom door, which was slightly ajar. His attention was arrested when he heard his mother crying. He moved closer to the small crack in the door, so as to hear what she was saying. She was crying over her son, expressing her concern about him to his father. "If he doesn't behave and learn his lessons well, what will become of him? How will he get along in the world? I am so concerned for his future because it seems that our son won't amount to much of anything."

The words his mother cried that night touched the young boy deeply. Right there, standing in the hallway outside his mother and father's bedroom, he decided to become the best student he could be. He decided that he would study, behave himself, and earn the respect of his teachers and his parents.

And that's exactly what he did.

Years later, after he had grown up and successfully completed his rabbinical studies, the Rabbi told an interesting story. He told of a vision he had experienced of an alternate life for himself, one in which he had not heard his mother crying that night. In that alternate life, after dying and going to heaven, the Rabbi had a conversation with God.

God asked him, "My child, where are all the books you have written?"

The man, feeling quite uncomfortable, timidly answered, "Dear God, I didn't write any books."

God then asked, "Well then, where are all of the students who have learned from you and made their lives better?"

"I didn't teach anyone."

Lastly, God asked, "Where is the outstanding reputation and legacy of spirituality you have left behind for others on earth?"

He responded with much concern and trepidation, "I didn't leave behind a great legacy."

God then said, "All of these things, and more, were within your potential to accomplish, and were indeed part of my master plan for your life. I gifted to you, when you were brought forth, everything you needed to accomplish your work."

God then showed the man a vision of all that he could have been had he lived up to his vast potential.

Happily, the Rabbi had lived up to his vast potential: he wrote numerous books, taught many others the way of spirituality, and established a name for himself as being a Godly man.

Some believe that when we leave this earthly life and arrive back at God's bosom, we will be shown two movies: the first movie is what our life actually was while we walked planet earth, the second movie was what our life could have been had we lived up to the vast potential God gave us when we were born.

I reflect on this story any time that I feel like not finishing something. My writing is a gift from God to me and the world. I am moved by writing, just as much as others are moved by what I write. God is working through me, as He is working through each of us, to accomplish great things.

I am like the little boy version of the Rabbi after hearing his mother crying over him. I have decided to apply myself, no matter how rough the road may be. I have decided that when I show up in heaven, if there are indeed two movies God shows me—one of the actual life I lived and the other of the life I could have lived had I used all the talent and gifts God gave me—the two will be identical.

Whether or not we see two movies in heaven is anybody's guess; we'll find out in the hereafter. Right now, while we are here, we've got work to do.

Not only do you have work to do, it is urgently important as you are on a time frame that is finite.

You are here to fill a very special purpose and mission that only you can accomplish. That's why you're here. We all need you and your contribution. Most importantly, our Creator desires to see you succeed in completing your purpose and passion and has given you everything you need to joyfully engage yourself in your life's work and offer your gifts lovingly to the world.

In life, we have one monumental and very simple—although not easy—task. That task is to give the world the best we have at any and every given moment, using all of our talents, abilities and God-gifts to the fullest potential. In every moment of every day, we are being divinely guided through the voice of God with regard to every aspect of how to accomplish our monumental task. We are always fully supported and divinely guided.

It is our joyful privilege to grasp readily everything God has so graciously and lovingly gifted to us and use it to transform ourselves, those around us, and ultimately the world.

Will you do that *NOW*?

If you've already started, I offer you one word with a mountain of love: *Finish!*

Namaste'
Valerie Love

E-mail: thepowerofloveworldwide@yahoo.com